The Tall Stranger

Barbie did not seem to be upset, or was she perhaps a little too cheerful? Amalie could not tell. She loved Edward and Barbie. It would make her happy if they married.

It was true she had been worried about this strange man who had set Barbie alight. Edward had said he was a 'menace', which sounded alarming. But the strange man had not turned up again, so that was all right – or was it?

D. E. STEVENSON

The Tall Stranger

Collins

FONTANA BOOKS

First published 1957
First issued in Fontana Books 1959
Second Impression June 1962
Third Impression July 1965
Fourth Impression July 1974

© D. E. Stevenson, 1957

Printed in Great Britain
C. Nicholls & Company Ltd.

The Tall Stranger is a work of fiction and none
of the characters are drawn from life. The
names of the people in the book have been
chosen at random and are not intended to refer
to any person who happens to bear the same
name.

CONDITIONS OF SALE:
This book is sold subject to the condition
that it shall not, by way of trade or otherwise,
be lent, re-sold, hired out or otherwise circulated
without the publisher's prior consent in any form of
binding or cover other than that in which it is
published and without a similar condition
including this condition being imposed
on the subsequent purchaser

PART ONE

CHAPTER ONE

For nearly a week London had been shrouded in fog. Today it had lifted a little (just enough for the half-choked inhabitants to see that there was a sun, still shining in the sky) but now it was settling down thicker than ever; it was for all the world like a dirty grey blanket.

Nell Babbington had finished her work for the day (she was secretary to a doctor in Kensington). She put on her coat and hat and took up the neat pile of letters which were ready for the post. Then she called out to Mrs Ridge, the doctor's housekeeper, to say she was going. Mrs Ridge was downstairs in the kitchen; her voice came up from the nether regions.

'The fog's awful,' yelled Mrs Ridge. 'I couldn't 'ardly find my way 'ome. Worse than ever, it is. You better be careful, Miss Babbington.'

'I'll be all right,' shouted Nell.

The fog was waiting for her when she opened the front door and surged at her like a billow of cold evil-smelling smoke. Certainly it was much worse than ever, there was something so sinister about it that she shut the door hastily with herself still inside. The reaction was instinctive, there was no sense in it, for sooner or later she would have to go out and find her way home . . . but all the same she lingered. The hall was warm and comfortable with its thick crimson carpet, solid mahogany furniture and grandfather clock (which ticked complacently and kept such admirable time). It was the sort of hall which gave one a feeling of security – and this was exactly what it was intended to do. Nervous patients were soothed by the atmosphere of permanence and stability, some of them were reminded of their grandparents' homes which they had visited in their childhood.

It's clever, thought Nell – but without surprise for she knew already that Dr Headfort was clever.

There were two other doctors, each of whom had a consulting-room in the house, but although Nell received their patients she really belonged to Dr Headfort. She had belonged to him for more than a year and liked the job for he was absolutely dependable and there was no nonsense about him; Miss Babbington was merely the young woman who received his patients, typed his letters and reminded him of his multitudinous engagements. Some young women might have resented this attitude on the part of their employer but Nell preferred it for she found it much more convenient to keep her business life and her social life in separate compartments. Until she came to Dr Headfort she had never been able to settle down in peace. No sooner had she settled into a congenial job and got used to her employer than the idiotic creature began to get silly. Nell's path through life was strewn with broken hearts. Of course it was not her fault; she had not made herself. Sometimes she *almost* wished herself plain and dumpy, but never *quite*. Life would have been a lot easier but not so exciting; besides, to be honest, Nell's looks gave pleasure to herself as well as to other people. Her smooth dark hair, which fitted her head like a cap, her gentian-blue eyes and creamy skin made a delightful picture whenever she looked in a mirror, and her slender figure would have graced a fashion-plate.

Nell was still dawdling in the hall when Dr Headfort came downstairs. Nobody could have called him good-looking, but he reminded Nell of her father, who was very good-looking indeed. Colonel Babbington would not have been flattered (the doctor was tall and gaunt with rugged features and a determined chin) but the likeness was there. It's when he smiles, thought Nell.

He was smiling now. 'Hallo, are you just going, Miss Babbington?' he inquired.

It was not really a question, for of course Nell was going – it was her usual hour of departure and here she was in the hall with her hat and coat on – but if nobody ever asked unnecessary questions there would be a good deal less to say.

'Yes,' said Nell. 'I'm going along to the hospital to see my friend – and then home.'

'I thought your friend was better.'

'They say she's better.'

Dr Headfort was shrugging on his overcoat but there was something in Nell's voice that made him pause. 'You're still anxious about her?' he asked.

'They say she's better,' repeated Nell. 'Her temperature has steadied, but she just lies there taking no interest in anything. I suppose it's silly to worry – '

'People always worry about their friends. It would be unnatural if they didn't,' declared the doctor. He opened the door as he spoke and the fog rolled in. 'Great Scott, it's worse than ever!' he exclaimed and like Nell he shut the door hastily. 'Look here,' he continued. 'You can't go home in this. You could never find your way to Covent Garden – that's where you live, isn't it? – the fog will be worse down there. Better stay here for the night. I'll tell Mrs Ridge to make up a bed for you.'

'It seems silly – '

'It would be silly to go. Honestly, Miss Babbington, it would take you hours – and what about the morning?'

Nell hesitated. She saw the point. If she could not get here in the morning it would be very inconvenient. The flat (which she shared with Barbie France) was empty; Barbie was in hospital, lying there and taking no interest in anything. There was no reason at all why Nell should not stay here for the night. Mrs Ridge would coddle her and she felt in the mood for a little coddling.

'Yes – well – perhaps – ' said Nell. 'But I *must* go to the hospital and see Barbie. I said I would.'

The hospital was only about ten minutes' walk from the doctor's house so it was agreed that Nell should go and see her friend and come straight back.

After that there was no excuse for dawdling in the hall so Nell went down the steps and turning to the left began to walk along the street. She knew the way well (she had called at the hospital every day for the last five weeks) but the fog really was awful. There are fogs and fogs. This was the worst Nell had ever experienced. She was choked and blinded (even when she walked close to the railings she could scarcely see them) and it seemed that she was deafened as well, for the roar of traffic, which is the accompaniment of life in London, had ceased. Although intrepid by nature Nell was definitely frightened and when she heard steps behind her it was all she could do to stifle a scream.

'It's all right,' said Dr Headfort's voice reassuringly. 'I'll come with you, Miss Babbington.'

'But aren't you – going somewhere?'

'I'm going to the hospital with you.'

Nell opened her mouth to object but by this time he had drawn her hand through his arm and they were walking on together – his arm was thin and bony but it felt very strong – so she changed her mind and said, 'It's very good of you. As a matter of fact I don't believe I could find my way, and Barbie will be expecting me.'

'That's all right,' he replied. 'I'll have a look at a couple of patients and we can come back together. Hold on a moment, we cross the road here.'

They crossed. Dr Headfort had a torch which enabled them to see the kerb and to find the railings on the other side.

Hitherto their relationship had been strictly professional, but this expedition was out of hours and as they walked arm-in-arm through the fog and darkness they began to converse in a more human way. You could not cling to a man's arm – however bony – and ignore the fact that he was a human being.

'It must be a bit lonely without your friend,' suggested Dr Headfort.

'It's ghastly,' agreed Nell. 'Barbie and I have shared the flat for years. We get on awfully well together.'

'Are you alike?'

Nell was surprised at the question. 'No-no,' she said doubtfully. 'At least not to look at. Barbie is rather plump; she has red hair and grey-green eyes . . . and I don't think we're alike in character either. I'm rather an easy-going sort of person, taking people as I find them, but Barbie is like the man in *Pilgrim's Progress*, Valiant for Truth.' Nell giggled and added, 'Sometimes her frankness is a bit devastating. I often wonder how she gets on in business.'

'What sort of business?' Dr Headfort wanted to know.

'Oh, she's in a big firm of Interior Decorators; she goes all over the country looking at houses and advising people about colour schemes.'

'Modern colour schemes?'

'Not for everybody,' said Nell quickly. 'Of course some people go in for bright colours and different-coloured walls, but it depends on the sort of house and the personality of its owner. I was just thinking Barbie would approve of your hall.'

'She would think it very old-fashioned.'

'She would think it very clever.'

Dr Headfort chuckled.

'You did it on purpose, didn't you?' asked Nell.

'You've guessed my guilty secret. When I took the house it was modern. I put back the clock a hundred years – yes, just about a hundred years.'

They walked on for a bit in silence and then Nell said, 'I wish you could see Barbie. I suppose she's getting better, but the last few days she seems worse – so feeble and wretched. She lies there looking like a ghost. It's so unlike Barbie.'

'She isn't my patient,' said Dr Headfort.

'Oh, I know,' agreed Nell. 'But I do wish – I mean I can't help wondering if the doctor understands. It's so awful to see somebody you're terribly fond of looking like that.'

For a few moments Dr Headfort did not speak. Then he said, 'Perhaps I might have a look at her in a friendly way.'

'Oh, please do!' exclaimed Nell. 'It's Dr Mills. He wouldn't mind, would he?'

'I'll see what I can do. No promises.'

Nell had not been bothering about the direction they were taking, she had left it to her companion in whom she had absolute confidence, so she was surprised when he stopped and said doubtfully, 'I believe we've missed the turning. We'll have to go back.'

They turned and went back, looking for the turning which should have been on their left, but most certainly was not. Presently the line of railings, which had been their only guide, gave way to a high brick wall which should not have been there at all.

'Where on earth are we!' exclaimed Dr Headfort. 'Look here, Miss Babbington. I'm most awfully sorry.'

'We can ask someone,' said Nell soothingly. She was sorry for Dr Headfort; men hate to bungle things, they like to be big and brave and clever.

'We'll have to ask,' admitted Dr Headfort. 'I'm awfully sorry, Miss Babbington. I thought I could have found my way to the hospital blindfold.'

Unfortunately there was nobody to ask. The street was deserted. Nell had a feeling that it was a narrow back street (one of those queer little rabbit-warrens which lead nowhere in particular and which you never notice on ordinary occasions) but of course she could not be sure. Dr Headfort's torch made a tiny cave of yellow light in the surrounding gloom. They might have been alone in the world, she and Dr Headfort.

'Perhaps there's something written on the wall – I mean the name of the street,' suggested Nell. 'We could see with your torch, couldn't we?'

They looked. There was no placard, but there was something written in yellow chalk: JACK LUVS MARLENE.

'And we pay millions every year for education!' exclaimed Dr Headfort in disgust.

'I know, but we've got to.'

'Why?'

'Because we might leave out somebody who could write another King Lear.'

'Do you think that's the best?' asked Dr Headfort. 'I think Othello. Anthony Quayle in Othello. I've never seen anything like it before or since.'

'Yes, but –' began Nell . . . and then she laughed for it was the craziest thing to stand here in the fog arguing about the respective merits of Othello and King Lear.

Dr Headfort laughed too. 'We must talk about it some time,' he declared. 'It's a very interesting subject. People who are moved by King Lear are usually those who are particularly devoted to their fathers –'

'And the Othello people have jealous dispositions,' suggested Nell. She was sorry when she had said it, for it sounded impertinent, but Dr Headfort did not seem to mind.

'I suppose I could be, if I had anything to be jealous about,' he said thoughtfully. 'But it's too cold to stand here. Shall we go on – or back – that's the question.'

'Wait, I hear someone coming!' exclaimed Nell.

They waited as the footsteps approached – two sets of footsteps in heavy boots – and as they drew nearer Dr Headfort called out, 'Hallo, can you tell us where we are, please!'

The footsteps stopped but there was no reply.

'Where are we?' repeated Dr Headfort urgently. 'We've got lost. Are we anywhere near the hospital?'

There was not a sound.

Quite suddenly Nell was nervous. She was all strung up. It was alarming to be aware that there were people – two men – quite close and not be able to see them . . . but they can see us, she thought; she was about to tell her companion to put out the torch when it happened. A hand caught her by the arm and seized her bag. At the same moment a burly figure pushed between her and the doctor and dragged him aside.

The assault took Dr Headfort by surprise. He staggered and almost fell but a wild scream from Nell brought him to his senses. He turned and grappled with his assailant; they swayed to and fro, stumbling over the edge of the pavement and continuing the struggle in the road. There was another scream – a hoarse scream like that of an animal in pain – and a torrent of blasphemy and with that the two thugs ran for their lives, their heavy boots clattering and skidding on the greasy pavement.

Dr Headfort was somewhat dazed. His torch had gone out and he could see nothing. He did not even know which way he was facing. 'Miss Babbington!' he cried. 'Are you all right? Where are you?'

'I'm here,' said Nell faintly.

He groped in the direction of the voice and found her leaning against the wall. 'Are you hurt?' he demanded.

'No, not hurt. He tried to get my bag – that's all.'

'Sure you're not hurt?'

'Yes, but – oh dear – I'm afraid I'm going to – to be sick.'

She was sick. It was terribly humiliating (why couldn't she have fainted gracefully like a Victorian young lady?) but fortunately her companion was a doctor.

'Natural reaction,' he murmured. 'Much the best thing. You'll be all right in a minute. Here's a bottle of smelling-salts, don't hold it too close to your nose.'

Nell had seen the little bottle before. It was a habit of the doctor's to carry it in his pocket and offer it to his patients when they required it, and he always said, 'Don't hold it too close to your nose.' She had seen, also, the startling effects upon patients who had sniffed the little bottle too enthusiastically; so she was careful to obey the instructions and sniffed carefully. The smell was curious but pleasant.

'Better now, aren't you?' said Dr Headfort comfortingly.

'Much better. I say, I'm awfully sorry – too frightful of me. Why couldn't I have fainted?'

'Thank goodness you didn't! What on earth should I have done if you had fainted?'

It certainly would have been awkward for him. Nell saw that.

At this moment there was a glow of orange-coloured light and a policeman arrived upon the scene. He was large and solid and, to the wanderers, an extremely pleasant sight. An angel straight from heaven would not have been more welcome to Dr Headfort.

'What's been happening here?' asked the policeman sternly. 'You haven't been annoying this young lady, have you?'

'Oh no, he's been marvellous!' cried Nell.

'The lady is suffering from shock,' explained Dr Headfort. 'We were attacked by two men – one of them grabbed her bag.'

'No wonder she was frightened,' said the policeman sympathetically.

'I wasn't frightened,' declared Nell. 'I was upset because – because I broke his arm. It was horrible. The bone snapped in two.'

'You broke 'is arm, Miss?' echoed the policeman in amazement. He looked at her more closely with his torch and added, 'You couldn't 'ave broken 'is arm – not possibly. Look, Miss, here's your bag on the pavement.'

'I know. He dropped it when I broke his arm.'

The policeman did not pursue the subject. He said, 'That's the worst of these fogs. All the riff-raff in the district are on the go. I s'pose you couldn't identify the men?'

'Not a hope,' replied Dr Headfort. 'I never even saw them. By the way I'm Dr Headfort. We were on our way to the hospital but we missed the turning and had to go back – and then we got lost. I expect you can tell us where we are.'

'You're there, sir,' said the policeman cheerfully. 'This is the back of the 'ospital. There's a door about twenty yards down the street. Better take the lady in that way. I'll show you.'

CHAPTER TWO

The fog had invaded the hospital, and although it was not so dense as it was in the streets it was thick enough to be extremely unpleasant. The windows had been shut all day so the atmosphere was stale; there was a constant sound of coughing. In the wide passages, where the nurses hurried to and fro, the fog curled and eddied; in the wards it stagnated until the door was opened and then swirled languidly.

There were two other patients in Ward 17 where Barbie France was lying. She had been in a small ward by herself, but they had moved her two days ago.

'It will be more cheerful for you,' said the Sister briskly. 'You're better now and it will be nice to have company.'

Barbie did not find it cheerful. She could scarcely see her two companions but their voices went on all day long, complaining voices. They talked about the awful price of food and the awful price of clothes and how they couldn't make ends meet no matter how they tried – but they both had 'tellies.' They talked about the awful way their neighbours' children were being brought up and about the inconsiderate behaviour of their husbands. One of them was pretty certain her husband was 'carrying on' with another woman. The other advised her to 'have it out' with him.

'I don't stand no nonsense with mine,' declared the complaining voice. 'Stick up for yourself, that's what I say. If you don't stick up for yourself there's nobody else is going to stick up for you.'

Barbie listened to the voices. She tried not to listen but she could not shut her ears.

Barbie had been taken ill suddenly. It was when she was talking to Mr Garfield about a contract for re-decorating a large and very luxurious flat in Kensington for a woman who seemed to have more money than taste. One moment she had felt perfectly well and the next moment Mr Garfield's office began to go round and round and Mr Garfield's face, with the big flashing spectacles (which gave him such an owlish appearance) dissolved before her astonished gaze . . .

and his voice faded out . . .

Barbie had never been ill before; she was an exceedingly strong, healthy young woman, so she was not a very good patient and the mysterious nature of her complaint was alarming. Every night her temperature soared sky-high and every morning it dropped like a spent rocket. It was 'a virus' the doctors said, but Barbie suspected that they did not know much about it. They had to say something. Evidently it was an unusual and interesting virus for quite a number of doctors had come to look at her and sounded her heart and tapped her knees and done other curious and uncomfortable things. Barbie had lain supine and allowed them to do what they liked. Her body was not her own any more. If it had been her body, only, Barbie would not have minded so much, but 'the virus' had invaded her soul. Yes, her very soul tainted with the poison so that she was not Barbie any more.

Barbie was usually cheerful and happy, vitally interested in life, vitally interested in her fellow creatures. It was not so now. She lay and gazed at the ceiling and wallowed in self-pity. 'They' told her she was better. 'They' said the virus had 'burnt itself out' but she did not feel better. She felt worse if anything. She felt like a rag. Nobody understood how ill she was – nobody cared. She did not care herself. What was life anyhow? Life wasn't worth living, it was just a senseless grind: getting up in the morning, going to work in a crowded bus; advising people about paint and paper and curtains; making out estimates with Mr Garfield; making little sketches for Miss Smithers; explaining to the girls in the work-rooms exactly what she wanted them to do! All quite useless and stupid, thought Barbie.

Two large tears formed themselves in Barbie's eyes and rolled on to her cheeks. She let them roll. Nobody cared. Even Nell did not care. Nell had promised to look in about six – it was long after six and Nell had not come. Why should Nell come? Nell obviously had found something better to do than visit a sick friend.

'Barbie!' said Nell's voice.

Barbie turned her head and there was Nell.

'Darling – you're crying!' exclaimed Nell in alarm.

'No, not really –'

'What's the matter?'

'Nothing. Everything. I don't know –'

14

'It's just that you've been ill,' Nell told her.

'Everything's miserable,' murmured Barbie. 'The day seems so long when the lights are on all the time. There's no difference between night and day – and those women talk – they're miserable too – and the fog makes my eyes water – '

'Of course you're feeling miserable, poor pet, but you're better, you know. The Sister says you're better.'

'I'm not better,' said Barbie . . . but she said it without conviction for you could not look at Nell and not feel better. Nell was so pretty and there was so much affection shining in her face.

'It's lovely that you're better,' declared Nell, sitting down and taking Barbie's hand. 'I've been terribly worried about you and the flat is an absolute desert – I can hardly bear it. Everybody has been worried. Your aunt has been ringing up every night to ask for you. Mr Garfield says – '

'Mr Garfield?'

'Yes, he says they miss you frightfully, but you're not to think of going back to work until you're perfectly fit. You're to have a long holiday – '

'What's the good?' said Barbie with a sigh.

'What's the good?'

'What's the good of anything? What's the good of getting fit? Fit for what? Fit to go back to the treadmill!'

'But you love your job!'

'Its so useless.'

'It isn't useless – making houses beautiful for people to live in. That's a worth-while job.'

'I don't know why you bother about me,' Barbie said.

Nell had been warned that Miss France was 'a little depressed' but even so she was alarmed. This pale languid invalid, lying in bed and being sorry for herself, was so un-like Barbie. There was no life about her; even her hair, instead of springing from her head in copper-coloured rings, lay dank and streaky upon her forehead. Her cheeks were as white as paper and there were violet shadows beneath her eyes. She looks iller than ever, thought Nell in dismay.

Aloud Nell said, 'We'll soon have you on your legs again.'

'I don't know why you bother,' repeated Barbie.

'Of course I bother.'

'I thought perhaps you weren't coming today.'

'You mean because I was late? It was the fog, darling. The

fog is frightful. We got completely lost.'

Nell hesitated. The Sister had said that Miss France would be 'all the better for a nice chat.'

'Tell her things that will amuse her,' said the Sister.

Would it amuse Barbie to hear about the adventure or would it worry her?

'You said "we,"' Barbie reminded her. 'Was somebody with you? Go on, Nell. Tell me.'

The other two women in the ward had stopped talking and were listening with all their ears, but the 'adventure' was private so Nell knelt down and whispered.

Barbie listened and was interested. 'Do you really mean you got lost?' she asked incredulously.

'My dear, it was like lentil soup. We couldn't see anything. We could hardly breathe. Dr Headfort had a torch, but that didn't help very much. We crawled along by the railings. Then he said we must have missed the turning so we went back . . . and then we were *absolutely* lost.'

'Were you frightened?'

'Not really,' said Nell in a doubtful voice. 'I don't know why – except that he's a very responsible sort of person. He's the kind of person who makes you feel safe.'

'I'd like to see him.'

'You're going to see him. I asked him to come and look at you and he said he would. You won't think much of him – I mean he's tall and thin and rather ugly, so don't expect to see an Adonis.'

'What happened next?'

Nell continued the story. She was a good raconteuse and the story lost nothing in the telling . . . and when she reached the point where she and her escort had been attacked by footpads Barbie was very interested indeed. So interested that she quite forgot herself.

'Two men!' exclaimed Barbie in horrified tones. 'Goodness, how awful! What were they like?'

'I've no idea. We never saw them. We just heard their footsteps approaching and Dr Headfort called out and asked where we were, but instead of answering they barged into us. One of them went for the doctor and the other seized my bag.' She paused and then added very, very softly, 'Barbie, I broke his arm.'

The policeman had received this statement with incredulity, but Barbie was aware that it might well be true.

Some time ago a little Japanese had come to lodge in the flat below that occupied by Nell and Barbie and had hung out a card advertising the fact that he was an exponent of ju-jitsu. The card caught Barbie's eye and she suggested to Nell that it would be rather fun. Nell had needed no persuasion – of course it would be fun – and they arranged to have lessons. Unfortunately they were induced to pay in advance and before they were half-way through the course their instructor vanished. He disappeared in the night leaving no address. For a time the two girls continued to practise together and then they discovered that they knew too little about it – or too much. Nell very nearly got her neck broken; it was stiff for days. Of course it was a mistake and Barbie was full of contrition. 'It's all right,' said Nell. 'But we'd better stop. "A little learning is a dang'rous thing."' They took up Country Dancing instead.

'Did you really – break his arm?' whispered Barbie.

'Yes, really. Of course I didn't *mean* to,' explained Nell. 'I was a bit excited – the creature had grabbed my bag – so I caught hold of his arm and held it – you know the way – and he struggled – and the bone went snap. He yelled like anything and dropped the bag on the pavement and ran for his life, Barbie it was horrible. It made me sick – yes, *absolutely* sick.'

'Nell, how awful!'

'Awful! I never was so ashamed in all my life. Fortunately the doctor is a doctor. I mean he didn't panic or make a fuss like any ordinary man would have. He just gave me his bottle of smelling-salts and said I would be better soon – and of course I was. It was the creature's arm breaking that made me sick. So horrible!' added Nell with a shudder.

'Don't think about it,' whispered Barbie. 'It was his fault, not yours, and perhaps it will be a lesson to him. Did you tell Dr Headfort?'

'I told the policeman but he didn't believe me. I suppose it does sound rather incredible,' said Nell thoughtfully.

They were silent for a few moments and then Barbie said, 'I think Dr Headfort sounds nice. You always say he's inhuman.'

'Not inhuman, just sensible. There's no silly nonsense about him. He treats me as a secretary ought to be treated, and that's what I prefer. I don't believe he's ever seen me,' added Nell in reflective tones. 'I'm just a piece of furniture in his consulting-room, like his desk and his filing-cabinet.'

'Perhaps it will be different now.'

'Different?'

'Well, he's seen you,' Barbie pointed out.

Nell chuckled. 'He saw me being sick in the gutter – if that's what you mean.'

It was – and it wasn't – but by this time Barbie was too tired to explain. The little chat with Nell had excited her, and for a few minutes she had felt better, but now the reaction was setting in and she felt worse than before.

'Darling, I've talked too much!' exclaimed Nell in alarm.

'Just – tired,' murmured Barbie. 'So – tired – '

Nell had risen to call the Sister when Dr Mills came in, followed by Dr Headfort.

'No, really, I'm only too pleased,' Dr Mills was saying. 'If you can suggest anything – '

'I've tired her,' said Nell quickly. 'They said I was to talk to her – so I did – but she isn't fit to talk. What a fool I am!'

Dr Headfort bent down and took Barbie's hand. For a few moments he stood there holding it and saying nothing.

Barbie had wanted to see Dr Headfort, but now she was too tired to speak to him, she was too tired even to see him properly – his face was a blur – but she managed to smile wanly.

'Couldn't you – give her something?' whispered Nell.

'Better not. Rest is what she needs.' He looked round and added, 'Don't you think Miss France would be more peaceful in a private ward?'

'Oh, she was in a private ward,' said Dr Mills. 'We moved her because Sister Smart thought it would be cheerful. Sister Smart has had a great deal of experience.'

Nell, listening to this, hoped Dr Headfort would press the matter for she agreed with his views, but he only nodded and said, 'Oh, yes. I see.'

After that the two doctors chatted for a few minutes about the patient's treatment and then they went away. Nell kissed her friend and followed hastily; she did not intend to let Dr Headfort out of her sight. He had said they could walk home together, but he might forget, and although

Nell had said she was not frightened she had no wish to walk back alone.

'I'm inclined to think it would be the best thing,' Dr Headfort was saying when Nell overtook them. 'As a matter of fact I'm getting all my patients out of town – all that can possibly be moved – not only the respiratory cases.'

'You think we're in for a spell of it?' asked Dr Mills.

'Looks like that to me. If Miss France has any relative in the country –'

'Her aunt would have her,' cried Nell.

The two men paused.

'Her aunt – Lady Steyne – she has a house in the Cotswolds – but Barbie couldn't be moved, could she?'

'I should be inclined to move her,' said Dr Headfort slowly. He looked at Dr Mills and added, 'But of course you know her condition much better than I do. It's merely a suggestion.'

Dr Mills hesitated. Miss France was a worrying case. Neither he nor anyone else knew exactly what had been the matter with her. Now that the temperature had steadied she ought to have been gaining strength, but she had begun to slip backwards. It would be a risk to send her . . . but it was a risk to keep her. He wished somebody else could make the decision.

'I think she could stand the journey in an ambulance,' said Dr Headfort.

Dr Mills nodded. 'Yes, I agree. Under ordinary circumstances I shouldn't care to risk it, but this fog is the very devil. Are you sure her aunt could have her?'

'I'm sure,' said Nell eagerly. 'I'll ring up Lady Steyne tonight. When can she go?'

'The sooner the better,' said Dr Mills.

The arrangements were made and Sister Smart (who was in charge of Ward 17) was informed that Miss France was being moved to the country tomorrow. Dr Mills told her himself and warned her that the ambulance would be ready about eleven.

Sister Smart was amazed. She thought it was crazy, but it was not her duty to make any objections so she held her tongue. As a matter of fact she would be glad to see the last of Miss France. Miss France was not the sort of patient she liked. Miss France had been very ill; she was better now but she was not trying to get well. She just lay and gazed at the ceiling. Sister Smart was not acquainted with young Mrs Dombey (if she had been she would have agreed with Mrs Chick), but she had known other 'cases' which could have recovered if they had made an effort to do so – and had died because they wouldn't try to live. Patients who behaved like that were no credit. Far otherwise.

Only yesterday morning Dr Mills had said, 'Miss France isn't making any headway. In fact she's lost ground.' He had said it in a grumbling tone of voice which had annoyed Sister Smart.

'Miss France is receiving every attention,' Sister Smart had replied.

'Oh, I know,' said Dr Mills hastily. 'I was just wondering if we were wise to move her into the larger ward.'

Wise to move her from one ward to another, and now he was sending her away to the country in an ambulance! Whatever next! thought Sister Smart. Miss France received every attention and if she did not get better here was it likely she would get better elsewhere?

Sister Smart's policy was to keep her patients in the dark. If you told them anything they fussed and objected and worked themselves up. As a matter of fact Miss France had seemed very low this morning and her pulse was weaker. The night Sister had reported that she had not slept and had complained that one of her companions snored. Sister Smart wondered whether she ought to tell Dr Mills but decided not to. He had said Miss France was to go and it was all arranged.

Miss France knew nothing of this. She was told nothing about all the plans which had been made on her behalf. She lay and gazed at the ceiling until suddenly two men appeared with a stretcher followed by Nell and Sister Smart. Nell had got leave from Dr Headfort to come to the hospital and see that all went well.

'You're quite happy about going, aren't you, darling?' asked Nell.

'Going!' exclaimed Barbie in alarm.

'Of course she's pleased,' declared Sister Smart. 'Who wouldn't be pleased to get out of this fog?'

'Where?' cried Barbie. 'Where am I going?'

'Haven't you told her?' demanded Nell. 'Why on earth haven't you told her?'

'Much better not. They only worry,' murmured Sister Smart.

By this time the ambulance men were ready and there was no time to be lost.

'You're going to Underwoods,' said Nell breathlessly. 'Dr Headfort thinks it's a splendid plan to get you away to the country. I phoned last night – it's all fixed – I thought they would tell you –'

Barbie said nothing. She allowed herself to be hauled out of bed, laid upon the stretcher and wrapped up in blankets.

'It's all right – really –' declared Nell in a strangled voice, for having accomplished her object she was almost in tears. She had spent hours telephoning and arranging for Barbie's departure and now she was not at all sure that it was the right thing to do. Was Barbie well enough to stand the journey? She looked ghastly – she looked as if she were going to die.

'Darling, it's all right,' repeated Nell. 'Lady Steyne is delighted. You'll get better much quicker. Barbie, say you're pleased – or something –'

Sister Smart had finished tucking in the blankets, the men had lifted the stretcher.

'Barbie, you love Underwoods!' cried Nell. 'It will be lovely for you – no fog! Sunshine –'

Barbie's lips moved. She said, 'You've forgotten something, Nell.'

'What?'

'The stamp,' said Barbie with the ghost of a smile.

The men moved off and carried her away.

'She was wandering,' declared Sister Smart.

'Oh no, she wasn't,' said Nell, trying to decide whether to laugh or cry. 'She wasn't wandering . . . and now I know it's all right. She's going to get better.'

Sister Smart said nothing in reply. She was watching the two young nurses tearing the sheets off the bed and preparing it for another occupant.

'Not like that!' she exclaimed. 'You know perfectly well that's not the right way to fold the corners – and do *hurry*! They'll be bringing her any minute –'

CHAPTER THREE

The fog was still very thick, though not quite so impenetrable as it had been last night. Traffic was moving slowly with a good deal of grinding and hooting but, considering everything, with remarkably few accidents and remarkably little bad temper. The ambulance nosed its way carefully through the streets. Its occupant lay upon the bunk with her eyes shut.

No use worrying, she thought. Parcels don't worry. You do them up and send them off and presently they arrive at their destination.

Barbie was not exactly worrying but she could not help wondering vaguely what Aunt Amalie would do when the parcel arrived. Aunt Amalie was a darling, there was nobody like her, but did she realise what a nuisance the parcel would be? Had Nell explained that the parcel contained a helpless invalid?

Poor Nell, thought Barbie. I should have been nicer. I should have said I was pleased.

The despatch had been so absolutely unexpected and so rapid that she had had no time to think, no time to examine her feelings, and of course she was not pleased. Indeed if she had been asked whether she would like to be hauled out of bed and sent to Underwoods she would have been horrified at the idea. All she wanted was to be left in peace. Peace, thought Barbie. Why can't people leave you in peace?

Presently the pace of the ambulance increased and Barbie realised that the atmosphere was clearing. They were leaving the fog behind. Fog, hospital, complaining voices and Sister Smart were all left behind. In front was Underwoods and Aunt Amalie. Something inside Barbie stirred and she drew a long breath.

The ambulance rolled along smoothly but already Barbie was at Underwoods. Her thoughts had arrived before her body. It was winter now, of course, but Barbie's inward eye saw the place as it was in summer-time.

The house was not large. It was a 'Queen Anne' house,

of rose-coloured brick with small-paned windows. Like so many houses of that period it had been built quite near the road so that its inhabitants might have the pleasure and excitement of seeing the world go by; the daily coach thundering past with its four horses; an occasional post-chaise; covered wagons and horsemen and all the rest. To be 'near the road' nowadays was less agreeable, but it was no longer a Main Road and there was not a great deal of traffic on it. A high wall and some well-grown trees gave the house sufficient privacy. When you opened the wooden door and passed beneath the archway you found yourself upon a rose-red brick path which led to the front-door with the brass knob in the middle and the fanlight overhead. Above and on either side were pink walls and windows with small leaded panes. The front garden was always a mass of colour; sweet-scented stock, wall-flowers, hollyhocks, sweet williams and tiny purple pansies and a host of other old-fashioned flowers which smelt delicious in the enclosed space. Behind the house there were lawns and flowering shrubs; beyond were the woods which gave the place its name.

Inside the house was beautiful and comfortable. There had been alterations of course, for modern ideas of comfort are somewhat different from those of the early eighteenth century and include such luxuries as electricity, bathrooms and central heating but the atmosphere of serenity remained. The drawing-room on the ground floor was L-shaped with an Adam fireplace and cushioned window-seats. It was rather a dimly-lighted room, owing to the small windows, but you looked out on to sloping lawns and sunshine. Here, too, there was a pleasing marriage of comfort with beauty. The comfortable chairs and sofa had made friends with the bow-fronted rose-wood cabinet displaying Dresden shepherds and shepherdesses; the rose-wood tables stood upon the reseda-green fitted carpet and seemed quite at home.

The house was full of lovely things but the loveliest was its mistress, Charlotte Amalie Steyne. She was over sixty now and her hair was silver, but her skin was smooth, her eyes bright and her movements as graceful as ever. She tired rather more easily of course; she could not dig in the garden as she used to do, and it took her a good deal longer to walk up the steep path to the top of the hill, but she accepted these signs of advancing age with equanimity.

There were people who said that Lady Steyne was spoilt; it was true that she had led a sheltered life with very few troubles, but she was so sweet-natured that no amount of spoiling could spoil her. She had been born at exactly the right moment (her parents already had two sons and were longing for a daughter) so the little daughter completed the France family delightfully and was as welcome as the flowers of spring. At that time Mr France owned a sugar estate in the Virgin Islands and it was in Charlotte Amalie, the capital, that the little daughter was born. Long before she had made her appearance in the world she had been named Charlotte Amalie.

'Charles, if it's another boy,' said Mr France.

'It isn't another boy,' said Mrs France confidently.

Mrs France was right, of course. It was Charlotte Amalie, and while she was a baby everyone called her by her full name, but as she grew older it became too much of a mouthful and the 'Charlotte' was dropped. There are many Charlottes in the world but few Amalies and the somewhat exotic name seemed to suit her.

Amalie spent her childhood in an earthly paradise of sunshine and flowers, warm blue seas and glistening white beaches. It was a lovely childhood and, although the family left the island of St Thomas when Charlotte Amalie was nine years old, she still remembered it clearly. She remembered the riot of bougainvillæa in the garden, and the pools where she had watched the tropical fish swimming amongst the corals, and she remembered the smiling black faces of the Negroes who worked on the estate. Oddly enough as she grew older she remembered even more clearly and it was one of her pleasures when she lay awake at night to evoke these childhood memories.

The France family came home to England to educate their children and bought a little property near Oxford. They made friends with their neighbours and there was a pleasant round of gaieties in which Amalie took part. One of her brothers went into the Army, the other was at Oxford and brought his friends home to be introduced to his family. It was surprising how many of them fell in love with his sister!

Amalie always said she did not want to marry, she was much too happy at home, but she changed her mind when she met Sir Edward Steyne. He was 'different' from her brother's friends. He was a good deal older than herself – older and wiser and full of integrity. She always thought of him as 'steel true and blade straight.' Some years before his meeting with Charlotte Amalie France he had lost his young wife in an accident; she had left him with a little son.

Sir Edward had always been called Ned by his family and his friends, but the little son was called Edward. Amalie fell in love with them both and she fell in love with Underwoods as well. The place, which had belonged to the Steyne family for years, was a most delightful home and Amalie settled down. Her life was sheltered and happy, it would have been perfect if she had had a child of her own, but that was not to be.

Fortunately she had little Edward to care for. She also had Barbie, her niece; for her elder brother (who had made the Army his career) died in India and his wife did not survive him very long. Barbie had had no recollection of her parents, she had come to Underwoods when she was an infant and it had been her home ever since.

Time was, when Underwoods had been run with a staff of four and it had not seemed too many, but now it was impossible to maintain a staff of well-trained servants and to tell the truth the house seemed just as comfortable without them, and much more peaceful. Amalie had a companion-housekeeper, Miss Penney, and a woman who came in daily from Shepherdsford village. Sometimes Amalie wondered what all those servants had done – except quarrel amongst themselves and make her life a burden. It seemed odd..

Of course Miss Penney was extremely capable. She had been at Underwoods only a few months but already she had become a fixture. She had fallen in love with Underwoods at first sight and also with Lady Steyne . . . and if Lady Steyne had not exactly fallen in love with Miss Penney in the same headlong manner she was certainly very fond of her now. Miss Penney was short and stout with a curiously flat face and pale-blue eyes and sandy hair. She was no beauty but for all that she was a treasure and worth her not inconsiderable weight in gold.

When Miss Penney had been at Underwoods for little more than a week her employer had asked permission to call her by her Christian name, explaining that it seemed more friendly.

'Just call me Penney,' said Miss Penney smiling.

Amalie hesitated. It was not what she had intended.

'Penney Plain,' explained Miss Penney. 'It suits me. When my parents decided to call me Diana they had no idea what I was going to look like when I grew up.'

Amalie was a diplomatic woman and seldom found herself at a loss but even she could find no suitable comment.

Usually Underwoods was a very quiet house but today there was a 'stir.' Penney had been busy getting the spare room ready; sweeping, dusting and airing the bed.

'You haven't seen her, have you?' said Amalie as they made the bed together. 'She's my elder brother's daughter, but she has always been like my very own child. She came to us when her mother died. She was such a sweet baby; so good and happy. It seemed dreadfully sad that she had no mother, but Ned and I both loved her so dearly. I don't believe even her own parents could have loved her more.'

Penney made a suitable rejoinder and then said, 'If you would just go and rest I could finish this quite easily.'

'I know you could, my dear. You're the most capable creature under the sun, and I don't know what I did without you, but honestly I'm not a bit tired and far too excited to rest. Of course she has been terribly ill. I wonder if we ought to get a nurse to look after her.'

'I could look after her,' suggested Penney. 'If we got a little more daily help I could manage quite easily; but you must do as you think best.'

'Yes,' said Amalie doubtfully. 'We had better wait and see how she is. Miss Babbington said . . .'

'What did she say?' asked Penney after a little silence.

'Such a lot that it was difficult to sort out,' replied Amalie in a puzzled tone of voice. 'She seemed awfully upset, and the line was not very clear. First she said Barbie was better and that her friend Dr Headfort thought she should be moved to the country – the fog in town is simply horrible – and then she said she was sure nobody realised how ill Barbie was . . . and then she began to sob and said "You won't let her die, will you? She's lying there like a rag doll. She's made up her mind to die." Then we were cut off and I couldn't get through again. There was no answer. I could hear the bell ringing and ringing in the flat but nobody answered it.'

'Perhaps Miss Babbington had rung up from somewhere else,' suggested Penney sensibly.

'I never thought of that!' exclaimed Amalie. 'I thought she was phoning from the flat.'

'You were worried and upset.'

'Yes, I was. It seemed so queer. Barbie is such a vital sort of creature. How could she have "made up her mind to die"?'

'People do, sometimes – when things get them down,' said Penney with a sigh.

By this time the spare room was ready and they were making Amalie's bed. Here, in Amalie's room, a coloured photograph of Barbara France stood upon the mantelpiece. Penney had seen it before – she saw it every morning when she was dusting the room – and the face had always fascinated her: not a beautiful face but certainly 'vital' with its wide generous mouth and broad brow and springing copper-coloured curls.

'So like her!' said Amalie.

You could tell that. The photographer had caught her leaning forward a little and the expressive eyes were full of humour – as if she had just thought of something very amusing and could scarcely wait to tell you about it, thought Penney.

'It was done by Arnold Fairbrother,' said Amalie. 'He did Edward too, but it isn't quite so good.'

The other photograph on the mantelpiece was of Amalie's step-son. Penny had seen him in the flesh for he had visited Underwoods not long ago. He was 'in business' and lived in London; an attractive young man, extremely good-looking and with most delightful manners. Edward Steyne had been friendly and kind to his step-mother's companion and she appreciated it greatly; some young men would not have bothered to be charming to a middle-aged spinster.

'They're both nice,' said Penney inadequately.

'Darlings,' agreed Amalie. 'Quite different of course. You see they aren't related to each other at all, but they grew up together as if they were brother and sister, playing in the garden and running about in the woods. I've always hoped and prayed that some day . . . but perhaps they know each other too well.'

It was at this moment that the front-door bell pealed loudly and the two ladies dropped everything and rushed downstairs to receive their guest.

CHAPTER FOUR

When the fuss and bustle of arrival was over and the guest safely in bed the two older ladies sat down to a belated tea. Penney noticed that her employer's hand was shaking so she poured it out herself.

'Don't worry too much,' said Penney. 'She looks fragile, but we'll feed her up –'

'Fragile!' echoed Amalie. 'It just – isn't Barbie. It's a ghost! Penney, I'm frightened.'

'I don't think you need be.'

'She couldn't even speak!'

'She was tired and upset. But after you had gone away and I had given her the milk she snuggled down and very next moment she was fast asleep – fast asleep and breathing like a child. I think she'll be a lot better tomorrow.'

'Dr Ladbrooke might –'

'Not tonight,' said Penney firmly. 'You can send for him tomorrow if you want to, but I won't allow her to be wakened tonight – not for any doctor under the sun.'

Amalie smiled a little tremulously. 'So you're taking over?'

'With your permission,' nodded Penney. 'I'll sleep on the sofa in her room – just in case she wants anything in the night – but I'm pretty certain she'll sleep for hours. That's what she needs.'

Penney hesitated, for she was a very reserved sort of person and never said more than was absolutely necessary, and then she decided that she really must go on talking. Perhaps if she went on talking it would help to relieve the strain.

'Hospitals are wonderful,' said Penney. 'They give you everything they can think of; they give you oxygen and blood transfusions and all the drugs in the chemist's shop, but they never seem to think of giving you enough sleep. I've often wondered why.'

Amalie was interested. 'Wouldn't it be difficult?' she asked. 'I mean there's so much coming and going, isn't there?'

'Oh, they can't help the noise and bustle but they could help wakening you at crack of dawn and washing your face,' said Penney bitterly.

Barbie was not wakened at crack of dawn to have her face washed. It was nine o'clock when she opened her eyes – and the room was full of pale winter sunshine. Barbie stretched herself luxuriously like a wakening cat – and yawned.

There was absolute silence. The window was open, and cool air drifted in, swaying the chintz curtains. For a few minutes Barbie lay there, not bothering about anything, not thinking about anything. Sweet fresh air and heavenly silence was enough. Then, far away in the distance she heard the chimes of a clock; it was the clock on the church-tower in Shepherdsford village.

Underwoods! thought Barbie. That's where I am! So I really did come; it wasn't all a dream. I'm here – at Underwoods!

The door opened and somebody entered very quietly. Barbie expected to see Aunt Amalie, but it was a strange face that bent down to look at her (yet not altogether strange for she had a vague feeling she had seen it before). It was a flattish sort of face framed in sandy hair. The face wore an anxious expression; truth to tell, Penney was beginning to be a little anxious about her patient, who had slept solidly for sixteen hours. Sixteen hours seemed a bit too much.

'Hallo!' said Barbie.

'So you're awake!'

'Only just,' said Barbie with another yawn.

'Well, please stay awake until you've had breakfast,' said Penny firmly.

Penney had said she was taking over the case and she did so in her usual capable manner. The bag, which had arrived with the patient, was found to contain a number of little boxes full of pellets and labelled with instructions. Some of the drugs were to be given at four-hourly intervals, others after meals. Penney had got up several times during the night and looked at her patient and wondered. Should she be wakened and given a pill – or not? But how could you disturb anybody sleeping so peacefully? Sister Smart could have done it quite cheerfully of course – but Penney couldn't. Penney thought sleep was – somehow sacred (it was one of God's greatest blessings to a weary world); so she left her patient sleeping and returned to her own not very comfortable couch.

In spite of her brave words to Lady Steyne, Penney had felt just a little bit frightened about the job she had taken on, but she had prayed that she might be guided and the prayer had been answered by an inflowing of confidence, firm and sure and peaceful. Prayers are not always answered, as Penney well knew, but this one had been answered in no uncertain manner. It was going to be all right.

Having given her patient a suitably light breakfast and tidied her up a little, Penney collected the boxes of pellets and putting them in the medicine cupboard locked the door. A young woman who could sleep for sixteen hours at a stretch did not need drugs; she needed rest and nourishment and fresh air and that was what she was going to get while Penney was in charge of her. No trained nurse would have dared to take the responsibility but Penney shouldered it without a qualm.

Barbie slept and woke and was fed and went to sleep again. She was washed (very efficiently) when she felt like being washed – sometimes in the morning and sometimes in the afternoon, but never at crack of dawn – and this extraordinary treatment suited her so well that by the end of the week she was able to sit up in bed, propped with pillows, to chat with Aunt Amalie for a few minutes and enjoy her meals. The meals were delicious and were brought to her upon a black plastic tray with a crisply-ironed traycloth, and the food was laid out temptingly upon delicate china plates. The most fastidious invalid would have been tempted and Barbie was not really fastidious; she polished off everything that was brought her and began to ask for more.

Another week passed and every day the patient's condition improved. There was an atmosphere of happiness in the house which affected everybody. Even Daphne the Daily felt it and sang loudly and cheerfully – though somewhat out of tune – as she went about her work. Occasionally Penney remonstrated with her in a tactful manner.

'You needn't bother,' said Barbie. 'At least not for me. I rather like to hear her singing "Cherry Ripe"; it's cheerful. I'm not quite so keen on "Parted." '

Penney shuddered.

'Oh, well, if you feel like that . . .' said Barbie.

Barbie was 'up' today for the first time, sitting in a chair near the window.

'You aren't cold, are you?' asked Penny anxiously.

'How could I be cold? You've wrapped me up like a mummy. No, don't shut the window, Penney; I like it open. The smell of flowers is delicious.'

'Flowers! There aren't any flowers; it's February.'

'Flowers,' said Barbie. 'Roses, stock, wall-flowers, and sweet peas; I can smell them all. Underwoods always smells of flowers, even in February. Perhaps it's their ghosts; the ghosts of all the flowers that have blossomed in the garden! If I had died my ghost would have come back to Underwoods.'

'What nonsense!'

'No, not nonsense, Penney. I believe I would have died if it hadn't been for Nell – and you – and I don't see why ghosts shouldn't come back to places they love and not only to places where they've been tortured.'

Penney was dusting the room (with a damp duster). She said, 'Why did you want to die, Barbie?' It was a question which had puzzled her considerably for she had got to know Barbie fairly well and Barbie was not the sort to lie down and die.

Barbie chuckled, she had a very infectious chuckle. 'Perhaps it was just to spite Sister Smart.'

'No, but honestly,' said Penney.

'Honestly?' said Barbie thoughtfully. 'Well, honestly I don't think I did actually want to die. I was just so tired that I didn't want to live. There's quite a lot of difference.'

Penney agreed that there was quite a lot of difference.

'How and where did you learn nursing, Penney?'

'By being a patient.'

'Oh, I see. By watching and noticing how to do things – and how not to do things.'

'Yes.'

'All nurses ought to be patients for a fairly long spell,'

declared Barbie with conviction.

'Yes.'

'It ought to be part of their training.'

'I think so too.'

'You do chatter, don't you?' said Barbie smiling.

Penney hesitated. 'I suppose I am rather – silent.'

'You listen and say nothing. I don't know anything about you at all. Perhaps I notice it more because Nell and I talk a good deal.' (Barbie was understating the case. When she and Nell got together they talked all the time, without stopping.) 'Why are you so secretive, Penney dear?' asked Barbie.

'Not secretive,' exclaimed Penney. 'It's just that people don't really want to know. My life hasn't been at all interesting, so why should I bore people by telling them about it?'

'Oh, I don't mean you should tell people the story of your life. I just mean you might let fall little bits of information occasionally; it would give you a background. You have no background, Penney. You're just a dear, nice, kind person – but not very real.'

Penney might have answered that companion-housekeepers are not expected to be real people with backgrounds. They are paid to do a little cooking and a little housework, to be there when they are wanted and to make themselves scarce when they not, but she did not say it because it would not have been fair; Underwoods was different. At Underwoods she was treated like a human being.

'For instance,' continued Barbie, 'when I said all nurses ought to have been patients you might have said, "I think so too – and that reminds me of the time I stayed with my grandmother at Brighton. She had a house there, and we used to walk along the pier every morning and sit in the sun." '

Penney chuckled.

'Oh, it isn't relevant,' admitted Barbie. 'But it might have reminded you – for some other reason or other – and I should have learnt painlessly that you had a grandmother who lived at Brighton.'

'She *did* live at Brighton,' said Penney. 'But she was far too busy to walk along the pier every morning. She ran a little school – just for tiny children – and taught them to read and write and do their sums.'

'Go on,' said Barbie encouragingly. 'You've got the idea.

It's still quite painless.'

'I lived with her,' continued Penney obediently. 'First I was a pupil and later a sort of pupil-teacher. She was a very clever, well-educated woman and taught me a lot. She wanted me to go to Girton, and when she died she left money to pay for my education – but I didn't go.'

'Why didn't you?'

This might be painless to Barbie, but obviously it was not painless to Penney. She was twisting the duster in her hands and her face had gone quite white. 'There was a good reason,' said Penney. 'My father was very badly off and I had two young brothers. It was more important that the boys should be properly educated.'

'So they went to school and you stayed at home?'

'Father said I would marry,' said Penney in a very odd sort of voice. Then she glanced at the clock and added briskly, 'You've been up for a whole hour. It's high time you were back in bed.'

Shortly after this Nell rang up to ask if she might come and see Barbie on Sunday, and was invited to lunch.

'But there will be two of us,' said Nell. 'Won't that be a bother? Dr Headfort has offered to bring me in his car. It would be quite easy for us to have lunch at the hotel.'

'Oh no, you must come here,' said Amalie, who was a very hospitable person. 'No bother at all. We shall look forward to having you, and please tell Dr Headfort it will be a great pleasure to meet him.'

'He wants to see Barbie,' explained Nell.

Barbie was delighted when she heard Nell was coming, but surprised at her choice of chauffeur. Having shared a flat for so long the two friends knew a great deal about each other.

'Perhaps she couldn't get anyone else to bring her,' suggested Amalie.

'She could have got half a dozen.'

'Half a dozen!' echoed Amalie.

'Nell has to keep them off with barge poles,' said Barbie darkly.

Strangely enough (or perhaps not strangely) this statement did not predispose Amalie in favour of Miss Babbington, so she was agreeably surprised when her luncheon guest arrived and proved to be a young friendly creature in tweeds and by no means one's conception of a femme fatale. She was attractive of course but not 'glamorous,' thought Amalie. (The truth is women do not always see that particular quality in another woman and are often puzzled when they see men buzz round one of their number, like bees round a honey-pot, and leave another to languish by the wall.)

Dr Headfort was 'ugly, but nice,' his hostess decided. The two of them had a very pleasant chat while Nell went bounding upstairs to see the invalid.

'Darling Barbie, you're you again!' cried Nell. 'Only more beautiful and – and interesting-looking than ever.'

'Yes, I'm me,' agreed Barbie. 'Not beautiful at all but quite human – thanks to you. If I'd stayed in that hospital another week I'd have been a beautiful memory . . . and I never said thank you for all you did. I never said I was pleased to go or anything. It was horrid of me.'

'You weren't pleased.'

'No, I wasn't really. I just wanted to be left in peace . . . not that there *was* any peace. It was pills and washings from morning to night and Sister Smart telling me to make an effort and get better.'

'Odious woman!' exclaimed Nell. 'Don't let's talk about her.'

Barbie agreed to the ban. 'Tell me things,' she said, making room on the bed for her friend to sit down. 'Tell me all. What have you been doing? Have you broken any more arms lately – or any more hearts?'

'I don't break things on purpose,' replied Nell with her sudden enchanting smile. 'How can I help it if things come apart in my hand? Oh Barbie,' she continued. 'There are new people in the Other Flat. It's a woman and a child; I met them last night on the stairs and she spoke to me. She's a widow, but very bright and hearty with yellow curls . . .'

Barbie listened to the account of the new neighbour without much interest, for there had been so many people in the Other Flat (which was just across the landing from the flat occupied by herself and Nell); so many different people and none of them very congenial. As a matter of fact there was something else Barbie wanted to know – and soon she found an opportunity to raise the question.

'Why Dr Headfort?' inquired Barbie. 'I mean you like to

keep business and pleasure in different compartments.'

'Oh, this is really business. He wanted to see you; he's interested in your virus.'

'But I haven't got it any more,' Barbie pointed out.

'He wants to ask you about it – and there was another reason too. You see I asked him for a day off to come down to Underwoods and he said if I waited till Sunday he would bring me in his car. Well, what could I say? Of course Roddy would have brought me –'

'Or Peter – or Phil –' murmured Barbie.

'But Dr Headfort offered, so I couldn't say no. Besides Peter has sold his car. Poor lamb, it died on him and he couldn't afford to have it mended.'

'There was still Roddy and Phil –'

'You don't understand,' declared Nell. 'This is a business trip. Dr Headfort wanted to know all about your virus – and he didn't want to give me a day off in the middle of the week. I don't know what you're getting at.'

'Nothing,' said Barbie hastily. 'But I still think it was nice of him – and of course I'll tell him anything he likes.'

CHAPTER FIVE

Spring came slowly to Underwoods. It was the most beautiful Spring Barbie had ever seen, for after lingering in the shadows so long she was in love with life – in love with the birds' song, and the tiny green leaves appearing on the trees and hedges. She was in love with the moist air which kissed her cheek and with the big white clouds which sailed slowly across the blue sky and disappeared over the hill. At first she could not go far, her legs were too uncertain, and she was content to dawdle in the garden until Penney came and fetched her in. As a child she had known the garden – every stone of it – and now she renewed her memories.

In all these years the garden at Underwoods had changed very little. Barbie was glad when she saw the old thorn-tree growing beside the gate which led to the woods. It had been old when she was a child, but it looked no older and was putting forth tender little buds of green. There was a rectangular lily-pond with a white-painted seat beside it, and behind the seat there was a high stone wall covered with grey and yellow lichen. Barbie greeted the wall as a friend and put her hand upon it; she remembered that she and Edward used to run along the flat top when they were children – it made her dizzy to think of it now. From this sheltered spot there was a lovely view of fields and trees and a silver trout stream which wound its way through the quiet English country to the far horizon.

Beyond the wall was the tiny paddock, tilted towards the sun like a square green handkerchief, lifted by one corner, and at the bottom end of the paddock was the little wooden shed where the donkey used to live. Barbie and Edward had called the donkey Amos – he knew his name and came to them when they called. The donkey had gone, of course, but the shed remained and the paddock was still starred with white daisies and golden buttercups.

In a little while Barbie was able to walk as far as the village – and that had not changed either. The street was crooked and on either side was a jumble of houses; houses of different heights and sizes, built at different periods, but somehow blending into a harmonious whole. Long ago the main road had run through the village and past the gate of Underwoods, but that was before Barbie's time. When the branch road had been made, and the new bridge built over the river, the village of Shepherdsford had gone to sleep. Occasionally in the summer it was awakened by the arrival of a bus which spilled out a strange crowd of visitors to lunch at The Owl Inn and wander round the old-fashioned shops buying postcards and little cheap brooches – made in Birmingham – and walk up the stony path to the ruins of Shepherdsford Abbey drowsing in a grove of ancient oaks . . . but the invasion took place very seldom, and did not last long, for to tell the truth there was not very much to see. There was just an old village with very poor shops and a pile of ruins in the woods!

In Underwoods itself life went smoothly and pleasantly. Barbie chatted to Aunt Amalie and helped Penney in the house and was busy altering her clothes. She had lost so much weight that everything she possessed had to be altered, and as she was determined to remain slim and elegant she went about the business with a will. In addition she was 'teaching Penney to talk' and in the process was learning a good deal about Penney's background. They had jokes together and sometimes were so overcome by mirth that they were obliged to stop in the middle of making a bed.

It was the end of April when Edward Steyne rang up and suggested coming for the week-end. Barbie answered the telephone and assured him that he would be welcome.

'How lovely it will be to see you!' she said. 'I haven't seen you for ages.'

'And I want to see you,' he replied. 'I'd have come down before this but I've been terribly busy. You know I've got a new job, don't you?'

Barbie knew this of course. Edward had tried several different kinds of jobs. He had been in a bank for a time, then he had gone to South Africa to an orange farm. Last autumn he had returned and become junior partner in a well-known firm of stockbrokers in the City. Barbie, who was in business herself, was aware that he could not have done so without capital and felt sure that Aunt Amalie must have provided this.

'Do you like your new job?' asked Barbie.

'Oh, rather,' replied Edward. 'It's very interesting. I'm settled now. I've done with roving – tell you all about it tomorrow.'

There were great preparations for Edward's arrival. Barbie lent a hand until she was chased into the garden by Penney to get fresh air, for although her patient was now convalescent Penney still ordered her about.

There was a huge cushion of primroses in a sheltered corner of the garden; Barbie had been watching it for days. She had seen the first delicate bud unfold and every day there had been more flowers – she had counted them as a miser counts his gold. Today the flowers were uncountable, the whole cushion was a solid mass of gold – and the scent was delicious beyond words. Barbie was kneeling upon the bank, enraptured, when she heard footsteps on the path and looking up saw Aunt Amalie.

'Look at them!' cried Barbie. 'Aren't they darlings? I really believe primroses are my favourite flowers . . . and of course primroses grow bigger and better at Underwoods than anywhere else in the world.'

'You love Underwoods, don't you?'

'Every bit of it! Every stick and stone! Even the snails,' declared Barbie looking up and laughing. 'I've been watching that snail on the wall – he's big and beautiful and his shell is full of rainbow colours. He isn't just an ordinary snail.'

Amalie was not very fond of snails and she was thinking of something else which had nothing to do with the creatures. 'Listen, Barbie,' she said. 'I've never told you, but I think the time has come when you ought to know. When I die Underwoods will come to you.'

Barbie gazed at her in astonishment. 'To me?' she asked incredulously.

'Ned left it like that in his Will.'

'But – what about Edward? I don't understand – '

'There were reasons.'

'Reasons!' echoed Barbie. 'Reasons why he should leave his beloved Underwoods to me – and not to his own son!'

'You were like his own daughter.'

'Oh, I know – and I adored Uncle Ned – but – but – '

Amalie sat down upon the corner of a nearby frame. She seemed to have some difficulty in explaining. 'I didn't want Ned to do it,' she admitted. 'In fact I did all that I could to persuade him not to. Edward was his own son and Underwoods should have been left to him. But there were reasons.'

'What sort of reasons?'

'It was when Edward was at Oxford. He got in with rather an odd crowd of young men. They had queer ideas about property. They thought people shouldn't own land. I don't think any of them owned land,' said Amalie with a little smile. 'So you couldn't blame them, really. Edward came home with his head full of the idea that land should be free. Young men get carried away by ideas.'

'Yes, but Edward – '

'Oh, with Edward it was just a phase. I never attached much importance to it, but Ned was rather upset. As a matter of fact I was right and Edward got over it quite soon. It was like chickenpox or measles – or any other childish complaint – but in the meantime Ned had altered his Will and left Underwoods in trust. It's mine as long as I live and then it goes to you.'

'Then it shouldn't come to me!' cried Barbie. 'It was all

a mistake. If Uncle Ned had known that Edward's views had changed he would have left it to him – not me at all.'

'Perhaps – or perhaps not. We don't know, do we?'

'Darling, we *do* know! Edward is terribly fond of Underwoods. He wouldn't dream of –'

'Underwoods is to be yours,' said Amalie firmly. 'Ned wanted you to have it. As a matter of fact I remember him saying at the time that it was better that way. I believe he might have left it to you even if Edward hadn't got those rather silly ideas. Ned had a theory that property is safer in a woman's possession.'

'Safer?'

Amalie nodded. 'He used to say "a home is more important to a woman than it is to a man." '

'That's true.'

'Of course it's true. A woman's home and children are the most important things in her life. Men don't grow roots in the same way. They're more vagrant. Even when people lived in caves the men went out hunting and the women stayed at home.'

Barbie smiled. It seemed funny to compare Underwoods to a prehistoric cave but all the same she saw the point. Human nature had not changed very much in its essentials.

'It's different if a place has belonged to one family for generations,' continued Amalie. 'But in that case it is usually entailed. Underwoods isn't entailed; if it belonged to Edward he could sell it.'

'He wouldn't want to!'

'I'm not sure,' said Amalie thoughtfully. 'Edward has a roving nature.'

'But that's all over,' Barbie declared. 'He's settled now and very interested in his new job. He said so himself.'

Amalie smiled at her vehemence. 'Oh, don't think I'm blaming Edward. I don't blame him in the least. It's natural and right for young men to be adventurous. There never would have been a British Empire if our young men had been content to settle down at home and not gone out to other lands to seek their fortunes. Of course it's the fashion nowadays to sneer at the British Empire – but what would the world be like today if there never had been a British Empire?'

'A good deal less civilised for one thing,' said Barbie after a few moments' thought.

'Yes,' agreed Amalie. 'It's an interesting speculation.' She laughed and added, 'I once asked a *very* clever young man (one of Edward's Oxford friends who thought he knew everything) what the world would be like today if there never had been a British Empire, and it sort of dried him up. He just gulped and said it was an interesting speculation.'

'I must remember that; it might be useful,' said Barbie.

'You must remember to look rather stupid when you put the question,' Amalie told her. 'I mean you must look as if you were terribly anxious to know. It works much better that way.'

Barbie said she would remember to look stupid – and they both laughed.

They had strayed quite a long way from Underwoods, but they had not forgotten the matter. It was in both their minds. So when Barbie frowned and said: 'What does Edward think about it?' Amalie was aware that she was not referring to the British Empire.

'He doesn't know,' replied Amalie quickly. 'I've never told him. There's no need for him to know.'

'I think he should be told.'

'No,' said Amalie firmly. She hesitated and then added, 'I'm quite sure it's better that Edward shouldn't know – in the meantime. I've thought about it a great deal, weighing up one thing against another, and I'm quite sure I'm right.'

'Why?' asked Barbie.

Amalie did not reply to the question. She said, 'Don't worry, dear pet. Edward will have money. He can buy a house if he wants to. It's all for the best. Just be happy about it and remember that Ned wanted you to have Underwoods – and I want you to have it when I'm gone.'

'Darling!' exclaimed Barbie. 'Oh goodness, I don't know what to say! I hope it will be a hundred years before – before – '

'Well, I don't,' said Amalie laughing. 'I've no wish to emulate Methuselah.'

CHAPTER SIX

Underwoods had been a house of women, and the advent of a man changed the atmosphere completely. The three women had been very happy together, but the male element was stimulating and life took on an added flavour. It was extremely pleasant – Barbie discovered – to hear a man's voice. She had not heard a man's voice for months (except doctors' voices inquiring about her symptoms, which didn't really count).

At dinner that night they were very gay. It was a 'party.' The food was excellent, Aunt Amalie had opened a bottle of hock and they had all dressed up for the occasion. It was the first time since her illness that Barbie had put on a pretty frock and she felt that she looked her best – which is always a pleasant feeling. They talked and laughed. Edward told them what he had been doing; it was mostly about his job but he made it entertaining. He told them about his Service Flat and the woman who came in and 'did' for him; he told them about a sale of furniture which he had attended with the object of buying a coal-scuttle and his subsequent discovery that he had bought two candlesticks and a picture by mistake.

It was part of Edward's charm that he noticed things. He noticed Barbie's frock and told her that the colour brought out the golden lights in her hair; he enjoyed the food which Penney had cooked, and complimented her on her skill, and added laughingly that if she ever found herself out of a job he would engage her at a fabulous salary; and he noticed a very lovely emerald ring which Amalie was wearing.

'I haven't seen *that* before,' said Edward.

'It's been in the bank,' explained Amalie. 'I was looking over some things in the bank and I decided to get it out and wear it occasionally. Ned gave it to me,' she added, taking it off and passing it round the table.

They all looked at it and admired it.

'It's a beautiful stone,' declared Edward. 'Father knew all about stones, didn't he? But look! It's a bit loose in

its setting. You ought to have that put right, Amie, dear.'
(He had always called her Amie. It was a childish mixture
of Mummy and Amalie and had solved one of the problems of
a step-mother. Pronounced as Edward pronounced it, in
the French manner, the little name meant 'friend,' and
that was exactly what Amalie had always tried to be to her
little step-son.)

Barbie examined the ring and saw that one of the little
claws which held the stone was broken. 'It's just as well you
noticed it,' she said.

'It wants cleaning too,' declared Edward. 'If you like
I'll take it with me on Monday when I go back to town
and get it put right.'

'I wish you would, if it isn't a bother,' said Amalie.

It was no bother to Edward; he liked doing things for
people. So the little white case which belonged to the ring
was fetched from Amalie's bedroom and Edward put it away
carefully in his pocket.

Barbie had been almost afraid to meet Edward, for in
spite of what Aunt Amalie had said she was not happy about
Underwoods and still felt she was defrauding Edward of his
rights. It would not have been so bad if Edward had known –
but he did not know, and she had no idea what he would
feel about it. Barbie liked everything fair and square. She
liked to know where she stood. She felt she was meeting
Edward on false pretences. Of course she could do nothing
about it (for Aunt Amalie had said 'No,' quite firmly) but
the feeling that she was defrauding Edward made her
especially kind to him that evening.

At nine o'clock Penney hauled her off to bed and Edward
was left to chat to his step-mother in the drawing-room.

'She's lovely,' said Edward after a short silence.

'Yes, she is,' agreed Amalie. 'Barbie always was lovely.'

'I mean she's lovelier. She used to be a little too fat,'
said Edward. 'It suits her to be slender. Oh, of course she
was always a dear pet, and very good fun, but there was
something a little off-putting about her.'

'Whatever do you mean?'

'Difficult to explain – exactly,' said Edward thoughtfully.
'She used to be a bit too sure of herself; she liked to run
things and thought she knew better than anyone else. There's
a new softness and gentleness about her.'

It was true, thought Amalie. Barbie had changed since her illness and had become more gentle . . . and, now that she was not so plump, she was almost beautiful. There was something very beautiful about the way her eyes were set and their constantly changing expression. Barbie's eyes could laugh when the rest of her face was sober; they could sparkle with anger or melt in softness. Her lashes were thick and soft; a deep copper-brown which was just a little darker than her hair. Her eyes were grey-green and bright like running water.

'Of course I haven't seen her for ages,' continued Edward. 'I've always been fond of Barbie, but I had forgotten what an attractive creature she is.'

'I've often wondered why you don't see each other more often,' Amalie said. 'You used to be great friends when you were children.'

'We still are!' exclaimed Edward. He paused for a moment and then added, 'Of course I know what you mean. It's my fault that we haven't seen more of each other. I couldn't see her while I was in South Africa but I ought to have looked her up when I got back. I meant to, but I never seemed to have time. I was busy settling in to the office and learning the ropes . . . and London is such a big place. You're apt to get in with a set of people and go round with them. It's a constant whirl. You never have time to see other people – outside your own particular set.'

'It seems a pity,' said Amalie.

'Yes. Yes, it is,' agreed Edward. 'We must meet in London. She might like to go to some dances. Meantime I shall be able to come down here for week-ends. Is Barbie going to be here long?'

'As long as I can keep her,' said Amalie smiling to herself.

Meanwhile Barbie had gone to bed and Penney was putting things ready for the night.

'I shall have to get out of my invalid ways,' said Barbie watching the usual preparations.

'Gradually,' agreed Penney. 'There's no hurry; you're still far from strong. For instance you're very tired tonight.'

She was tired – too tired to sleep – and there was a great deal to think about which did not help matters. First of all there was Edward. It was so long since she had seen him that she had forgotten how attractive he was . . . or perhaps he was more attractive now than he had been in the past. We must ask him to the flat, she decided. I wonder what Nell would think of Edward . . . and what he would think of Nell. It would be fun if they fell for each other . . . Edward has much more in him than all those silly boys who trail after her . . . and he's very eligible.

Thinking of all this made her think of Underwoods, which was to belong to her in the dim and distant future – to her and not to Edward. She had been so upset at the idea that she had wondered if she could give the place to Edward when the time came, but now she began to realise that it would not be right. Uncle Ned was wise and kind; he had wanted her to have his beloved Underwoods, to make it her home and keep it as it should be kept. (She wondered if he had left her any money for its upkeep – if not it would be difficult – but probably he had done so, for he was a sensible man.) This being so she must accept the responsibility and enjoy it and be happy about it – as Aunt Amalie had said. Barbie went on thinking about the future: perhaps she would marry and have children and bring them up here, in these lovely surroundings. They would play in the garden and in the woods and they would climb the trees and run along the top of the wall. Curiously enough Barbie's future husband was nebulous but her children seemed quite real: a girl and a boy with fair hair – not red – and blue eyes. I'll get them a donkey, thought Barbie. He must be called Amos.

It was her last thought before she went to sleep.

There was a very good golf course at Shepherdsford, and on Saturday morning Edward went off with his clubs saying he wanted some exercise and fresh air. He would be sure to find somebody who wanted a game. He would lunch at the club and be back about five if that would suit Amie.

It suited very well.

The house seemed quiet after Edward's departure – at least it seemed quiet to Barbie – but soon after he had gone Mrs Mainwaring dropped in to see Aunt Amalie and to chat about her daughter's wedding which was to take place quite soon. The Mainwarings lived at Melville Manor about two miles the other side of Shepherdsford; they were near neighbours and had been friends for many years. Of course Barbie had known Elsie Mainwaring when they were both children but she had not seen much of her since.

'You must meet Elsie, now that you're better,' said Mrs Mainwaring. 'You must come over to lunch one day and see all her presents – and of course you must come to the wedding. It was meant to be a quiet wedding but it has grown and grown. George says we must have a marquee in the garden.'

'You'll have to,' declared Amalie. 'You could never get all those people into your house. Have you fixed up about the catering?'

Barbie left them talking and went to find Penney, who was in the kitchen preparing delectable food. She was beating up white of egg and on the table beside her were several large oranges and a pile of castor sugar.

'Orange meringues!' exclaimed Barbie in delight.

'Yes,' nodded Penney. 'We had them last time Mr Steyne was here and he liked them. Did you want me for something?'

'Just to talk to, that's all. Aunt Amalie and Mrs Mainwaring were talking about The Wedding – and I was bored. I wonder what Elsie is like now. She was a silly child so I expect she's a silly young woman.'

'She's very pretty,' said Penney. 'Not as pretty as Miss Babbington but much the same colouring.'

'Nell *is* pretty, isn't she?'

'I think she's beautiful,' said Penney simply.

'Go on,' said Barbie smiling encouragingly. 'You were going to say more and then you stopped.'

'It was silly, really; I was going to say she reminded me of Sweet Nell of Old Drury – pretty, witty Nell – but how could she?'

'It's the association of ideas,' Barbie pointed out. 'Nell, Covent Garden and oranges . . . and Charles falling for her in a big way. People are always falling for Nell in a big way.'

'I don't blame Charles if she was like that,' said Penney beating furiously.

'You do talk funny,' said Daphne the Daily who had

come into the kitchen for her elevenses. 'It beats me 'ow you know what each other means. Are you 'aving a cuppa, Miss Barbie?'

Barbie said she would. She sat down at the kitchen table and shared a pot of dark brown tea with Daphne. Penney, who liked her tea very weak, took one look at the brew, and said she wouldn't bother – she must finish making her meringues.

'You're missing something,' declared Barbie, putting her elbows on the table and sipping with obvious enjoyment. 'This is what I call tea, Penney. It's got body.'

Daphne was still brooding over the conversation which she had overheard. 'It beats me 'ow you know what each other means,' she repeated. 'I s'pose it's edjucation. I never 'ad edjucation – didn't want it *then* but I'm sorry *now*. I get books from the lib'ry, but there's lots in them I can't make 'ead or tail of. Gets my goat sometimes.'

'You went to school, didn't you?' asked Barbie, who was vitally interested in the affairs of her fellow human beings.

'Only when I 'ad to,' admitted Daphne. 'There was six at 'ome, all younger than me, and I liked 'elping. Besides school doesn't teach you things like I mean. It's edjucation does that.'

Barbie pondered the matter. It was a curious point of view and she could not make up her mind whether there was anything in it – or not. Could you go to school, and learn what they taught you, and yet not be 'edjucated' sufficiently to understand books out of the 'lib'ry'?

Meanwhile Daphne was swilling the dregs of her tea into the slop-basin and examining the residue of tea-leaves in her cup.

'Ow!' she exclaimed. 'That's a fish, that is. Means a letter coming from overseas! That's a ring at the bottom – the only ring I'm likely to get is the door-bell – but it ain't no fun reading your own,' added Daphne meaningly.

'Who taught you?' asked Barbie, swilling out her cup and passing it across the table to be read.

'My grannie. She could tell you! It made your 'air curl the things she told you – knew all the patter, she did! I can't do it proper.' Daphne took the cup and added, 'It's just fun, you know, Miss Barbie.'

Barbie agreed it was 'just fun' and promised not to be

unduly elated nor depressed when she heard her fortune. After this somewhat unpromising opening she did not expect much from Daphne and was somewhat surprised at the result, for Daphne was quite an impressive seer and it was obvious she had had a lot of practice.

Peering into the cup Daphne discovered 'a tall stranger' (there is always a tall stranger in everybody's tea-cup).

'See, Miss Barbie, there 'e is,' said Daphne. 'And there's a little cross quite near 'im. That means trouble.'

'Trouble?' asked Barbie, playing up.

'Some sort of trouble – it's a sort of warning. You'll rue the day. You've got to beware of 'im – see?'

Barbie nodded solemnly.

'There's wedding-bells,' continued Daphne. 'That'll be Miss Mainwaring's wedding most likely . . . and there's an important letter from the north that'll change your life. You'll lose something – it'll be something valuable – but you'll find it again all right. There's a ring – see, Miss Barbie, it's down there at the bottom of the cup. There'll be trouble about money . . . and you'll go a journey and a voyage across the water . . .'

There was quite a lot more – in fact all the usual prophecies – and, as Barbie was an inveterate 'fortune-hunter' and always made a bee-line for the gipsy's tent at a fair, she had heard it all before; but this morning she was more interested than usual. Daphne had said it was 'just fun' but her face was intent and serious; it really seemed as if she believed in all the nonsense herself.

And what nonsense it was, thought Barbie. Everyone met tall strangers – at one time or other – and received important letters and went on journeys and crossed the water, and lost their belongings and found them again!

When the fortune-telling was over Barbie pressed half a crown into Daphne's hand and only then remembered that they had been wasting Aunt Amalie's time, as well as their own, for Daphne was paid by the hour.

'Cut along, Daphne,' said Barbie rather guiltily. 'I'll wash all these dishes for you.'

CHAPTER SEVEN

Some days after this Barbie was invited to lunch at Melville Manor to renew her acquaintance with Elsie and see the wedding presents. Amalie passed on the invitation and was surprised to discover that Barbie would have preferred to stay at home.

'Not go!' exclaimed Amalie. 'I thought it would be a nice change for you – and you used to be great friends with Elsie!'

Barbie remained silent. It would not be a nice change and she never had been great friends with Elsie. It was true that she and Elsie had played together when they were children, but it had not been of Barbie's choosing; Aunt Amalie's friendship with Elsie's mother had thrown them together – that was all. The friendships of one generation seldom extend to the next, and the mere fact that she was expected to love Elsie dearly did not help matters.

'I don't see what excuse you can give,' added Aunt Amalie with a worried frown.

Before her illness this would not have weighed with Barbie, but now it did. She said quickly, 'Darling, don't worry. Of course I'll go. Perhaps Elsie isn't as silly as she used to be.'

Unfortunately Elsie was just as silly and even more intolerable. She displayed her presents with smug complacency and then lured Barbie upstairs to display her trousseau.

'We must have a good talk,' declared Elsie. 'It's so nice for me to have someone like you to talk to. You're so clever, Barbie.'

'Clever?' said Barbie. 'I don't think – '

'Oh well, I don't mean clever. I just mean you've been about the world and seen things, that's all.'

Barbie was slightly annoyed. It was quite illogical to be annoyed for she did not think she was clever – and had been about to say so – but it is one thing to say this yourself and quite another thing when another person says it . . . especially if the other person happens to be Elsie.

'There are all sorts of things I want to know,' continued

Elsie, sinking on to a chair in an elegant manner. 'I'm just a Home Bird. I don't know anything about marriage.'

'I've never been married either,' Barbie pointed out.

'But I expect you *know*,' said Elsie in significant tones. 'You've lived in London and had so much Experience of Life.'

Barbie could not make up her mind whether to laugh or be very angry, but looking at Elsie sitting there, wide-eyed and innocent, she decided to be wide-eyed and innocent too. 'I've had a good deal of experience at Garfield's if that's what you mean,' said Barbie solemnly. 'We do Interior Decorating.'

'Interior Decorating?'

'That's my business,' explained Barbie. 'I tell you what, Elsie. If you want my advice about decorating your house I'll give it to you free – for old times' sake.'

'But I don't want a house,' declared Elsie. 'At least not just at once. Walter and I are going to New Zealand for our honeymoon. We shall be away for six months at least. Perhaps when we come back we might have a flat in Town but I haven't made up my mind.'

'What does Walter want to do?'

'I don't know – really. He talks about buying a farm, but I shouldn't like that. Think of me on a farm!' she added with a little laugh. 'Can you see me milking the cows?'

Barbie could not.

'You know, Barbie,' said Elsie confidentially. 'Sometimes I feel I just want to stay at home with Daddy and Mummy and not marry Walter at all. What do you think I should do?'

'It seems a little late to change your mind.'

'Oh, I haven't!' cried Elsie. 'At least not really. I mean it would break Walter's heart. It's just that I'm so terribly sensitive and sometimes I wonder if Walter *understands* . . .'

If Elsie had been in real trouble she would have found help and sympathy in Barbie, but she was not in trouble at all. She had no doubts about marrying Walter; she had him in chains and would keep him, come weal come woe.

After this somewhat unsatisfactory talk Barbie was anxious to see the prospective bridegroom (he must be a fool of course but one could not help being sorry for the creature); so she made a point of being at home when he was brought to Underwoods to be introduced to Aunt Amalie. She formed the opinion that Walter was 'nice.' He was not particularly brilliant nor was he handsome, but he was much too good for Elsie. Barbie did not speak to him much but she glanced at him several times while Elsie was talking to Aunt Amalie and decided that he was not completely happy. In fact Walter looked as if he were beginning to have qualms about his marriage; already the chains had begun to chafe.

Barbie had said she was bored with Elsie Mainwaring's wedding – at least that was what she had meant – and she was even more bored with it before the Great Day arrived. Nobody seemed to be able to talk about anything else and Mrs Mainwaring dropped in nearly every morning to discuss the arrangements with Aunt Amalie and to ask in doleful accents what on earth they would do if it happened to be wet. Mrs Mainwaring was sure it would be wet, the marquee would leak and the guests would bring in lumps of mud and tramp them into her new drawing-room carpet. Or, even if it were fine, something else would happen to mar the occasion: Elsie's dress would not be ready in time; one of the bridesmaids would be ill or perhaps the organ in Shepherdsford Church – which everyone knew was somewhat temperamental – would suddenly cease to function. As the day approached Mrs Mainwaring became increasingly worried and even Aunt Amalie, who was an extremely patient and sympathetic friend, began to get a little tired of her.

Fortunately Mrs Mainwaring was wrong. The day was warm and sunny; not a cloud marred the brilliant blue sky. When Barbie looked out of her bedroom window in the early morning she decided that if anything the day would be too hot . . . but of course she could wear the new frock which Aunt Amalie had given her. It was very pale-green nylon and would be pleasantly cool.

Edward was coming to Underwoods for the wedding – which would be nice, thought Barbie – and it was pleasant to think that after today there would be no more talk about the boring affair, for it would be over and done with.

Barbie leaned out of her window and sniffed appreciatively; there were real flowers in the garden now – not only their ghosts. She reflected that she would be terribly homesick for all this beauty when she returned to London and her job. She was fit now, or very nearly, but Dr Ladbrooke who was rather an old fuss had told her to take another month. That would be the beginning of July – and the tenth of July was Aunt Amalie's birthday, so she would wait and go back after that. She *must* go back after that; she must turn a deaf ear to all persuasions and objections from Aunt Amalie and Penney – dear pets that they were!

The day became hotter and more brilliant. Edward arrived in his car and said London was like an oven – and ran upstairs to change. He took so long over the business that they were all ready and waiting for lunch when he came down . . . but he had not wasted his time, thought Barbie. The formal clothes suited Edward; he looked marvellous. He looked more like a bridegroom than a wedding guest.

'Are we going in my car or in yours?' asked Edward as he sat down and unfolded his table-napkin.

'Both,' replied Amalie. 'You've got to be there early, so – '

'Good lord!' exclaimed Edward. 'I forgot I was ushering! I'll have to be quick.'

'If you're going to eat soup quickly you had better tuck in your table-napkin,' said his step-mother warningly.

He smiled at her and did so, as if he had been a small boy. 'How right you are, Amie!' he said. 'A grease spot would be a disaster.'

The meal was finished without any disaster and Edward rushed off in his car. The others followed more slowly.

Shepherdsford Church was a beautiful old building in the Norman style; usually it was rather cold and bleak and, (sad to say), half empty; but today it was *en fête* with its bells ringing joyfully and a red carpet at the door; it was full of flowers and the scent of flowers; full of a fashionably-dressed throng of people who had come from far and wide to see Elsie Mainwaring married to Walter Summers.

It all went off splendidly – none of Mrs Mainwaring's fears were realised. The bride was beautiful in her white satin and lace, the bridesmaids were in attendance and the organ pealed out the wedding march at the right moment. When it was over, the chains securely welded, the guests found their cars and went on to the reception at Melville Manor – and here, too, everything was as it should be.

A marquee is usually hot and stuffy and today it was

hotter and stuffier than usual for the sun had been beating down upon it for hours. Barbie lost Aunt Amalie in the crush and was hemmed into a corner and, what with the heat and the noise, she began to feel rather queer. Quite suddenly she could not bear it a moment longer. Fortunately there was a loose flap in the tent and she was able to pull it aside and slip out. She was sure nobody would notice her absence, for they were all too busy talking, and in any case it was better to slip out quietly than to faint and cause a commotion. It was hot outside of course, but the air was sweet and after a few deep breaths she felt better and was able to walk across the lawn to a seat beneath a tree.

There was nobody about; not a creature. They were all herded together inside that stuffy tent! Afterwards they would groan and moan and say the tent was like a furnace and the noise was awful and the speeches were dull – but at the moment they all seemed perfectly satisfied with their entertainment.

People are odd, thought Barbie. It would be so much more pleasant to walk about the garden. Not one single creature has thought of escaping, except me . . . but apparently one other creature had had the same thought as Barbie. He emerged from the loose flap – just as she had done – and was coming towards her across the grass, carrying a small tray with two glasses and a piece of cake. He was a big man with broad shoulders, and was dressed in a grey flannel suit (not in traditional wedding garments) and, as he came nearer, Barbie noticed that his hair was thick and brown, he was clean-shaven and had very blue eyes. She had never seen him before but she was sure he was a sailor.

'I hope you don't mind,' he said. 'I saw you slip out and I thought you might be feeling a bit faint.'

'Yes, I did,' replied Barbie. 'I've been ill, you see. I just felt I couldn't bear it a moment longer.'

'I thought it might be something like that.'

'I'm all right now.'

He nodded and said, 'A glass of fizz will complete the cure.'

Barbie smiled and agreed.

Apparently he took this as an invitation and putting the tray upon the seat beside her he sat down at the other end. 'My name is Buckland,' he said. 'Henry Buckland. I'm a friend of Walter's. He and I were at school together. I'm

52

staying at Shepherdsford Golf Club for a week's leave . . . I say let's drink our fizz before the bubbles go off.'

'We don't deserve it. We ought to be in there, listening to the speeches and drinking their healths.'

'I know, but we can drink their healths here, can't we?'

They drank, touching glasses and saying, 'Walter and Elsie,' quite seriously. (Why do sailors always have such very blue eyes? wondered Barbie.)

'There,' he said. 'We couldn't have done it half as well in all that crowd. It meant something, didn't it?'

She nodded. It really had meant something but she was not quite sure what it had meant.

'I wouldn't have come if I had known it was going to be so posh,' continued Henry Buckland. 'I'm feeling a bit out of the picture – no wedding garments, you see – but I didn't know I was coming until yesterday and there was no time to do anything about it. Walter said it didn't matter, I was just to come.'

'You look nice and cool,' she told him.

'Women score heavily,' said Henry Buckland, glancing at her. 'I mean they can be nice and cool and look absolutely right.' He paused for a moment and then continued, 'Walter is an awfully good fellow. Do you think – I mean he seemed a bit depressed. Not quite my idea of a happy bridegroom. Am I imagining things?' He looked at her anxiously and waited for her answer.

'I've known Elsie for years,' began Barbie, and then she stopped for it was impossible to say she was sure Elsie would make a good wife. But she had to say something, so she said, 'Elsie is beautiful, don't you think so?'

'Yes, beautiful – but that isn't everything you want in a wife. At least I don't think so. Of course I should want my wife to be beautiful, but I should want her to be a friend and a partner as well.'

'And a good cook,' suggested Barbie with a chuckle.

Henry Buckland did not laugh at the joke and Barbie felt sorry she had teased him. She said hastily, 'It's nice here, isn't it? I'm glad I managed to escape.'

'So am I,' he agreed.

They were silent for a few moments. It was very peaceful sitting in the shade. The marquee looked like a hive of bees – and sounded like it too – people were buzzing round it, going in and coming out, but none of them left it for very long. The hive was the centre of attraction.

'I saw you in the tent,' said Henry Buckland suddenly. 'You're Edward Steyne's cousin, aren't you? Somebody told me that's who you were.'

So he had asked who she was! 'Well, not really,' replied Barbie who was quite used to this mistake. 'Lady Steyne is my aunt and Edward is her step-son. That's how it is.'

'Then you're Miss Steyne? No, of course not. How silly of me!'

'Barbara France,' said Barbie. She was rather amused at the way in which he had made her disclose her name. 'Do you know Edward?' she asked. He had mentioned Edward so it was a natural question.

'Not very well,' he replied. 'I've met him at the Golf Club, but we've never had a game. He's a lot better than I am. Tigers don't play with rabbits. Why should they?'

They went on talking. He told her that he had been abroad for two years and had just got back; his next job was to be in London, at the Admiralty (so he *was* a sailor!). He was not looking forward to it much. Sitting in an office was not his idea of bliss – and unless you had a home near London it might be a bit lonely. He had a married sister in Scotland but no other relations at all. In return Barbie told him that normally she lived in London, in a flat which she shared with a friend, but at present she was staying with her aunt recovering from an illness.

'We might meet in London,' he suggested.

Barbie replied vaguely. If she had been Nell she would have 'clicked' but Barbie was more cautious.

There was nothing brilliant about the conversation but Barbie was conscious of an undercurrent. Their two voices chimed together pleasantly. Henry Buckland's voice was deep; it was a real man's voice. He had lived so much with men and was so intensely masculine that he made her feel very feminine. They were silly words – masculine and feminine – thought Barbie, but she could find no others to describe the sensation he gave her.

'What about the cake?' he said at last, looking at the slab of wedding cake which lay on the plate between them. 'I should have brought a knife, shouldn't I?'

'Sailors always have knives in their pockets.'

'This one hasn't – not in these trousers!'

'Little Tom Tucker,' said Barbie without thinking.

The blue eyes looked at her quickly. 'You mean the chap that sang for his supper. Didn't he have a knife?'

She shook her head.

'Go on,' he said. 'Tell me about him. I only know that he sang for his supper. What happened after that?'

Barbie hesitated for a moment and then she said:

'Little Tom Tucker
Sang for his supper.
What did he sing for?
White bread and butter.
How can I cut it without a knife?
How can I marry without a wife?'

Henry Buckland nodded. 'How could he, poor devil? Perhaps he was a Naval Officer and hadn't much chance of finding a wife.'

'I thought they had a wife in every port,' smiled Barbie.

Her companion abandoned the subject. 'I shall have to break it,' he said. He took the piece of cake and broke it in half and, as he did so, a tiny packet fell on to the plate. It was a golden bell, very small but perfectly shaped with a little tongue inside.

'How pretty!' exclaimed Barbie. 'I've never seen one like it before.'

'Yes, it's nice,' he agreed. 'Would you like it fixed on to your bracelet? I could do it in a minute.'

Barbie took off her bracelet and handed it over. There were other charms on the bracelet and each one had a history: the tiny jade pig was a gift from Nell for her birthday; the golden slipper was from a 'satisfied customer' – a woman at Guildford whose house had been redecorated under Barbie's direction. The woman had wanted to 'give her something' and had been told that she did not accept money. Aunt Amalie had found the little gold rose among her treasures. All these charms meant something to Barbie and the new charm would mean something too. It would remind her of a delightful interlude, of very blue eyes and a deep voice.

Barbie watched her new friend fixing the new charm. It took a full minute to fix so she was able to look at him properly for the first time: the brown hair, short and thick; the strongly-moulded neck and the well-set ear. He really *was* rather nice.

'I've seen other girls wearing this sort of bracelet,' said Henry Buckland. 'Do you buy them with the charms attached?'

'No. At least I didn't. It's more fun to pick up the charms as you go along. Nell and I each bought a bracelet with some money we won on E.S.B. in the Grand National. Nell has nearly a dozen charms on her bracelet. Nell is the girl I share a flat with,' added Barbie.

'She picks up charms indiscriminately?'

Barbie did not answer that, for the fact was Nell picked up charms from her admirers – from Peter and Phil and Roddy and all the rest. Barbie did not approve of this and they had argued about it more than once. Nell had pointed out that if the creatures wanted to give her something for her birthday or for Christmas (which of course they did) it was much better that they should give her a little charm for her bracelet than waste their substance upon flowers. ('A few flowers are nice, but too many flowers are frightfully depressing – like a funeral or something,' declared Nell. 'Besides it saves their pockets. You can buy quite a nice little charm for seven and six, and flowers cost the earth.') All this was true, of course, but still Barbie did not approve . . . yet here she was, doing the same thing herself!

But it isn't the same – not really, thought Barbie. The little bell fell out of the cake. He didn't buy it for me.

It was absolutely different, but Barbie was blushing when she took the bracelet and fastened it on her wrist.

'We ought to go back,' said Barbie rising from the seat.

'Why ought we?' asked her companion. 'They're quite happy without us; we'll never be missed. As a matter of fact I don't think we *ought* to go back. The marquee will be hotter than ever by this time and you might feel faint again, you know.'

Barbie pointed to the stream of people moving across the lawn towards the house. 'Look,' she said. 'They're going to see the presents.'

'Do you want to see the presents?'

'I've seen them,' said Barbie. 'But you haven't . . . and anyhow I really must go. Aunt Amalie will be wondering what's become of me.'

He rose with reluctance. 'But look here, Miss France, we're not just going to say good-bye. I mean I'm staying at the club for a week. Couldn't we meet – somewhere? Couldn't I call?'

'Call?' said Barbie doubtfully.

'I could call on your aunt. That would be all right, wouldn't it?'

Barbie hesitated.

'She wouldn't mind, would she?'

'She wouldn't mind in the least,' said Barbie with a sudden smile. 'Aunt Amalie is the most hospitable person in the world.'

'Tomorrow afternoon?'

Barbie nodded. 'Come to tea. Aunt Amalie will be delighted to see you. It's Underwoods. Do you know where it is?'

'I can find out,' said Henry Buckland.

The words were perfectly simple but the tone was so significant that Barbie was slightly alarmed. He was going too fast. She felt quite breathless – as if she had been running.

'Au revoir!' said Barbie and ran across the grass into the house.

CHAPTER EIGHT

The wedding reception was nearly over by this time. Aunt Amalie had felt tired, so she and Penney had gone home. Edward had been invited to dinner and an informal dance, so Barbie stayed to throw a handful of confetti at the bride and bridegroom and then went home by herself. She found Aunt Amalie resting quietly in the drawing-room.

'Well, how did you get on?' asked Aunt Amalie. 'It wasn't as boring as you expected – at least you don't look as if you had been terribly bored.'

'I wasn't bored at all,' replied Barbie laughing. 'As a matter of fact I met a rather nice man and I've asked him to tea tomorrow. He's a sailor and his name is Henry Buckland. I hope you don't mind.'

'Of course I don't mind. It will be very pleasant to meet a nice man – and he must be very nice indeed to make you look like that,' added Amalie smiling.

Barbie blushed. She said hastily, 'Oh well, perhaps it was the fizz – or something' (which was nonsense because she had had only one glass). 'Anyhow it was a good party,' added Barbie. 'Elsie looked really beautiful and none of Mrs Mainwaring's doleful prophecies came true.'

They talked about the wedding – who was there and who was not – and the frightful heat in the marquee. Aunt Amalie thought Mrs Mainwaring's hat was 'rather a mistake'; Barbie thought it was a disaster. Aunt Amalie thought the bridegroom had 'looked a little pale'; Barbie thought he had looked absolutely miserable. In fact the two ladies were in perfect agreement.

Barbie was tired that night. She went to bed early and was asleep and dreaming long before Edward returned; but Amalie had waited up for him. Amalie never slept very well so it was no use going to bed early. She sat and read in the quiet drawing-room until she heard Edward's car.

'Not in bed yet, darling!' exclaimed Edward dropping a light kiss on the top of her head. 'Sitting up waiting for the roisterer's return – and reading – let me see – Ayala's Angel! How often have you read Ayala's Angel?'

Amalie smiled. 'Oh, I know it isn't supposed to be one of his best, but it appeals to me. Ayala is so human. Real people behave like that.'

'Like what?' asked Edward, who had not read the story.

'Misunderstand each other and make a mess of things.'

Edward hesitated and then he said: 'Just what do you mean by that, Amie dear?'

Amalie did not reply. Perhaps she was not quite sure what she had meant.

'You meant something, didn't you?' asked Edward. 'You were just thinking about the book. If you were thinking about Barbie and me you needn't worry. We understand each other all right.'

'Are you sure, Edward?'

'Yes, of course.'

There was a little silence. Amalie was remembering Barbie's face when she came back from the wedding.

'Look here,' said Edward. 'You know what I feel about it. I practically told you – and I could see you understood.'

She nodded.

'Amie! You don't mean there's somebody else?'

'Goodness, no!' exclaimed Amalie a little too vehemently. 'I just mean – what I said.'

'There *is* somebody else.'

'No, Edward. It's just that I'm not sure –' she hesitated.

Edward sat down beside her and took her hand. 'Look, darling,' he said. 'You had better tell me. You want us to get married, don't you? It would be a pity if there was a misunderstanding and we "made a mess of things" when a little plain speaking would clear it all up. Of course Barbie and I aren't engaged officially – or anything like that – but we've always been sweethearts since we were children. We drifted apart a bit when I went abroad, but that was just – well, it was just temporary. I've always felt sure of Barbie, if you know what I mean.'

Amalie knew exactly what he meant; he was free to wander where he liked and Barbie was supposed to sit and wait for him! It was not often that she was cross with Edward, for she loved him dearly, but this was really a little too much. She said with some asperity, 'I'm quite sure Barbie doesn't feel "engaged" either officially or unofficially, and she's very attractive – you said so yourself.'

'Darling, don't be cross with me. Of course Barbie is attractive. She's a little like you.'

'She isn't in the least like me.'

'Not in colouring of course, but there is a look of you in Barbie. You both have the same lovely eyes. I bet you had lots of admirers when you were younger.'

'The best butter,' said Amalie, but she was smiling.

'It's true,' declared Edward. 'Not butter at all – but never mind. Tell me about Barbie's admirers.'

'I don't know anything,' she replied. 'I was just trying to warn you that you may not be the only pebble on the beach.' She laughed and added, 'For instance there's a young man coming to tea tomorrow afternoon.'

'Who?'

'Oh, there's nothing in it – just a young man called Buckland. Barbie met him at the wedding and –'

'Buckland! Good lord, he's an absolute menace!' exclaimed Edward in dismay. 'What on earth is Barbie thinking of to take up with a fellow like that?'

'She hasn't "taken up" with him. He's just a casual acquaintance. I only mentioned him to show you that other people probably find her attractive, that's all.'

'Buckland – coming here to tea!'

'You're making far too much of it,' declared Amalie. 'Why shouldn't she ask a young man to tea? It's dull for her here.'

'You won't like him.'

'Well, it doesn't matter. I suppose I can be pleasant to him and give him a cup of tea even if I don't like him much. You won't be here (you're going back to town tomorrow) so it won't matter to you.'

'I wish I were going to be here,' declared Edward. 'Buckland really is a menace. They call him Force Eight Buckland – that shows you the type of fellow he is.'

'Force Eight?'

'Means a gale,' explained Edward briefly. He rose and added in quite a different tone of voice, 'You're tired, Amie darling, and it's frightfully late. I shouldn't have kept you talking like this. You run upstairs and pop into bed and I'll lock up everything.'

Amalie did as she was told. She was tired – and also a little worried. She had not intended to tell Edward about Barbie's new friend but just to warn him that Barbie was an attractive young woman and if he really wanted to marry her he had better do something about it soon. It did not take her long to 'pop into bed'; she was in bed when Edward looked in to say good night.

'Don't worry,' said Edward, who seemed to have regained his usual cheerfulness. 'Everything will be all right. I've got to go back to town tomorrow but I'll come down next week-end. Things are very quiet just now so I can get away quite easily.'

Barbie had gone to bed feeling at peace with the world. It would be amusing to see Henry Buckland again. She was looking forward to it. Of course there was nothing 'special' about it; he had said he would call and she had asked him to tea – she could scarcely have done less – but somehow by the morning her feelings had changed and she wished she had not asked him. In the cold light of day she realised that it was not just a casual invitation to a man she had met at a party. It meant more. She was not sure that she wanted it to mean more.

The morning passed very slowly. Edward went off in his car and Penney was busy as usual. Penney made a coffee cake for tea.

'Men always like coffee cakes,' said Penny cheerfully. 'I've made some scones as well. You won't mind doing the tea, will you? Lady Steyne said I could go out and I thought I might take the bus to Cheltenham.'

'Yes, of course,' said Barbie.

'If you'd rather I stayed in and –'

'No, of course I can do it. Off you go!'

Aunt Amalie rested in the afternoon, so Barbie had ample time to wander round the deserted house and tell herself she had been a fool, but when she had laid the tea and changed into a new and very pretty cotton frock her mood changed again and she began to feel pleased and excited. It was quite ridiculous to feel excited but somehow she was – just a little. She was sure he would come early so she was all ready at four o'clock, but at half past four when Aunt Amalie came downstairs he had not arrived.

'We'll just have tea,' said Barbie. 'No need to wait.'

'We had better wait a little,' said Aunt Amalie. 'Something may have delayed him – or he might have thought we had tea at five. Lots of people do.'

They waited until five but there was no sign of the expected guest, nor any message, so Barbie made the tea.

'Something must have happened to delay him,' said Aunt Amalie for the third – or fourth – time.

'He could have phoned.'

'Perhaps he couldn't find the house.'

'He could have asked. Anybody could have told him.'

Amalie looked at her. There were two bright spots of red in her cheeks and her eyes were blazing. It was obvious that Barbie was very angry indeed. Like most 'redheads' Barbie's temper was somewhat fiery. Amalie knew this, but all the same she was surprised. 'I expect he'll ring up later and explain,' she said in a soothing voice.

'I expect he's forgotten all about it,' declared Barbie with a little laugh that did not ring quite true.

'Barbie, it doesn't matter. I mean you don't really mind –'

'No, of course not. Why should I mind? He was merely

a chance acquaintance. I asked him because he seemed to want to come.'

'You're upset, darling.'

'No. At least I am, in a way, because it's so rude – I hate people who are rude.'

'There may be some reason –'

'Oh, for goodness' sake don't let's talk about it any more!' exclaimed Barbie.

They talked about other things in a desultory manner and Barbie calmed down a little – at least outwardly. Inwardly she was still very angry. The man had made a fool of her; he had buttered her up and wangled an invitation to tea – and then not come. He had made her look an absolute fool. All that fuss! A special cake baked for him; a special frock put on! All that fuss!

When Penney returned she naturally inquired how the tea-party had gone off and was informed that the visitor had not come.

'Oh, what a pity,' said Penney in a matter-of-fact voice and proceeded to talk about her own doings and the convenience of the bus service . . . but even Penney's tact was annoying.

After dinner the telephone bell rang and Barbie went to answer it. She was prepared to be perfectly cool. She was prepared to say that it did not matter in the least. She was prepared to listen to his explanations and to tell him that she was sorry but it was impossible to fix another day for him to come . . . but it was not Henry Buckland. It was Nell's voice, warm and sweet and friendly, to ask how she was ('You aren't doing too much, are you, darling?') and to suggest that Nell might come to lunch on Sunday if that would be convenient.

'Yes, of course,' said Barbie. 'I'm sure it will be all right. Who is bringing you?'

'Rupert,' said Nell. 'Oh, he's just a man I met the other day at a cocktail party. He's going to play golf at Shepherdsford, so he can have lunch at the club and pick me up in the afternoon. It will all fit in beautifully.'

This conversation soothed Barbie and she felt a good deal better when she put down the receiver. It would be lovely to see Nell on Sunday – and Edward would be here. Barbie had been wondering how to arrange a meeting between her two friends, a quite natural sort of meeting, and now it was going to take place without any bother at all.

The next few days passed quietly and pleasantly. Nothing was heard of Henry Buckland and nothing was said about him; but that did not mean the incident was forgotten. Amalie could not get it out of her mind. She thought about it as she wielded the hoe in her garden and picked off the heads of the violas. The whole affair was so unlike Barbie that she was puzzled. Barbie was really a level-headed creature; it was unlike her to fall for 'a chance acquaintance' and if he were merely that – and nothing more – why had she been so angry when he did not come? Amalie wondered whether she should suggest ringing up the club and finding out the reason, but decided not to. Presumably if Barbie really wanted to see the man, she would think of that herself.

Being of the older generation Amalie was apt to 'fear the worst' and, if any of her friends or relations failed to appear when she expected them, she immediately conjured up frightful visions of sudden illnesses or motor accidents or other calamities, but she was aware that young people are exempt from this folly. She also was aware (when she thought about it seriously) that if the man had had a motor accident and been killed they would have heard. Shepherdsford was a small place and anything exciting was a topic of conversation for days. Daphne would have heard every detail and certainly would not have kept the news to herself.

Barbie did not seem to be upset. She seemed much as usual – or was she a little too cheerful? It was hard to tell. How good it was to be old! thought Amalie. How peaceful to live for one's garden – 'all passion spent'! She was fond of her friends and she loved Edward and Barbie. It would make her happy if they married. If they married and had a child she would feel like a grandmother (like two grandmothers really, thought Amalie, smiling at the ridiculous idea). It would be delightful if things went like that; but if they did not she would accept what came and make the best of it. She would not worry – or at least she would not worry much. It was true that she had been just a trifle worried about this strange man who had set Barbie alight. Edward had said he was 'a menace' which had sounded somewhat alarming. But the strange man had not come, so that was all right – or wasn't it? wondered Amalie.

Edward arrived at lunch-time on Saturday. They had expected him to play golf in the afternoon and had arranged a shopping expedition to Cheltenham but instead of playing golf as usual he declared his intention of coming with them.

'It will be fun,' he said. 'I haven't been to Cheltenham for years. I'll take you over in my car and we can have tea at the George Hotel.'

'Barbie and I have shopping to do,' said Amalie in warning tones, but even this failed to deter him and the expedition was a great success.

CHAPTER NINE

The meeting between Edward and Nell took place in the hall at Underwoods. There was nothing in the least dramatic about it; they were introduced and acknowledged the introduction in a perfectly ordinary way. Barbie had thought about this meeting so much that she was a little disappointed – but what had she expected? She could scarcely have expected that her two friends, meeting for the first time, would fly into each other's arms.

At lunch the conversation was general, Edward and Nell spoke to each other quite naturally, neither more nor less than occasion demanded. Nell talked about what she had been doing in town; Edward said town was uncomfortably warm and he wished he were a farmer.

'Lots of people wish that – in the summer,' said Nell.

Half-way through the meal Edward suddenly remembered something. He rose and went round the table and put a little white case beside Amalie's plate.

'Oh, my ring!' she exclaimed.

'Your ring,' agreed Edward. 'It's taken a long time to do but here it is at last.' He opened the little case, took out the ring and held it up for them to see. The emerald sparkled and flashed green fire in the sunshine.

'What a lovely ring!' cried Nell.

'What a difference the cleaning has made!' exclaimed Penney.

Edward smiled. He took Amalie's hand and kissed it and slipped the ring on to her finger. 'There,' he said. 'You've always been my very dear Amie; now we're officially engaged.'

Amalie tried to laugh but the laugh was a trifle shaky and she saw the green stone winking at her through a haze of tears. She had always tried to be Edward's friend; it was wonderful to know that he appreciated it. Sometimes he had caused her anxiety but he was a dear boy, her own dear Edward. She would have liked to say something of what was in her heart but she could not trust herself to speak . . . and in any case she could not have said much with the others sitting round the table listening.

'I think the chap has done it quite well,' Edward was saying. 'He's a working jeweller – an awfully decent fellow. He says it's a particularly fine stone. Well, we knew that before, didn't we? If you want anything else done I can give you his address.'

After lunch they all went out and walked round the garden which was now a blaze of colour. It was nearly the end of June and a spell of bright sunshine had brought on the flowers in a rush. Nell adored flowers and ran from one bed to another exclaiming in admiration and delight . . . and of course her hostess began to pick them for her, saying: 'You would like some freesias, would you, Miss Babbington? And what about a few sweet peas? Delphiniums look lovely in a tall vase . . . and you must have some of these pink asters to go with them.'

Nell accepted them all.

A new rose-bed was being prepared at one end of the garden and Amalie explained that she intended to have an espalier put up, but it was difficult to get hold of 'the man.'

'I'll do it,' said Edward. 'You get the wood and I'll put it up in half no time. It's the sort of job I like.'

Having settled this matter satisfactorily they moved on to the kitchen-garden and admired the rows of peas and beans and lettuces, and once again Amalie claimed Nell's attention and led her to the cold frame where an enormous marrow was to be seen; it was growing larger every day and ripening for the Shepherdsford Flower Show.

'Dear thing, it's just like a baby!' exclaimed Nell rapturously . . . and then, noting the surprised expression of its owner, she added, 'Oh, I don't mean it looks like a baby, I just mean it's behaving like one. All good babies put on weight and grow enormously. My sister has four, so I know all about it. Her letters are always full of how many ounces the new one has gained in a week. Barbie hasn't gained many ounces, has she?'

'It isn't my fault,' said Amalie smiling. 'Nor Penney's fault either. Barbie has decided to remain slender, and I must admit it suits her.'

Nell agreed – though somewhat reluctantly. Barbie certainly was much prettier since her illness but Nell was so fond of her that she would have liked to see her exactly as she was before. (It is a strange quirk of human nature that if we are very fond of people we like them to be plump.)

When the marrow had been sufficiently admired Amalie sent off the two girls to have a chat. Of course Barbie wanted to talk to Nell so she could not complain but it seemed a pity that Edward and Nell had had so little of each other's society.

'Who is Rupert?' asked Barbie when they had gone upstairs and settled down comfortably in Barbie's bedroom.

'Oh, just a man,' said Nell. 'Rather sweet, but not terribly special. Rupert was coming to Shepherdsford to play golf. He belongs to Shepherdsford Golf Club. He said he knew Edward and had played with him several times. This afternoon Rupert had fixed a match with a man called Henry Buckland. Of course Phil would have brought me but he would have had to come to lunch, so it was much more sensible to come with Rupert, wasn't it?'

Barbie agreed. She hesitated for a moment as if she were going to ask something and then decided not to.

'What were you going to say?' asked Nell.

'Nothing important. How is Dr Headfort?'

'He's all right,' replied Dr Headfort's secretary. 'Terribly busy of course. He's got a whole lot of new patients.'

'Have you seen any more of him unprofessionally?'

'Oh well! As a matter of fact we went to Othello the other night – it was just to clear up an argument. My dear, it was too shattering! It isn't just a play; it's an experience. I say, you've got a new little charm on your bracelet. Where did you get it?'

'I got it out of Elsie's wedding cake.'

'Nice,' said Nell. 'I haven't seen one like it before.'

'What else has happened?' asked Barbie.

'That woman I told you about, who has taken the Other Flat, is getting to be a nuisance. She trips in to see me at all sorts of inconvenient moments – and now she's asked me to call her Glore.'

'Glore!'

'Short for Gloria.'

'Oh Nell!' exclaimed Barbie with one of her infectious chuckles.

'I suppose it *is* rather funny,' agreed Nell. 'But the fact is Glore has got beyond a joke.'

'Don't tell me she's a borrower!'

Nell nodded. 'Yes, and I can't refuse to give her milk, because of the child. I mean you can refuse milk to a grown-up person but not to a child.'

For several minutes they discussed the principles of borrowing with not a little bitterness for they had suffered from borrowers before. It was all very well for Polonius to say 'Neither a borrower nor a lender be' (they could not have agreed more with this admirable advice); but they had found it well-nigh impossible to refuse a neighbour who appeared upon their doorstep late on a Saturday night with an empty tea-caddy and a request for 'just a few spoonfuls – if you can spare it – to tide me over till Monday.' It was all right if it happened only occasionally, and only with small things like tea and bread and potatoes, but borrowers have borrowing in their blood and when they discover a lender they go from small things to large. Presently they begin to borrow money!

'Polonius didn't live in a flat,' said Nell with a sigh. This seemed the final word upon the matter.

'What do you think of Edward?' asked Barbie. Perhaps it was not very wise to ask, but she simply had to know.

'Means business,' said Nell, smiling.

'Means business?' echoed Barbie in bewilderment.

'Yes, my dear innocent. Edward's intentions are obvious – and strictly honourable. In other words he's simply waiting for a favourable opportunity to propose.'

'You mean – to me?'

'Who else?' asked Nell, giggling. 'You didn't think it was me, did you? I only met the man today and I haven't exchanged a dozen words with him. I may be a fast worker, but really – '

'Me?' repeated Barbie, gazing at her, wide-eyed.

'Didn't you know? Barbie, you really are a donkey!'

'You're wrong, Nell.'

'My dear, if you had seen his face when he was putting the ring on Lady Steyne's finger! It was your finger he wanted to put it on – ' She smiled mischievously and added, 'Aunt Nell has had *lots* of experience. Aunt Nell knows all about it.'

'But we've known each other all our lives! I mean we're friends. We're just like cousins.'

'But you aren't cousins,' Nell pointed out. 'And you haven't known each other all your lives. He's been away for years, hasn't he? Now he's come home and fallen in love with "the girl next door." '

Barbie was silent.

'Perhaps I shouldn't have told you,' continued Nell in a much more serious tone. 'I wouldn't have said anything, but I know you so well – and you really are such an innocent – and it's better for you to know what's coming than to be taken aback like an early Victorian heroine. At least I think it's better. I know I would rather.' She hesitated and then added, 'You can make up your mind beforehand whether to say yes or no or perhaps.'

'It will be no,' said Barbie hastily. 'I mean if he really does – '

'Are you sure?' asked Nell. 'It would be a pity to say no without considering it seriously. Edward seems to me a most engaging creature and I think you're very fond of him. I think you're sort of blinded by this "friends and cousins" idea. Why don't you put all that out of your head and give the man a chance?'

Barbie said in a dazed voice, 'I don't know. I never thought – '

At this moment a small red car drew up at the gate and hooted in a gentlemanly manner.

'It's frightfully unselfish of me to have warned you,' declared Nell, seizing her hat off the bed. 'The very last thing I want is for you to go and get married. The flat is so empty – and lonely – and so absolutely beastly without you that I believe I shall have to think of getting married myself.

There,' she added as she settled the hat at the most becoming angle, and turned her head this way and that, and looked in the glass. 'Don't you think it's rather a duck of a hat? Parks and Spender – fourteen and eleven – you'd never believe it, would you?'

Barbie said in a dazed voice that you never would believe it – unless you knew Nell – but knowing Nell you could believe it quite easily, for every hat Nell put upon her head looked as if it had come straight from Paris.

The hoots from the gate had become imperative.

'That's Rupert! I must fly!' cried Nell. 'Men are so frightfully impatient, aren't they? Good-bye, darling. Be good.'

She kissed Barbie and flew.

The last fortnight of Barbie's long stay at Underwoods passed very quickly. She had decided quite definitely to return to London immediately after Aunt Amalie's birthday and despite all persuasions she stuck to her decision. She burnt her boats by writing to Mr Garfield to say she was coming and received a letter from him by return of post. After saying he was delighted to hear she was better, and that 'everyone in the place' was looking forward to seeing her, he went on to explain that Miss Brown (her temporary substitute) was inefficient and spent most of her time stirring up trouble and quarrelling with Miss Smithers, who was in charge of the girls in the work-rooms. Several important orders had been lost and two old and valued customers were dissatisfied. Mr Garfield enclosed some correspondence from a certain Mrs Albert Bray who lived about twenty miles from Shepherdsford and asked if Miss France would go and see her while she was in the district and 'try to smooth her down.'

On reading the enclosures Miss France discovered that Mrs Bray would take a good deal of 'smoothing down,' for apparently her order for chair-coverings had been completely muddled and the lady was very angry indeed.

Barbie took the letters to Aunt Amalie and explained.

'I'll go tomorrow,' said Barbie. 'I can get a bus and go over in the afternoon.'

'I wouldn't go if I were you,' said Aunt Amalie. 'She sounds so angry. Her letters are quite rude.'

Barbie smiled. 'But that's business,' she declared. 'Sometimes people are nice and sometimes nasty. In business you have to take the rough with the smooth . . . and in any case I must go because Mr Garfield has asked me to do it and he's my boss.'

Obviously all this was an eye-opener to Aunt Amalie. 'I don't like it,' she said. 'Why should people be nasty? I'm never nasty to girls in shops.'

'Everybody isn't like you, darling.'

'I don't like it,' repeated Aunt Amalie, with a worried frown. 'I thought Garfield's was a nice job. It was silly of me but I never realised you would have to put up with rudeness and unpleasantness. However I suppose when you're there yourself there are no muddles, so the customers have no reason to complain.'

Barbie laughed – but said nothing. It was just as well for Aunt Amalie to be comforted by this extremely pleasant idea. As a matter of fact Barbie had found that customers were often rude and disagreeable when they had made the muddles themselves and therefore had no just cause for complaint. She had discovered also that it was these people who were the most difficult to pacify – these people who were uncomfortably aware that the whole thing was really their own fault.

'Oh well, you'll be leaving Garfield's soon,' added Aunt Amalie with a sigh of relief.

'Leaving Garfield's!'

'Oh, I just mean perhaps you might think of it,' said Aunt Amalie hastily – and began to talk of something else.

It was perfectly clear to Barbie what Aunt Amalie meant.

Mrs Albert Bray was tall and dark and elegant; she swept into the little room, where Barbie had been put to wait for her, and began without preamble to state her case.

'I'm furious,' she declared – quite unnecessarily, for her fury was obvious – 'I don't know why you've come. Any woman who can write such impertinent letters isn't fit to speak to – and I don't intend to listen to any excuses at all. The covers are hopeless, they aren't the pattern I chose and they look perfectly frightful in my drawing-room. I shall send them all back and I won't pay for them – not a penny – you can sue me if you like. I shall put the whole matter into the hands of my lawyer . . .'

'I just came to apologise,' said Barbie, when she was able

to get a word in edgeways.

'It's too late for apologies. I've waited weeks for the covers – I'm sick and tired of waiting – and now they're all wrong. Someone told me that Garfield's was a good firm to deal with but I've never dealt with a worse one – and I've never had such impertinent letters in my life.' She paused and looked at Barbie. 'I suppose you're Miss Brown?' she said.

'No,' replied Barbie meekly. She was not in the least annoyed with Mrs Bray, for although she had a temper which was apt to flare up at inconvenient moments she felt pretty certain that the lady had good cause to be enraged. Besides this was 'business' and Barbie rather enjoyed dealing with difficult customers. It was a sort of game to Barbie; a game which required tact and diplomacy and an understanding of human nature. To tell the truth Barbie rather liked Mrs Bray.

'You're not Miss Brown?' asked Mrs Bray in surprise.

'No,' repeated Barbie.

'Well, why on earth have you come?'

'Just to apologise, that's all.'

Mrs Bray was slightly deflated. It was impossible to go on raging at a nice-looking young woman who put up no defence – and, now that Mrs Bray had time to look at her properly, she became aware that the young woman was very nice-looking indeed. In fact she was quite beautiful, with that most unusual colouring and those expressive eyes!

'You had better come and see the covers,' said Mrs Bray.

Barbie followed Mrs Bray to the drawing-room.

'There!' said Mrs Bray, throwing open the door. 'I put them on the chairs, just to see. Of course I knew directly I opened the parcel that they weren't what I chose. I chose a very pretty rose-pink brocade which toned with the curtains – and that's what you sent!'

'They're ghastly,' said Barbie with conviction.

'Absolutely ghastly,' agreed Mrs Bray. 'They make the curtains look faded and they scream at the carpet. What do you propose to do?'

'Make new ones,' replied Barbie promptly.

'And keep me waiting for weeks and weeks, I suppose.'

'We'll put them in hand at once.'

Mrs Bray looked at her suspiciously.

'You see,' said Barbie. 'The mistake has arisen because I was ill and Miss Brown was acting for me in a temporary capacity. I know Mr Garfield will be very upset when I tell him about it, and will do all he can to put things right. I'm going back to Garfield's on Tuesday and I'll attend to your order myself.'

After that Barbie had no trouble at all with her 'difficult customer.' She was invited to stay to tea – and stayed – and she was taken to see Mrs Bray's bedroom and given an order for new curtains and a bedspread to match.

And this was not all, for they had now become so friendly that Mrs Bray confided to Miss France, as a dead secret, that in a few months' time she might possibly be thinking of turning the spare bedroom into a nursery, and she wondered whether Miss France had any suggestions to make. Miss France immediately replied that turning a spare bedroom into a nursery was one of her favourite jobs and offered several suggestions, all extremely sensible; and it was agreed that the moment Miss France got back to Garfield's she was to look out some books of pictures and patterns and make some little sketches which would be helpful to anyone who was thinking of such a thing.

In fact all was 'gas and gaiters,' and as Barbie went home to Underwoods in the bus she decided that 'business' was extremely pleasant. She had almost forgotten how pleasant it was – and how satisfying.

CHAPTER TEN

Amalie's birthday was on the tenth of July and Edward came down the night before to celebrate the occasion. He was staying at Underwoods over the week-end and returning to London on Monday morning. This fitted in perfectly with Barbie's plans, for Edward could give her a lift back to London.

The weather had been rather unsettled but the birthday was as sunny and warm as anyone could have wished. The sun streamed in through the open windows on to the breakfast table.

Amalie opened her parcels and letters and birthday cards; she was delighted with everything, in fact almost too delighted. Birthdays are strangely moving as one gets on in life, for one is apt to think of the past rather than the future.

After breakfast Barbie set out for the village to do the shopping and Edward ran after her and took the basket out of her hand, and fell into step beside her.

'Aren't you playing golf this morning?' she asked him.

'It's too hot for golf,' he replied. 'I'd rather come to the village with you. You look delightfully cool in that pretty white frock. Have you much shopping to do?'

Barbie thought Edward looked 'delightfully cool' in his pale-grey flannels and a white shirt, open at the neck, but she did not say so. Instead she explained that there was not much shopping and suggested that they should have a cup of coffee together at the new restaurant which had just opened in the village.

'Coffee on a day like this!' exclaimed Edward.

'Lemonade?'

'No, nor ice-cream,' said Edward scornfully. 'What we want on a day like this is beer.'

'But Edward –'

'Beer,' declared Edward, smiling at her. 'I tell you what, Barbie; we'll go to that nice old inn near the village. You like beer, don't you?'

She admitted that she liked beer.

'Why say it in that apologetic tone of voice? It's sensible to like beer. I like people that like beer,' said Edward.

Twenty minutes later Barbie and Edward were leaning upon the counter of The Owl Inn and drinking beer out of tall glasses. There was nobody in the bar except themselves and the innkeeper, who was busy polishing glasses and setting them in orderly rows. Barbie had been somewhat dubious about the amenities of The Owl, she had never been inside the place before and her recollection of it was that it was a dilapidated old building, not very clean and perhaps not very reputable, so she was pleasantly surprised at its air of prosperous comfort.

'I've been here two years,' said the innkeeper in answer to a question. 'It was a bit dirty, but me and the missus soon put that right, and we soon got a lot of new customers too. People like things clean and nice. It used to be tankards,' he continued, pointing to a shelf where a dozen or so pewter tankards stood in a line. 'Tankards are all very well in their way but you never know if they're really *clean*, that's what I say. A clean glass, nicely polished – well, it's high-jinnick.'

Barbie agreed. The glasses were beautifully polished, they winked and glittered in the rays of the sun.

'If they wants pewter they asks,' said the innkeeper. 'But glasses for me, every time – that's what I say.'

'Have one with us,' suggested Edward.

'Well, I don't mind if I do. It's hot this morning. Thank you, sir.'

Edward's own glass was refilled. 'You've had your sign repainted, haven't you?' he said. 'This place used to be called The Owl Pack. I've often wondered what it meant. Owls don't go in packs, they're solitary birds. Why Owl Pack?'

'Now you're asking,' declared the innkeeper, grinning from ear to ear. 'That was what my missus said when we came. "Why Owl Pack?" she said, "it's silly." Of course nobody called it that – none of the local people – it was just "The Owl." So when we had the sign repainted my missus said to change it and put "The Owl" – and that's what we did. Well, now I don't know whether to have it painted again – or what.'

'You mean your customers objected?' asked Barbie.

'Bless your heart, no! There wasn't one of them noticed. They call it The Owl – and The Owl it was.' He stepped back and shouted, 'Tom! Tom, are you there? You bring up that old sign what we found last week at the back of the cellar!'

'An old sign!' exclaimed Edward.

'Old as old,' nodded the innkeeper. 'You'll see.'

A big red-faced boy staggered in with the sign and propped it against the counter. It was broken and weatherbeaten and the chains which dangled from it were red with rust, but you could see the ghostly outline of a picture on the wooden boards.

'Is that an owl?' asked Edward. 'I suppose it's meant to be an owl, but it looks more like a sack tied at the corners.'

The innkeeper grinned and turned the sign round so that they could see the other side. There was lettering on it, almost too faint to read; some of the letters had been completely obliterated:

TH WO L PA K

'Whatever is it?' exclaimed Barbie.

'Got me beat,' said the innkeeper chuckling. 'But my missus guessed it. She's the clever one – does Crossword Puzzles.' He took a piece of chalk and added the missing letters. There were only three missing letters and when they had been added the legend was clear: THE WOOL PACK.

'It's easy when you know how,' declared the innkeeper. 'This inn was called The Wool Pack – sensible name – nothing silly about it. There used to be thousands of sheep in these here parts and the shepherds brought their wool down from the hills on mule-back. That's history, that is. The village was called Shepherd's Ford – there wasn't no bridge in those days – and this here inn was The Wool Pack. See?'

'It's very interesting,' said Edward, gazing at the board. 'It all fits in and you can even see how the name got changed. Some fool of an artist who was asked to paint a new sign thought it was Owl – wrongly spelt. I bet he thought he was clever!'

'And nobody noticed,' added Barbie. 'Nobody noticed because in those days people couldn't read.'

The innkeeper nodded. 'Well, there you are,' he said.

'You should change back to the old name!' exclaimed Barbie impulsively.

'I'd like to – but the missus says no. She says The Owl's better – more romantic – and she says the customers wouldn't like it if we changed the name. This place has been The Owl for years and years, so why change? That's what she says.'

'She's right, you know,' Edward declared.

'She's usually right,' admitted the innkeeper.

Barbie was silent. To her mind 'The Wool Pack' was more romantic; the name took you right back into the past; it evoked the picture of shepherds in smocks sitting on the oaken settles drinking their ale out of pewter tankards. They would discuss the weather in slow deep voices and compare the state of their flocks. Outside in the courtyard there would be sacks of wool waiting for transit across the ford. 'The Owl' was commonplace in comparison and it meant nothing.

But whether or not it would be good policy to change the name was a different matter. Barbie was a business woman and was aware that it is never good policy to change the name of a well-known concern.

'We talk about it,' said the innkeeper as he removed the glasses and polished the bar counter. 'We argue about it – friendly like. I'm apt to be a bit impulsive, but my missus keeps me on the lines. That's the way to do when you're married.'

It was time to go home now, so Edward paid for the beer and they walked up the hill together. There was a short cut to Underwoods over the hill and past the ruined Abbey. They rested for a few minutes sitting upon one of the fallen stones.

Barbie knew what was coming for Nell had warned her; once warned, she realised how blind she had been. In a hundred little ways Edward had made it clear that he loved her. So far she had kept it off, but you could not do that for ever. Sooner or later it would have to come. She had given it a great deal of thought; she had tried to do as Nell suggested and 'give the man a chance' and, in so doing, she had discovered that she was very fond of Edward. They had been friends all their lives; they had shared memories and shared jokes and shared interests. Aunt Amalie wanted her to marry Edward. Nothing had been said, but Barbie knew it and it weighed with her quite a lot for she adored Aunt Amalie. Then there was Underwoods. If she married Edward they would share Underwoods and the problem would be solved in the most satisfactory manner. She and Edward both loved the dear old place, and the prospect (far-off she hoped) of living at Underwoods and sharing it with Edward was exceedingly pleasant. They would share the joys and the responsibilities.

Barbie had thought of all this and she had decided to say 'yes,' if and when Edward asked her to marry him.

It was very quiet in the ruined Abbey. Barbie and Edward knew the place well for they had often come here when they were children. It had been fun to climb on the stones and to play at being 'alpine climbers.' It had been fun to 'seek for treasure.' Edward had been so certain that the monks of the Abbey had buried their valuables somewhere in the ruins that the two of them had spent hours digging and searching amongst the rubble, but they had never found anything of the least value.

Barbie glanced at her companion and wondered if he remembered.

'That innkeeper – he's a happy man,' said Edward after a long silence. 'I don't know why I toil and moil in a crowd when I could have an inn like The Owl – and live in peace.'

'You'd soon get tired of it.'

'No, I shouldn't. Not if I had you to "keep me on the lines."'

'You're talking nonsense.'

'Yes, about keeping the inn, but not about you.' He slipped his arm round her waist. 'Barbie, darling, you will, won't you? You'll marry me and "keep me on the lines." We've always loved each other, haven't we? We've always been sweethearts. D'you remember we cut a sixpence in half and each took a piece?'

Barbie remembered. She had kept her half of the sixpence for years, and then somehow she had lost it.

'I've still got my half,' said Edward. 'I've knocked about the world – here, there and everywhere – but I've always kept my half of the sixpence and I've always had you in my heart. I've always thought that some day you and I would get married and settle down together and be happy. Some fellows have wander-fever, you know. I had it for a bit, but that's all over. I just want a home – and you.'

'I don't know . . .' began Barbie in a breathless voice.

'You don't know! But Barbie, darling, we've loved each other since we were children!'

Barbie had made up her mind to say yes, but now that it had come to the point she was not quite sure. 'Couldn't we – leave it for a little?' she murmured.

'But why? Dearest girl, why leave it for a little when you know quite well you're going to say yes?'

She hesitated. It was strange that just at this very moment she should think of Henry Buckland. She had put him out of her mind in anger – he had made a fool of her! She had seen him once and spoken to him for half an hour and yet for some absurd reason she remembered his face so clearly that if she had had the skill she could have drawn a portrait of him. It really was absurd because she knew nothing about him – nothing except that he did not keep his word!

'You can trust me, can't you?' said Edward gently.

Barbie was almost frightened. It seemed as if Edward had read her thoughts.

'You can trust me,' repeated Edward. 'We know each other so well. I've been a bit of a wanderer but that's all over – and, honestly, I've loved you all the time. You believe that, don't you?'

'Yes,' said Barbie. She did believe it – that was what she meant – but Edward took it to mean a great deal more.

'Darling!' he cried joyfully. 'I'm so happy I could jump over the moon!' He drew her into his arms and kissed her.

Somehow this settled everything. Barbie's doubts vanished and she too was happy. I love him, she thought. I've always loved Edward. I loved him when we were children, and played together in these very same ruins, and I still love him.

They sat there in the sunshine for some time. Edward's arm was round her and she felt secure. Edward's voice went on talking, telling her over and over again how he had always loved her, always wanted to marry her, and how he had come to Underwoods and seen her and immediately fallen in love with her all over again in a different kind of way.

'You understand, don't you, Barbie?' he said anxiously. 'I want you to understand.'

She understood.

'It's perfect,' declared Edward. 'It's so – right, if you know what I mean. We're absolutely made for each other, you and I. We'll be so happy doing everything together. Of course we can't be married for some time. I mean I must get properly settled into this job, and we shall have to find a flat.'

'There's no hurry at all,' Barbie agreed. 'I shall have to go back to Garfield's. They've kept the job open for months, so I must go back until Mr Garfield can find someone really capable to take over.' She hesitated and then added, 'Of course I could go on with my job at Garfield's.'

'Goodness no!' cried Edward. 'I shouldn't like that at all. I shall want you all to myself when we're married. It will be lovely to come home and find you there, waiting for me, and of course you can be the greatest help to me in my business. You see, darling, one of the most important things in a firm like ours is going about and making contacts and doing a little entertaining in a quiet way; making friends with the right people. It will be tremendous fun doing it all together, won't it?'

'Yes, of course,' agreed Barbie, but not very enthusiastically, for to tell the truth the picture Edward had painted did not appeal to her greatly. She liked going about and meeting people and she liked parties, but she had a feeling that after a bit one might get a little tired of 'all play and no work.' Perhaps she would not have felt this so keenly if her visit to Mrs Bray had not been such a success; Barbie, after her long holiday, had tasted the sweets of office and was looking forward to her return to Garfield's. It was enjoyable work and she knew she could do it well. There was satisfaction in looking round a shabby, down-at-heel house and transforming it into a beautiful, comfortable dwelling-place . . . but I can do our own house, thought Barbie. That will be fun.

'We must go home,' said Edward. 'It's beginning to get a bit cold and you've only got on that thin frock. It's my job to look after you. I shall look after you always. Besides we must tell Amie.'

He drew her arm through his and they walked home together.

CHAPTER ELEVEN

Amalie was not surprised at the news for she had seen the two go off to the village and had thought: *perhaps it will happen today.* She was not surprised, but she was delighted beyond measure. The happiness of seeing her dearest wish come true was almost frightening.

'My two darlings!' exclaimed Amalie. 'Nothing could be lovelier. It's the best birthday present of all!'

Penney was delighted, too; she kissed Barbie fondly, and offered her good wishes and congratulations, and of course Daphne was thrilled.

'Oh, Miss Barbie!' cried Daphne. 'I dunno when I've been so thrilled. I do wish you all the best. Such a nice gentleman 'e is – so 'andsome and gay – just like a film star!

And it's all coming out like it was in your cup; wedding bells, I said, didn't I? You remember?'

Barbie could not help smiling, for if she remembered rightly the seer had said the wedding bells were 'Miss Mainwaring's, most likely' and had gone on to warn her to 'beware of a tall stranger.' Edward was not very tall and certainly, by no stretch of imagination, could he be called a stranger . . . and then it crossed her mind that she *had* met a tall stranger and had *not* been wary of him, and he had let her down with a bump.

For a few moments Barbie felt quite uncomfortable.

'And I said there was a ring, didn't I, Miss Barbie?' continued Daphne eagerly. 'Well, you'll be getting a ring, won't you? And I said you'd be going across the water – and of course you'll be going abroad for your 'oneymoon.'

Barbie laughed and said, 'Oh, we haven't fixed anything like that yet, Daphne.'

The day passed in a whirl but after dinner the excitement died down and they began to discuss future plans. Penney left them to talk, and the three of them sat by the window and watched the light fade.

Barbie leaned back in her chair and let the others do most of the talking. For days she had struggled with the problem of whether to say yes or no to Edward. Now it was decided and she felt peaceful and happy and secure.

'A small flat in town,' said Edward. 'That's my idea. I should hate to live out of town and travel every day. I've always been sorry for fellows who lived out of town . . . and if it wasn't too far from the office I could go home to lunch. It would have to be a service flat – the sort of place you can walk out of and turn the key whenever you feel inclined.'

'Just what I thought,' agreed Amalie. 'You could come down here for week-ends, couldn't you? We must try to find a really comfortable service flat.'

'They're rather expensive,' said Edward doubtfully.

'My dear, don't worry about that! I can help you – '

'But Amie – '

'I'd like to help you. It's far better that you should have the money now, when you need it, than wait until I'm dead. I've got nobody else to think of – just you two.'

Barbie listened to them talking about where the flat was

to be, and wondered what she would do all day while Edward was in the office.

'What do you think, Barbie?' asked Amalie.

'I don't mind, really,' she replied. 'I'd like it to be in a very bad state of repair – that's all.'

They looked so surprised that she had to laugh. 'So that I could do it up and have it exactly as I wanted,' she explained.

'Oh, of course,' agreed Edward. 'But you can do that even if it isn't in a bad state of repair. You shall have it exactly as you want it.'

Barbie began to think about colour schemes. Of course she could not make definite plans until she saw the place, but it was rather pleasant to think about it. When she returned to earth she discovered that her companions were talking about something else.

'It isn't for myself,' Edward was saying. 'It's for a pal of mine called Tony Chancellor. I knew him at Oxford. As a matter of fact we shared digs for a bit. I don't suppose you remember him, do you?'

'Was he tall with dark hair?' asked Amalie doubtfully.

'No, you're thinking of Tony Armstrong. This fellow is small and fair. The fact is poor old Tony is in a bit of a hole. He's getting married soon and they've found a house but they've got to put down a hundred pounds. If they don't do that the agent will probably sell it to someone else. Tony asked me if I could help him and I didn't like to say no. They've been looking for a suitable house for ages. I intended to raise the money by selling out some shares, but if you could lend it to me –'

'Yes, of course I can,' said Amalie. It was too dark to see her face but Barbie could tell by her voice that she was smiling.

'I say, you are a brick, Amie,' said Edward gratefully. 'You've given me so much already – but of course this isn't for myself. I'm getting along splendidly, but it just so happens that I haven't got the cash at the moment and he must have it soon – on Monday if possible.'

'I suppose he will pay you back?' asked Amalie.

'Good lord, yes. He's quite well off, really – at least his parents are. They happen to be abroad at the moment or they would have given it to him like a shot.'

'Couldn't he have explained that to the agent?' asked

Barbie, chipping into the conversation.

'Oh, he did,' declared Edward. 'But you know what these house agents are. The agent said he had several people after the house . . . but it doesn't matter,' added Edward. 'I mean if it's the least bit inconvenient for you I can easily sell out those shares. I was going to do it on Monday and then I thought if you happened to have some loose cash in the bank it would save a lot of bother.'

'Don't sell your shares,' said Amalie quickly. 'It would be a pity to do that. I can let you have a cheque tomorrow.'

'You are a brick,' repeated Edward. 'You really are! It's wonderful to have somebody like you to depend on. You understand, don't you, Amie? It will only be for a short time. Tony will stump up when he gets the money from his parents.' Edward rose and added, 'I'll give him a ring, if you don't mind, and tell him that he can have it on Monday. It will relieve his mind no end.'

'Edward is kind,' said Amalie, when he had gone to ring up his friend. 'He's a little too kind, really. He can't say no. I don't suppose for a moment that the young man will repay the money.'

'But he'll have to!' cried Barbie in alarm. 'A hundred pounds! Of course he'll have to repay it. I mean it would be frightfully wrong to borrow money and not pay it back –'

'My dear, don't worry,' said Amalie. 'I'm so happy to-night that I would give anyone a hundred pounds – willingly.'

The next two days were busy. Barbie rang up Nell and told her the news and received her congratulations.

'I told you so,' declared Nell. 'I knew you were fond of him. I do hope you'll be terribly happy, darling pet. When are you going to be married?'

'Oh, not for ages,' said Barbie. 'I must give Mr Garfield a chance to get somebody suitable – that woman they got temporarily while I was away seems to have been an absolute wash-out – and of course we must find somebody nice to share the flat with you.'

'Yes – well – we can talk about that when you come. You're coming on Monday, aren't you? It will be lovely to see you.'

Barbie had her packing to do and a whole lot of little odds and ends to arrange. She had been at Underwoods for so long that she had got thoroughly dug in – and the digging out took time. Some of her clothes were so much too large for her new slender figure that she gave them to Daphne, who declared that they would do her a treat. Meanwhile Edward was busy in the garden putting up the espalier in the new rose-bed, and Amalie spent her time holding the poles and handing the nails and directing the operations.

They're happy together, thought Barbie as she listened to the voices in the garden. We must come often to Underwoods. She's so good and sweet and unselfish. We must never take her for granted. She shall have more of Edward – not less – when we're married.

CHAPTER TWELVE

'Barbie!' shouted Edward. 'Come on, Barbie!'

It was Monday morning and he was waiting for her at the gate. They were going up to town together and had arranged to have lunch at a small restaurant in Covent Garden not far from the flat which Barbie shared with Nell. Barbie was a punctual person, her suitcase had been packed and stowed in the car and she herself was ready. She had not intended to keep Edward waiting, but somehow it took longer than she expected to say good-bye to Aunt Amalie and Penney and thank them for 'everything.' There was so much to thank them for that it was impossible to find words.

'You must go, darling,' said Amalie, giving her a last fond hug. 'Edward is getting impatient. I'll see you again soon.'

'Not next week-end, but the one after – '

'Yes, I know. It will be lovely. Darling, you must go!'

There were tears in Barbie's eyes when she looked back and saw Aunt Amalie standing on the doorstep. Barbie did not know why she was upset; it seemed silly when they were coming back again so soon.

'We'll be seeing her again in less than a fortnight,' Edward said.

'I know, but she looks tired.'

'It's the heat, I expect – and all the excitement. She's awfully pleased about our engagement, isn't she?' He hesitated and then added: 'It's nice to make people happy. I like everything to go smoothly.'

Barbie knew this already. He liked to make people happy – and why not? She thought of Tony Chancellor who was to have his path made smooth by the loan of a hundred pounds.

'Are you going to see Mr Chancellor this afternoon?' asked Barbie.

'Who?' exclaimed Edward in surprise.

'Your friend, Mr Chancellor.'

'Never heard of him.'

'Edward!' cried Barbie. 'I mean the man who wants the hundred pounds!'

'Oh, that bloke!' said Edward with a chuckle.

For a little while Barbie was silent, and then she said, 'How could you have forgotten his name? Edward, how could you?'

Edward was passing a big lorry filled with sheep; it was a manœuvre which required concentration, and he did not answer the question.

'Edward, there's no such person!' cried Barbie. The words burst from her. She heard herself uttering them with astonishment, but the moment she had uttered them she knew that they were true. 'Edward, there's no such person,' she repeated. 'You made it up! All that about the house agent and having to put down the hundred pounds or the house would be sold – and – and – '

'Rather good, wasn't it?'

Barbie glanced at him and saw that he was smiling. 'Good!' she cried in horror-stricken tones. 'It was frightful!'

'My dear girl, why go up in flames about nothing? It was just a joke.'

'A joke?'

'Well, not exactly a joke; just a sort of bed-time story. There was no harm in it.'

'No harm! Getting money out of Aunt Amalie on false pretences!'

'Oh, nonsense, Barbie,' said Edward in a gently reproachful tone. 'You know perfectly well that if I'd asked Amie for the money for myself she'd have given it to me just the same.'

'Then why didn't you?'

'Because it sounded nicer the other way. If I'd asked for a hundred for myself she'd have wondered what I wanted it for – she would have worried about it. As it is she's perfectly happy.'

'Lies!' cried Barbie. 'You told her a string of lies.'

'But, Barbie darling, everybody tells lies. The world couldn't go on if we all told the truth, the whole truth and nothing but the truth. When somebody you don't like asks you to lunch and you say you're sorry you can't come, owing to a previous engagement – '

'I don't – ever,' declared Barbie. 'And anyhow that's utterly different.'

He drew in to the side of the road and turned and looked at her. 'Darling, you're really upset,' he said in surprise. 'What's it all about? I could have raised a hundred quite easily in the City – that was what I meant to do – and then I remembered that Amie had hundreds in the bank, lying idle, and I thought it would be ever so much better to borrow it from her. It gives people a bad impression if you start borrowing small sums. The money is nothing to Amie. Of course I shall pay it back, but even if I didn't she'd never miss it.'

'It isn't the money.'

'What is it then?'

'The lies.'

'But I've explained about that already. If I'd asked Amie for the money for myself she would have worried. She would have thought I was in some sort of scrape – don't you see? So I just made up the little story about Tony What's-his-name. It came to me all in a moment.'

Barbie's hands were lying in her lap. Edward leant forward and put his hand over them. 'You understand now, don't you?' he said.

'No,' said Barbie in a breathless voice. 'No, it's horrible.'

She remembered every detail of the incident: the long story about the house and the house agent, and Edward's grave face as he told it. She remembered how Aunt Amalie had believed every word, and had thought him kind. 'Too kind, really,' she had said with an indulgent smile.

'It's horrible!' repeated Barbie, tearing her hands from his grasp. 'You deceived her! All those lies about his parents being abroad – and everything.'

'Don't let's talk about it any more, darling.'

'We must talk about it. It's important.'

'It isn't important. I'll pay it all back on Saturday – every penny of it. I promise you faithfully.'

'On Saturday?'

He nodded. 'Listen, Barbie,' he said eagerly. 'I know a fellow who lives at Newmarket and he gave me the tip. April Cloud is an absolute snip for the 3.30 on Saturday. This chap has seen the horses being exercised and he says April Cloud *simply can't lose*. It's an absolute snip – and it's twenty to one!'

'Edward, you don't mean –'

'Yes, honestly. I shall win two thousand. It's money for jam. Of course the first thing I'll do is repay Amie – and I'll get her some books as well – that Alpine Flower book she was talking about – Hatchard's is sure to have it. Don't worry, Barbie. It will be all right, I promise you.'

'We don't understand each other,' said Barbie helplessly.

She could not understand him. Quite suddenly Edward had become a stranger to her – even his face looked different. She watched him take his cigarette-case out of his pocket and light a cigarette and throw the match out of the window.

'We'll have to go on or we'll be late,' he said. 'Let's talk about something else.'

He drove on. Barbie heard his voice talking but she was too upset to listen to what he said. Presently they approached London and the houses closed in – thousands and thousands of houses and streets and shops, thousands of cars. He parked the car and they went into the restaurant together.

Barbie went to the ladies' room to leave her coat and tidy her hair. It was small and rather sordid. She looked into the mirror; her eyes, wide and frightened, looked back at her blankly.

I mustn't panic, she thought. It's silly to panic. I look awful.

For a moment she hesitated and then she took out her lipstick and rubbed it on the palm of her hand. She mixed it with some cold cream and touched up her cheeks. The slight colour made her look better – and she felt better too. She felt ready to face Edward now.

He was sitting waiting for her at a little table in the corner and he looked up and smiled at her in his usual engaging way. 'You've been ages,' he said. 'I ordered an omelette and mushrooms. You like that, don't you?'

'Yes,' said Barbie. She sat down opposite to him at the table.

'Darling, it's all right, isn't it?' he said. 'You're not really angry with me. You know I love Amie dearly – every bit as much as you do.'

'I'm not angry. I'm frightened,' said Barbie.

'Frightened?'

'I've discovered that I don't know you.'

'What on earth d'you mean?'

She began to rearrange the flowers in the vase which stood on the table between them. She said, 'I mean I can't marry you.'

'Barbie, you must be mad! Just because I borrowed that money from Amie!'

'No, not because of that.'

The waiter came with their omelette and for a few moments they could not continue the conversation.

When he had gone Edward said, 'What's made you so prudish all of a sudden? I seem to remember you used to like a flutter on a horse yourself. You got quite a nice little packet when E.S.B. won the Grand National, didn't you?'

'I won five pounds,' said Barbie in a flat voice. 'It was just for fun. I'm not against betting in a mild way –'

'April Cloud is a snip,' declared Edward. 'This fellow *knows*. He sees the horses exercising –'

'It isn't that,' said Barbie. 'I wouldn't mind if you put everything you've got on the horse – and it came in last.'

'Barbie! What a frightful idea!'

'It wouldn't matter.'

'What is it then? What are you worrying about?'

She did not reply.

'Because I told Amie a little fib?'

'Because you did it too well,' said Barbie gravely.

There was a short silence.

'Don't let's quarrel,' said Edward at last. 'I'll say I'm sorry and you'll forgive me. Do you remember how we used to do that when we were children? Kiss and be friends?' He raised his eyes and smiled at her.

'It isn't for me to forgive or not to forgive,' she told him.

'You don't mean you're going to tell Amie?'

'No, of course not. It would hurt her dreadfully. Besides it isn't my business. I was just – just an onlooker. It's between you and Aunt Amalie.'

'Yes,' he agreed. 'Then that's all right, isn't it? We'll say no more about it. I'll give up betting altogether when we're married – honestly I will.'

'I can't marry you, Edward.'

'Barbie, listen – '

'I can't,' said Barbie desperately. 'I'm terribly sorry – but it's off.'

'I don't understand you – ' he began.

'I know – that's why,' she declared. 'It's no good people getting married when they don't understand each other.'

'Let's leave it,' Edward said. 'We're both a bit het up. Let's talk about it some other time. Please, Barbie.'

She shook her head.

'Please, darling Barbie! You're making me terribly unhappy – and Amie – what about Amie? You know what she feels about it. You can't throw it all up like this.'

'I can't marry you.'

'And what are you going to tell Amie?'

'I don't know,' said Barbie in a strangled voice. 'I haven't thought. I just know I can't marry you – that's all.'

She rose and groped for her bag and gloves and went away.

CHAPTER THIRTEEN

When Barbie opened the door of the flat she saw that it was full of flowers. There was a huge bowl of mixed flowers on the corner table, which looked very gay, and there were roses on the gate-legged table upon which they had their meals. In Barbie's own room there was a vase of sweet peas which filled the air with fragrance.

Nell was not there herself, she was not due to return from Dr Headfort's until after tea, but the flat was *en fête* for Barbie's homecoming, that was obvious; Barbie, who already was exceedingly upset, sat down and wept.

Presently the peace and quiet and the familiar surroundings pacified her feelings and she pulled herself together and made tea and ate some biscuits; she had had no lunch. (The mushroom omelette which Edward had ordered had been left upon the plate.) After that she felt a good deal better. She was busy unpacking when Nell arrived home, laden with parcels of food.

'Darling!' cried Nell, flinging her arms round Barbie's neck and kissing her fondly. 'Oh joy, it's almost too good to be true!'

'It's good to be back –'

'And you're looking quite fit – or very nearly. How lovely it is to see you. What a lot we shall have to talk about! Of course I know it's only for a time,' continued Nell, 'but you aren't going to be married immediately, are you?'

'I'm not going to be married at all.'

'You mean it's off?' asked Nell incredulously.

'Yes, it's off,' replied Barbie.

Nell said no more – there was something in Barbie's manner that precluded questions – but Nell was sure she would hear about it later. Meanwhile there was a lot to be done. Nell was a wonderful cook; supper – on Barbie's first night – was to be very special. She had run to half a bottle of champagne, which was to have been drunk in honour of Barbie's engagement, but there was no reason why it should not be drunk in honour of Barbie's return.

It was not until supper was finished and the two friends had settled down comfortably for the evening that Barbie felt able to unburden herself to Nell.

'About Edward,' she said suddenly, interrupting Nell in the middle of rather an amusing story about the vagaries of the woman in the Other Flat.

'Yes?' asked Nell.

'You'll probably think I'm mad, but I just suddenly found I didn't know him.'

Nell grunted sympathetically. She was aware that Barbie had known Edward since she was a child, but that was neither here nor there of course.

'I can't tell you the whole story,' continued Barbie thoughtfully; 'but I must talk to somebody about it or I'll burst. You know what you said when you came to Underwoods to lunch? You said "give him a chance" and so I did – and then I realised that you were right; I was very fond of him. He's very charming and attractive, and he was so specially – nice – to me that I couldn't help seeing . . .'

'It was obvious,' said Nell.

'So when he asked me to marry him I couldn't say no. It's difficult to say no to Edward. Everything seemed to – to push me into it. Aunt Amalie wanted it – I knew that – and there was another reason why it seemed the right thing to do. It all seemed as if it were *meant* that I should marry Edward. So I said yes and I was very happy about it. Everybody was happy and everything in the garden was lovely.'

'Then something happened?' suggested Nell.

'Yes, something happened. He told Aunt Amalie a lie. I can't make up my mind whether it was an important lie or not, but he told it so well and with so many details that it took us both in completely. It was only this morning coming up in the car, that I discovered the whole story was untrue . . . and when I asked him about it he just laughed and said it was a joke!'

'Perhaps it was a joke,' suggested Nell, who was puzzled.

'It isn't my idea of a joke,' declared Barbie.

There was a short silence.

'You'll either have to tell me or not tell me,' said Nell.

Barbie had realised this ten seconds before her friend. Five seconds later she realised that already she had told Nell too much to leave her guessing; besides she wanted Nell's judgment. The story did not take long to relate and Barbie related it with admirable impartiality, for not only was she Valiant for Truth, but she had a passion for fair dealing.

'You see,' said Barbie earnestly. 'You see Edward's idea was that there was no harm in telling Aunt Amalie "a bedtime story" – that was what he called it – because if he had told her the truth he would have got the money just the same. That was his idea. I had no ideas at all; I just knew I couldn't marry him.'

Nell was more experienced in the ways of the world. She said, 'I don't like lies either, but lots of people tell lies.'

'You think I'm making a mountain out of a molehill?'

'It isn't a question of mountains and molehills; it's a question of feelings. If you feel you can't marry him that's that.'

'What would you feel?'

'I don't know,' said Nell thoughtfully. 'If I loved him

frightfully I don't think it would have put me off – but I'm different from you.'

'It didn't change me; it changed him,' declared Barbie. 'I suddenly discovered that I didn't know him. The man sitting next me in the car wasn't Edward; he was a complete stranger – and I didn't like him.'

There was quite a long silence after that. Nell broke it. She smiled at her friend with her sudden delightful smile and said, 'Well, obviously you aren't heart-broken.'

'Heart-broken?' said Barbie doubtfully. 'No, I don't seem to – to mind very much. It's funny, isn't it? But I'm afraid Aunt Amalie will be heart-broken. What am I to say to Aunt Amalie?'

Nell saw the difficulty. The truth could not be told, and Barbie could tell nothing but the truth. 'You'll just have to say you've changed your mind, that's all,' said Nell thoughtfully. 'If she knows you – which I suppose she does – she'll realise that there's some good reason, but you can't help that. Don't write at once. Wait a few days until you've calmed down a bit.'

'You needn't think I shall change my mind!'

Nell did not think so, but there was no harm in waiting. 'I should wait,' said Nell. 'People are always so keen to rush and tell other people bad news.'

Barbie's reception at Garfield's was cordial and affectionate. They were all pleased to see her, from Mr Garfield himself down to the youngest girl in the work-rooms whose monotonous duty it was to sew on buttons and to put in zips. Of course they might not have been quite so enthusiastic in their welcome to Miss France if her temporary substitute had not been rather an unpleasant person and difficult to work with. Miss France realised that, but she was touched all the same.

The first thing Miss France did was to arrange about the chair-covers for Mrs Bray and to put them in hand immediately . . . and she looked out the pictures and patterns and sketches for the transformation of Mrs Bray's spare bedroom and despatched them without delay. As she did so she thought of the irate lady who had turned into a friend, and of various other 'difficult customers' who had been placated just as easily.

This is my job, thought Barbie. This is the thing I can do. Even if Edward were different it would be a mistake for me to marry him. I shall never marry anyone, thought Barbie.

It was lucky that she had not written to Mr Garfield and told him of her engagement. She had thought of it and then had decided that she would tell him when she saw him. Now there was no need; she could slip back into her old place and settle down.

With Nell it was easy to slip back into her old place. They talked and talked about everything under the sun – or almost everything. Strangely enough they each had one secret unsuspected by the other. Barbie's secret was the fact that some day in the distant future Underwoods would belong to her. To tell the truth Barbie was not happy about it. Her engagement to Edward had solved the difficulty, but now the problem of Underwoods had begun to bother her again.

The two friends talked and talked, calling out to each other from the kitchen to the sitting-room – or wherever they happened to be – and it was all just the same – or very nearly.

So far Barbie had not seen the woman in the Other Flat, but had heard quite a lot about her. Apparently she had no job but lived there with her child. She was a widow, so presumably she had a small pension.

'There's a man,' said Nell. 'He comes to see her quite often. I've met him on the stairs. He's a smooth man, if you know what I mean; smarmy sort of manners and patent-leather hair. She hinted to me one day that "Mr Banks" wants to marry her. I wish he would.'

'Would it be a good thing?' asked Barbie in surprise, for Nell's description of the prospective bridegroom did not sound attractive.

'They would go away,' exclaimed Nell. 'That would be a very good thing. You see I was so frightfully lonely without you that I gave her a footing. I gave her an inch and she took an ell – she's that sort of person. Now, I can't get rid of her. I don't like to cast her off completely. As a matter of fact it would be difficult to cast her off. Glore has a hide like a rhinoceros . . . and then there's Agnes,' added Nell and paused.

'Is she a nice child?' asked Barbie.

'Oh, it isn't that,' said Nell. 'She's a very uninteresting child and never says a word (of course it's a bit difficult to get a word in edgeways when Glore is holding the floor). It's just that I'm sorry for the child and sometimes a bit worried about her. Perhaps I'm an ass but you do read such awful things in the papers.'

'I don't know what you mean,' declared Barbie in bewilderment.

'Wait till you see Glore,' said Nell.

These confidences prepared Barbie for the worst.

The second night after Barbie's return, when she and Nell had just settled down for the evening, there was a knock on the front door. It was a curious sort of knock and Nell immediately sat upright and looked at Barbie in dismay.

'It's Glore!' she exclaimed.

'Glore?'

'She always knocks like that. Oh blow!' exclaimed Nell inelegantly. 'Why did she have to come tonight? She'll come in and talk.'

'We'll get rid of her quickly – or shall we pretend we're out?'

'She can see the light,' declared Nell. 'I've tried that before and she just goes on knocking. I shall have to let her in.'

Barbie had not expected to like Glore so she was not disappointed when the door was opened and the lady appeared. The odd thing was that Glore was exactly as Barbie had imagined. Usually, when one hears a lot about people, one discovers that they are quite different from one's mental picture. One imagines them to be tall and thin, and discovers them to be short and fat – or vice versa. Barbie had imagined Glore as a smartly-dressed woman, rather heavily made-up, with a stout body and very thin legs . . . and she was.

'We had to come,' said Glore, tripping in gaily. 'We couldn't wait a moment longer to see Miss France. We mustn't stay long, but we just *had* to come. You see, Nell told us so much about you, Miss France. Poor Nell has been *so* lonely without you, but we've tried to cheer her up, haven't we, Agnes?'

Barbie saw then – but not before – that she had a child with her.

'This is Agnes,' added Glore. 'You wouldn't think she was my child, would you?'

'She isn't very like you,' admitted Barbie rather uncomfortably.

'Goodness no!' Glore exclaimed. 'She takes after her father's side of the house – plain and mousy.'

It was difficult to know what to say with the child standing there. The child was not attractive so one could not praise her looks (or at least Barbie could not). She was small and thin and pale with dark hair, scraped back from her forehead and tied in a 'pony tail' with an old piece of brown ribbon – a most unsuitable style of hair-dressing for a little girl.

They had hoped to get rid of their visitor quickly but by this time she was in the sitting-room and looking round.

'Oh Nell, what lovely flowers!' she cried delightedly. 'From one of the boy-friends, I suppose.'

'I bought them,' said Nell.

'Oh, you extravagant creature!' squealed Glore.

Having admired the flowers – and called upon Agnes to admire them – Glore subsided into a chair. 'So tired,' she explained. 'So terribly tired – and your chairs are so comfortable. There aren't any really comfortable chairs in my flat. I've just taken it furnished and put all my own nice little bits and pieces into store until I can look about and decide what to do. Of course if it wasn't for Agnes I could get a job quite easily – but I expect Nell has told you all my problems.'

'Er – yes,' said Barbie. It was not strictly true, for she and Nell had had far more interesting things to talk about but she could hardly explain to Mrs Evans.

Fortunately Glore did not bother about what people said, she liked to do the talking herself, so she went on talking about her problems; about the price of food and the price of clothes and she invited Nell to guess what she had paid for the nylon stockings she was wearing – and incidentally displayed her neat ankles. It was nearly ten o'clock when she rose to go home and Agnes had gone to sleep in a chair and had to be awakened.

'She ought to have been in bed long ago,' said Barbie, as she watched the child being dragged away.

'Oh, I know,' agreed her mother. 'But she won't be left alone in the flat – so ridiculous for a child of eight years old! I don't know what she thinks could happen. Come on, *do*,' she added to the child. 'You heard what Miss France said – and Nell thinks so too – you ought to be in bed.'

'She's horrid,' said Barbie when they had bolted the door behind their unwanted guests.

'Yes, I told you she was horrid.'

'I mean she's horrid to the child.'

Nell hesitated for a moment and then said, 'I know. That's what I meant when I said I was worried. I've often thought . . . but it's no good thinking about it. Agnes is her own child, so what can one do?'

'Do you think she ill-treats her?'

'Oh no,' said Nell quickly. 'At least she doesn't beat her – or anything like that – she just neglects Agnes and – and shows her quite clearly that she's a nuisance.'

Nell was surprised that Edward had not rung up, nor called, nor written, but perhaps he had accepted his fate. To tell the truth Barbie, too, was surprised. Each time the telephone bell rang she expected it to be Edward, but it was Phil or Peter – and once it was rather a deep voice that called itself Will.

'That's Will wanting to speak to you!' Barbie shouted to Nell who was in the kitchen – and she added, 'Who's Will – ' for Will was unknown to her.

'Oh – just Will,' replied Nell, rushing madly to the phone.

Barbie did not inquire further (for of course if Nell wanted her to know about Will she would disclose his identity), but she was interested to learn that Will had asked Nell to go to the theatre with him on Friday night to see a new production of Romeo and Juliet.

On Friday morning Glore's usual knock was heard at breakfast time and Glore was discovered on the landing with an empty jug in her hand.

'Just a teeny drop of milk – for Agnes,' said Glore with a brilliant smile. 'So silly of me to run out of milk – but you're always so kind. I don't mind a bit drinking my tea without milk but Agnes is so faddy. Oh, and I wondered if you could have Agnes to supper. Could you possibly? I've simply got to go out tonight; it's very special.'

'I'm going out myself,' said Nell.

'Oh, Nell, need you?' asked Glore. 'Couldn't you put it off? I mean you can go out any night, can't you? Agnes won't be any bother, and you can make her wash up the dishes.'

Nell hesitated.

'Oh, please!' cried Glore. 'Dear Nell, please say yes. It really is terribly important. I wouldn't ask you if it wasn't terribly, terribly important to poor little me. I'd do the same for you any day. You know I would.'

Nell did not see how Glore would do the same for her – and in any case she had discovered that Glore would make the most extravagant promises and forget all about them in a few hours. Friendship with Glore was a very one-sided affair.

'Look here,' said Nell. 'I've told you I've got a date tonight. I'm going to the theatre with a friend, so –'

'But you could put it off, couldn't you?'

'I suppose I could.'

'Dear Nell, you are so kind!'

'But when will you be home?' asked Nell. 'Last time you asked me to have Agnes to supper you didn't come home till after twelve o'clock.'

'Oh, I know,' agreed Glore. 'But that was because I missed the bus. I went to supper with some friends at Welwyn – and I missed the bus. I couldn't help it, Nell. This time is quite, quite different. You *will* say yes, won't you? Please Nell –'

'All right,' said Nell ungraciously.

'You see how it is,' said Nell to Barbie as she shut the door.

Barbie saw how it was but she was surprised. 'Do you really mean you're going to put off your date?' she asked incredulously.

'I've done it before and I'll probably do it again,' declared Nell. 'I don't trust Glore. She might go out and leave that child locked up in the flat alone – and supposing something happened? I wouldn't enjoy myself; I'd be wondering all the time. Will won't mind – or at least he won't mind very much,' added Nell, trying to be strictly truthful.

'I'll have her,' said Barbie. 'You go to Romeo and Juliet with Will – whoever he is – and I'll look after Agnes.'

They argued about it in a friendly manner: Nell declaring that it was her pigeon – it was she and not Barbie who had got mixed up with the Evans family – and Barbie declaring that she would stay in and look after Agnes and probably wash her hair.

'My hair needs washing,' said Barbie, running her fingers

through her copper-coloured curls. 'I'll kill two birds with one stone.'

Eventually Nell was persuaded and went out to her date looking even more ravishing than usual, and Barbie had Agnes to supper and washed her copper-coloured curls.

CHAPTER FOURTEEN

All this time not a word had been heard from Edward but on Saturday night Nell answered the phone and shouted, 'Barbie, it's for you! It's Edward!'

'I don't want to speak to him,' shouted Barbie.

'But what shall I tell him?'

'Just that I would rather not speak to him – that's all.'

Nell was unwilling to convey the message (and who could blame her?). She said, 'Come on, Barbie, you had better hear what he has to say.'

Very reluctantly Barbie took the receiver and put it to her ear.

'Is that you, Barbie?' asked Edward. 'Darling, I didn't bother you before. I thought I'd wait and see what happened – it's marvellous news! April Cloud simply romped home. Isn't it grand? Of course I knew he would (I told you he was a snip, didn't I?) but all the same it's marvellous and I'm terribly excited. I've just this minute got back, and I had to ring you at once because I knew you'd be so pleased.'

Barbie had almost forgotten about April Cloud – which was odd because in reality April Cloud was the cause of all the trouble – and, now that she remembered, she did not know whether to be pleased or displeased at his victory. She supposed that Edward would pay back the money he had borrowed (which was all to the good), but it would have satisfied Barbie's sense of justice if April Cloud had been a non-starter.

'You *are* pleased, aren't you?' said Edward's voice in her ear. 'It's all right now, isn't it, darling? I'm sending the cheque to Amie this very minute.' He paused.

Barbie said, 'Yes, you should.'

'This very minute,' repeated Edward. 'And Barbie, listen:

I want you to come shopping with me on Monday. I'll call for you at Garfield's. Can you arrange to get off early – about four? We'll go and choose a ring – an absolutely super ring – expense no object – see? Would you like an emerald – like that ring of Amie's? I just thought when I put it back on her poor old finger that it would be perfect – for you.'

'No, Edward.'

'All right. If you'd rather have diamonds, we'll – '

'No, Edward!' cried Barbie. 'Don't you understand? I meant what I said; we aren't engaged.'

'Oh, Barbie,' said Edward's voice reproachfully. 'It isn't a bit like you to go on like this. Listen, darling, I'll come along tomorrow and see you and explain everything. I've got something to show you – '

'I shall be out!' cried Barbie frantically. 'It's no good coming. I shall be out all day.'

The line suddenly went dead and she had no idea whether he had heard her or not, but having said she would be out all day it was necessary to be out. She explained this to Nell.

'Yes, of course go out if you want to,' said Nell. 'I shall be out all day too, so if he comes there won't be anyone here . . . but I wouldn't worry if I were you.'

'Not worry!'

'There's nothing to worry about. Edward can't marry you against your will,' said Nell, smiling at her friend's anxious face. 'What do you think he's going to do? Abduct you or something?'

'No, of course not. It's just – so odd. I mean I've been quite rude to him. Why does he keep on badgering me?'

Nell looked thoughtful. She said, 'Because he wants you, of course, and I have a feeling that Master Edward usually gets what he wants.'

'That's just why I'm a little bit – frightened.'

'What nonsense!' exclaimed Nell.

'It's just a feeling I have,' said Barbie doubtfully. 'If I saw him he might persuade me. That's why I don't want to see him. And I don't want to see Aunt Amalie either. I shall write to her tonight.'

'Perhaps you had better,' agreed Nell. 'Why not go to Green Beech Cottage tomorrow? You haven't seen the Kirks for ages.'

This was an excellent plan for, next to Nell, David and Jan Kirk were Barbie's greatest friends and were always delighted to see her.

Barbie went to church in the morning (she liked going to church and was a regular attendant); then she lunched at a small restaurant and caught her bus.

It was a hot steamy day; London had been uncomfortably warm and the bus overcrowded; but when she got out of the bus at Grimble's Garage, and, leaving the main road behind her, began to climb the steep lane which led to her friends' house, the air was quite different – fresh and sweet. It was one of the charms of the little place (this sudden transition from noise to peace, from the bustle and hurry of the arterial road to the leisure of the unspoilt country) but there were other charms as well, and when Barbie pushed open the green gate in the green beech hedge and saw the little house she was struck afresh by its perfection. It was quite small but its proportions were admirable and it was built of rose-pink brick – a gem of a house in a delightful green setting!

When David Kirk had inherited the property from an old aunt it had been neglected for years and the garden was little better than a jungle, but he had set to work with a will and had got it cleared, and now it was tidy and well cared for. The same had happened inside the little house – as Barbie had reason to know, for she had helped Jan with the redecorations.

Barbie had often thought that Green Beech Cottage was like a nest. Set on the side of the hill it looked out over the tops of the trees towards London. On a clear day you could see the winding Thames and masses of buildings but more often there was a haze over the great sprawling city which veiled its ugliness and turned it into a city of dreams.

David was working in the garden. He looked up when he heard the gate. For a moment he hesitated and then he waved and shouted joyfully and came towards her holding out his hands.

'Barbie, is it really you!' he exclaimed. 'This is a grand surprise. How are you? Let me look at you properly. You're a lot thinner – '

'You're fatter,' said Barbie smiling.

'I know,' agreed David. 'It's Jan's cooking – and being

so well looked after. Come in, Barbie. Jane will be delighted, she was just talking about you this morning and wondering how you were. And you must see Matthew James. He's grown-up now. He's a person. You won't know your godson – '

Matthew James was not quite grown-up yet (except in the eyes of his parents), for he was just two years old, but during the seven months since Barbie had seen him he had developed from a somewhat uninteresting baby into an amusing and delightful little boy. His godmother was pleased with him and astounded at his intelligence – for the intelligence of a two-year-old who spends his whole life with intelligent parents is often astounding to people who are not used to children.

'He's going to write books – like his father,' Barbie declared.

'Well, I don't know,' said David. 'I thought it would be nice for him to be an admiral, but Jan is absolutely determined he's to be Prime Minister – a second Churchill, no less.'

'David, don't be silly!' exclaimed Jan, laughing.

'He used to be very like Sir Winston,' continued David, with a perfectly serious face. 'He's not quite so like him now – and I'm just wondering if Jan is right. She's usually right, of course,' added David . . . and he smiled suddenly and very sweetly at his wife.

The time passed quickly for they had a great deal to talk about (not only the future career of Matthew James) and Barbie was shown various improvements in the house and the garden and called upon by her godson to admire his guinea pigs. The more she saw of the little family the more pleased she was, for she had had a good deal to do with the 'making' of it. If the marrige of David and Jan had turned out badly she would have felt responsible, so there was reason to be delighted that it was so thoroughly satisfactory.

Once or twice Barbie found herself looking at David and comparing him with Edward. He had not Edward's charm, but he was a better man in every way; solid and safe and extremely considerate; and he still had that air of boyish unself-consciousness which she had always found so endearing. In spite of his very real success in the world of letters David Kirk was completely natural and unspoilt.

That's the best thing I ever did, thought Barbie as she shut the gate of Green Beech Cottage behind her and walked down the hill to catch her bus.

Nell, also, had been out all day. She and her companion had lunched at an old inn on the South Downs and then had decided to take a walk to stretch their legs and fill their lungs with fresh air. They parked the car in a convenient spot and set off up a steep path which led over the hills . . . and at three o'clock in the afternoon (when Barbie was opening the gate of Green Beech Cottage and being greeted rapturously by David Kirk), Nell and her companion were sitting resting in a little hollow in the shade of an old thorn.

'You do understand, don't you?' Nell was saying. 'I can't leave her now – all in the middle of her troubles. She's frightened.'

'That's nonsense.'

'I know. I told her it was nonsense – but she is. It seems odd because Barbie is a very brave sort of person in most things, but she really is scared. So we can't be engaged.'

'We are engaged – '

'No, Will,' said Nell firmly. 'If we were engaged I'd have to tell her. We tell each other everything. I simply couldn't keep a secret from Barbie.'

Will was silent for a moment. He was a little puzzled, for it seemed to him that Nell *was* keeping a secret from her friend, but he was aware that he was merely a man and that the curious workings of the female brain were mysteries which no mere man could hope to unravel.

'You understand, don't you?' said Nell anxiously.

'You said you would marry me – '

'Because I thought she was engaged to Edward.'

'Then you mean – '

'I mean I'll marry you when things come right for Barbie – if they do come right. In the meantime – '

'In the meantime you'll run about all over the place with Phil,' said her companion clenching his teeth. 'Oh yes, I know I'm jealous. I told you I could be jealous if I had anything to be jealous about, didn't I?'

'Dear Othello, it's rather thrilling,' said Nell in a dreamy voice.

She was lying back upon the soft turf and Will turned and looked at her. He put his hands very gently round her neck.

'Rather thrilling,' repeated Nell softly.

He leant over and kissed her.

She had thought him ugly. Perhaps he was – but it didn't matter.

'Darling Will,' said Nell. 'You haven't anything to be jealous about. They're all just boys. It's fun having them as friends.'

'Give them up.'

'Why?'

'Would you like it if I had half a dozen women friends?'

'I'd rather you had half a dozen than just one,' replied Nell, giggling at the idea of her tall gaunt doctor surrounded by a bevy of adoring females.

He had to smile, and when he smiled (as Nell had noticed before) he was not in the least ugly, but rather the reverse.

'You must smile a lot,' she told him.

'I shall smile when we're engaged – not before.'

'What a pity!' said Nell sadly. 'You see I love you so much more when you smile.'

'I love you all the time – better and better every moment. It all began that night in the fog. D'you remember what was written on the wall?'

'Somebody Luvs Somebody,' said Nell vaguely. 'You were so cross because love wasn't spelt properly – and then those men attacked us – and I was sick. You couldn't possibly have fallen in love with me *then*.'

'Yes, that was when it began. I remember *everything* about that night – every smallest detail. For instance I've often wondered why you told the policeman you had broken the man's arm.'

'Because I did.'

'But Nell – '

'Yes, honestly. The bone snapped. It was horrible.'

'You couldn't have done it.'

'Ju-jitsu,' said Nell nodding significantly. 'Barbie and I had some lessons from a little Jap. We were getting on quite nicely and then he suddenly disappeared in the night. You don't have to be stronger than the other person,' explained Nell. 'You just hold their arm and they do it themselves.' She giggled and added, 'It wouldn't be as easy as you think to strangle me. That was one of the first things he taught us – how not to be strangled.'

'You are a most extraordinary girl,' declared Will Head-fort.

Nell was pleased. What girl doesn't like to be told she is extraordinary?

After a bit Will said, 'I've been thinking about that child – the child you're so worried about.'

'Agnes?'

'Yes. I think I could arrange for her to be put into a Home. Of course I'm not particularly keen on putting children into Institutions, but the Home I know about is in the country and there's an exceedingly nice matron. It might be better for her than her present mode of life.'

'Almost anything would be better!'

'Or we could adopt her ourselves,' added Will Headfort, throwing out this amazing suggestion in a casual manner.

'Oh Will, you are good!' exclaimed Nell in astonishment. She pondered the matter and then continued, 'Of course we should have to think about it very seriously. She isn't a very attractive child – poor little scrap – but I dare say she would improve. Do you really mean you wouldn't *mind*?'

'Why should I mind?' he asked, smiling at her. 'There's plenty of room in the house and Mrs Ridge is a good soul. She would help. Anyhow you can think about it.'

'Yes,' agreed Nell. It was obvious that already she had begun to think about it very seriously indeed.

It was peaceful and quiet on the hill; not sunny, but pleasantly warm. A soft haze was spread all over the sky and the light was silvery. They sat there for quite a long time and presently they began to play their 'special game' which consisted of bandying quotations of Shakespeare. It was rather a silly game, really, but it was fun to be silly together and Nell had found it a good way of keeping her Will in check when he became slightly unmanageable. He was more conversant than she with the works of his namesake, but Nell was making it her business to read, mark, learn and inwardly digest some of his favourite plays so as to be up-sides with him.

So when Will – after a little silence – suddenly exclaimed:

'Lord, who would live turmoiled in a court,
And may enjoy such quiet walks as these?'

Nell laughed and replied: 'But "Here's the lord of the soil come to seize me for a stray, for entering his fee-simple without leave!"'

The 'lord of the soil' was merely a South Down sheep, which had wandered round a rock in search of succulent pasture and, far from seizing the trespassers upon its fee-simple, stood for a moment regarding them with an expression of horrified amazement before it turned tail and fled with a loud 'baa-aa.'

When they had finished laughing Nell said it was time to go home so they walked back together to the place where they had left the car. They walked arm-in-arm, as they had done in the fog, and anyone seeing them might have jumped to the conclusion that they were engaged to be married – but of course they were not.

CHAPTER FIFTEEN

Underwoods seemed very quiet without Barbie, but there was plenty to do in the garden and Amalie was not lonely The garden was now at its best; wistaria rioted over the south wall, its branches bowed down with their weight of blossom, and the willow-gentian in its cool shady spot was beginning to come into flower. Soon the little bushes with their slender stems would bear narrow bells of deep blue flowers, and the corner of the garden where they grew would look like a pool of blue water. Amalie was very fond of these gentians, she had grown them herself from a few seeds gathered on a visit to Switzerland. She had been told that they would not grow here in the Cotswolds but they had liked their new home and had thriven and multiplied under her care.

Amalie was in no hurry for them to flower. She would have held back the garden if she could . . . for, as each plant flowered and faded, she knew that it was gone for a whole year. The longest day was long past and not until next year would she see the may-tree smiling like a bride in the sunshine, nor the glowing lamps upon the rhodies nor find the scatter of golden primroses upon the bank beneath the ash. Next year was such a long time to wait . . . all through the dead winter. Summer days passed too quickly, thought Amalie; and then she thought, but there are still the chrysanthemums to come and the dahlias and the proud upstanding gladioli and the gold of ripe corn in the harvest fields and the flames of the autumn leaves!

And there was planning to do. Now that the espalier had been erected she must make up her mind about climbing roses. Which to have! There were so many different kinds and all so lovely.

Perhaps Amalie's favourite spot, amongst all the enchantments of Underwoods garden, was the rectangular lily-pool surrounded with flowering shrubs which had been made long ago by her husband. Beside it was the wooden seat, and several large urns which were always full of roses. The trees had been cut back a little to give a vista of surpassing beauty, of a green valley and a silver river and small farms. She and Ned had often sat here together and enjoyed the peaceful scene; to Amalie it was 'Ned's seat'; the place where she could best evoke the memory of their companionship.

Amalie had expected 'bread and butter letters' from Edward and Barbie but it was a week before they arrived. They came the same morning at breakfast time and Amalie opened Barbie's letter first. She was a little surprised to see it was so short, for Barbie usually wrote long letters full of amusing details; she would have been more surprised if she could have seen the condition of the waste-paper basket when the final draft was completed. After the usual expressions of thanks Barbie continued:

'I'm afraid this is going to hurt you a lot but I can't help it. I have decided I can't marry Edward. I made a mistake about my feelings. The only thing to do was to tell him. I expect Edward has told you about it. Later on I hope we shall be "just friends" as we were before, but in the meantime it will be better for us both if we do not meet. So I shall not be coming to Underwoods for the week-end. Dear Aunt Amalie, I am very sorry.

Ever your loving
BARBIE.'

Amalie felt a little dazed as she put down Barbie's letter

and opened Edward's. His was very much longer and not nearly so clear for he had written in haste and without revision. It began by saying that he and Barbie had had 'a little tiff' but he was sure it would all come right so Amie was not to worry. There was quite a lot about 'Barbie's red-haired temper' and how the disagreement was 'all about nothing.' He went on to say that he had done all he could to bring her round; he had rung her up and tried to explain but she had been 'horrid' to him and refused to listen: he had gone to see her at the flat but had not been able to get in. He did not know whether she was really out, or 'was inside, sulking.' It was absolutely the limit, declared Edward. He had done all he could. Barbie must be crazy. If she thought she could treat him like that, and get away with it, she could think again. He then said that he would not come to Underwoods for the week-end because Barbie would be there and it would be unpleasant for everyone and anyhow it was better to 'let her stew for a bit in her own juice.' He had been asked by some friends to go yachting on the Broads and he thought he would just go and leave Barbie to stew until he returned. Perhaps she would be more reasonable by that time. He finished by imploring his dearest Amie to write to Barbie immediately and persuade her to see him so that he could explain everything and put things right before he left for his holiday, otherwise he would not enjoy it at all.

The postcript said, 'Enclosed is the money from Toby Chancellor with many thanks for the loan.'

'Is it bad news, Lady Steyne?' asked Penney in concern.

'Yes. At least – it's a disappointment,' replied Amalie. 'Look, my dear, I should like you to read the letters and see what you make of them. Read Barbie's first.'

While Penny was reading Barbie's letter Amalie read Edward's again. There was nothing to be learnt from it except that he was angry and upset (which of course was quite natural) but there was something odd about the postscript which in spite of her perturbation caught her eye. There was something wrong about it . . . Toby Chancellor? Edward had said his friend's name was Tony.

I must have made a mistake, thought Amalie as she passed the letter across the breakfast table for Penney to read . . . and then she thought, but I didn't make a mistake. Edward said Tony Chancellor! I know he did.

The more she thought about it the more certain she became, for she had thought at the time: another Tony! Such a lot of Tonys! And Anthony is a nice name. And she had thought of St Anthony of Padua, who preached to the fishes. She would never have thought all that if the young man's name had been Toby, which was probably short for Tobias – not a nice name at all and nothing whatever to do with St Anthony of Padua!

She frowned, trying to solve the mystery. It was a silly little mystery and it didn't matter in the least – or did it?

'Oh dear, I *am* sorry,' said Penney. 'I don't know what to say. They seemed so happy, and you were so pleased about it.'

'Do you think it will come right, Penney?'

'Well, I may be wrong, but somehow – '

'I don't either,' said Amalie. 'Barbie may be a little hot-tempered at times but she wouldn't – do that – without a good reason. There must be something – but what could it be?' She paused for a moment and then continued, 'It all seemed so safe and secure, didn't it? I was so very pleased because I'm so fond of them both, and also because it settled a matter which had been troubling me . . .' and she went on to tell Penney about Ned's will and how he had insisted on leaving Underwoods to her niece instead of to his own son. But she told Penney a good deal more than she had told Barbie – more about her own feelings – and she told Penney the reason why she had been so anxious that Edward should not know. 'I thought it would be better if he married Barbie entirely for herself, with no thought at all of Underwoods,' explained Amalie.

'But surely you never imagined – ' began Penney aghast.

'Not really,' said Amalie. 'All the same a thing like that might have influenced him – a little. You never can tell. It was more for my own comfort that I didn't want him to know that Barbie would have Underwoods – eventually. It was just a feeling I had. Feelings are difficult to explain, aren't they?'

Penney agreed that feelings were very difficult to explain, but she thought Lady Steyne had explained her feelings very clearly.

Presently Penney said, 'It seems a pity that neither of them is coming for the week-end. You could have one of them, couldn't you? I've ordered a chicken and – '

'I think not,' said Amalie with a little sigh. 'I think we'll just leave them both to "stew in their own juice," and you and I will stew in ours – quite quietly and peacefully. We'll have the chicken hot and we'll go on eating it cold until it's finished. There are lots of lettuces coming on and what could be nicer than cold chicken and salad?'

Amalie was very disappointed, of course, but she was by no means broken-hearted. Strangely enough she was not even very much surprised. As she put on her old garden hat she tried to diagnose her own feelings. I must have known, deep down, that it wasn't really going to happen, thought Amalie.

The week-end was as peaceful as anybody could wish. Amalie and Penney, who were both rather tired, enjoyed it. They sat in the summer-house most of the time, knitting and chatting. Penney had profited from Barbie's lessons and had learned how to chat – or perhaps it would be more true to say she had unlearned the lesson of silence which she had taught herself during her years of bondage. At any rate Amalie found her an extremely interesting companion.

'There's something worrying me, Penney,' said Amalie. 'It's a very small thing and not a bit important, and I wouldn't mention it to anyone else, but you're so understanding – and safe.' And with this introduction she proceeded to tell Penney the queer mistake about Mr Chancellor's name.

'It's silly, isn't it?' said Amalie when she had explained the whole thing. 'It's ridiculous to worry about it – but for some reason I can't get it out of my head.'

'I don't think it's silly – or unimportant,' said Penney thoughtfully.

'Don't you?' asked Amalie. 'Well, what do you think happened? Could Edward have made a mistake about the man's name?'

'You said they shared lodgings at Oxford.'

Amalie nodded. 'Yes, so it isn't likely he could have made a mistake.'

There was a short silence and then Penney said, 'You ought to ask him, Lady Steyne.'

'You really think I should?'

'It isn't fair not to,' said Penney with conviction. 'He ought to be given a chance to explain. I mean if I were he . . . I mean that's just the way misunderstandings arise. I remember once . . .' She paused. There was a time to speak of her own experiences and a time for silence. This obviously was a time for silence. Lady Steyne was looking very thoughtful indeed.

'Yes,' said Amalie doubtfully. 'Of course I see your point, but it seems such a very small thing. It doesn't seem worth bothering about.'

> 'It is the little rift within the lute
> That by and by will make the music mute,'

said Penney. She smiled and added, 'So hackneyed, but so horribly true.'

'Oh, I wouldn't let it – influence me,' declared Amalie.

Penney thought it was already influencing Lady Steyne – just a little – so she did not reply.

'You were going to tell me something you remembered,' said Amalie.

'Oh, it was just – something that happened. It was when I was with Mrs MacBrayne. She misunderstood what I said and instead of telling me she brooded over it. Her manner changed completely and everything became very uncomfortable – so uncomfortable that I couldn't bear it and I said I must leave. Then she told me,' said Penney with a sigh. 'She told me and I explained and it was all put right in a few minutes. If only she had told me before it would have saved me a great deal of misery – and not a few sleepless nights.'

Although Amalie had never been in a position of that kind (balanced precariously on a tight-rope with nothing but the goodwill of an employer to depend upon) she was so sympathetic that she understood a great deal more than she had been told.

'Poor Penney,' she said gently. 'We shall never fall out like that. You must stay with me until I die – because I couldn't possibly do without you – and I may as well tell you now that I've left you a pension in my will.'

After that Penney's gratitude (which seemed to Amalie out of all proportion to the promised boon) put an end to the conversation about Edward's friend, but afterwards when Amalie thought it over she realised the connection between Penney's story and her own small problem. Probably there are few people in the world who have not had the same kind of experience, thought Amalie. It was not quite the same (for of course she had no intention of changing her manner to Edward) but she was aware that the mystery had slightly changed her feelings. The suspicion that Edward had not been quite open and above-board was unpleasant to say the least of it. The whole matter was too stupid for words because if Edward had asked straight out for the money she would have given it to him unquestioningly; she had helped him out of a good many scrapes before now.

Amalie finally decided that Penney was right; she must clear up the mystery by asking Edward about it, but of course she could no nothing until she saw him (it was not the sort of thing you could ask in a letter) so meantime the matter was shelved.

Amalie replied to the two letters in a temperate manner; saying to Edward that she was sorry but she did not feel justified in interfering, and to Barbie that of course she must do as she thought best. Both letters were quite cheerful and full of local news (news about the bridal couple who were on their way to New Zealand, about Daphne's latest sayings and the condition of the garden) and both letters surprised their recipients. Edward had expected sympathy and active support; Barbie had feared persuasions.

CHAPTER SIXTEEN

After being away for so long Barbie found it more difficult than she had expected to settle down at Garfield's, and it took some time to gather up all the threads. Miss Brown had muddled things considerably, so much so that one almost suspected the skein had been tangled on purpose! This suspicion was strengthened when Joan Waghorn let fall the information that Miss Brown had hoped to remain at Garfield's permanently.

'Oh yes, she thought she was going to stay,' said Joan Waghorn. 'She was only engaged temporarily – I know that because I saw the letter – but she thought you wouldn't be coming back. It gave her a bit of a jolt when Mr Garfield told her you were coming back in a fortnight and she must look for another job. She'd been bad enough before – interfering with everyone and keeping back letters she ought to have given me to answer – but after she got her notice she was awful. I scarcely dared to speak to her she was so cross. Of course she hated you from the very beginning,' added Joan.

'How could she hate me when she'd never even seen me?' asked Barbie in bewilderment.

'People talked about you,' explained Joan. 'Everyone in the place talked about you and wondered how you were and asked Mr Garfield if he had heard from the hospital – and of course everyone kept on telling her that you always did this and never did that. You know the sort of thing.'

'Poor Miss Brown!'

'Yes, I suppose it must have been rather galling,' agreed Joan. 'But it was her own fault, really. I did my best to help but she wouldn't listen and she was so horrid that I gave up the attempt. She really was horrid, Miss France. If anything went wrong she blamed everyone but herself. You were just the opposite. I've known you take the blame for things that weren't your fault at all.'

'I think you might have been a bit more tactful,' declared Barbie. 'It can't have been easy for the woman coming into a job like this without any preparation at all.'

'Well – perhaps – ' said Joan doubtfully. 'But, honestly, I think everyone would have helped her if she had been nice. She started off wrong the very first day – went up to the work-rooms and found two of the girls going off ten minutes early to catch their bus. Miss Smithers had given them permission because they'd been asked to a party – and of course they were going to make up the time next day. Miss Smithers said you always let them do that, and Miss Brown said she wasn't you, and Miss Smithers said That was Obvious (you know how she talks!). Golly, there was a row,' declared Joan, her eyes widening at the recollection. 'They went at it hammer and tongs. Some of the girls giggled and the others cried and everyone was late getting away. After that Miss Brown made a point of going up to the work-rooms to see that nobody left early. Of course Miss Smithers was furious – I mean the work-rooms are under her charge and always have been – so you see how it was, Miss France.'

Miss France saw.

'It made things awfully difficult for everyone, but specially for me,' continued Joan. 'Sometimes they didn't speak to each other for days and I had to take messages and everything got muddled. If Miss Smithers said one thing Miss Brown said the other. It really was hopeless.'

Miss Smithers had the same tale to tell and told it even more emphatically. 'Impossible Woman,' declared Miss Smithers. 'Quite Impossible to Work With. She gave Orders to the girls Behind My Back and did all she could to Undermine My Authority. She went to Mr Garfield with Stories!'

'How dreadful!' murmured Barbie.

'Yes, it was Dreadful,' agreed Miss Smithers. 'At first he was Completely Taken In – so much so that I decided to Resign – but happily he Found Her Out before I had actually written and Tendered My Resignation. I can't tell you about it Now, Miss France,' said Miss Smithers earnestly. 'It would Take Too Long, but some day when we are not so busy I should like to tell you the Whole Thing.'

'Yes, of course,' said Barbie.

'It was all so very Disagreeable,' said Miss Smithers. 'That Woman Poisoned the Whole Atmosphere of Garfield's. She Set Everyone by the Ears. We have always been so Happy at Garfield's, but while She was here it was Quite Different,' and with that Miss Smithers proceeded to unburden herself of her story, quite forgetting that she had said it would Take Too Long.

Of course it took Far Too Long (or so Barbie thought as she listened to the tale of grievances and pin-pricks and petty persecutions); but there was no stopping Miss Smithers once she got started and as Barbie knew she would have to listen to it some time she thought it better to listen now and let poor Miss Smithers get it off her chest.

'You can say what you like, Miss France,' declared Miss Smithers (rather unfairly, for Barbie had played the part of sympathetic listener). 'You can say what you like, but That isn't the way to get the Best Work out of girls. Snooping after them to see if they're doing their work and Snarling at them. Snooping and Snarling,' repeated Miss Smithers, her eyes blazing at the thought. 'Wearing rubber-soled shoes, so that nobody could hear her coming, and Pouncing like a Tiger . . .'

Fortunately, just at this very moment, Joan Waghorn interrupted the conversation to say that Miss France was wanted on the phone, so Miss France was able to escape to her own small office and laugh in private.

Barbie had been back at Garfield's for more than a month before she caught up with arrears of work and got her books in order, and during that time she had been too busy to think about much else. She was aware that Edward was yachting with friends on the Broads – Aunt Amalie had mentioned it in her letter – and this fact contributed greatly to her peace of mind. If Edward had been in town he might have called, or she might have met him somewhere. She was still a little scared of meeting Edward.

It was towards the end of August when one morning Barbie had occasion to see Mr Garfield. She tapped on the door of his office and entered, for she was a privileged person and had access to him at any hour of the day.

'Mr Garfield, are you busy?' she inquired.

'Never too busy to see you, Miss France,' said Mr Garfield gallantly.

'I'm afraid this is rather a serious matter,' Barbie told him.

He held out his hand and she gave him a letter which had just arrived by post. It was short but by no means sweet and was written in large bold writing upon thick white paper.

Oddam Castle, Ryddelton,
Scotland.

Mrs Scott will be obliged if Messrs Garfield & Co will let her know by return of post whether they received her letter of 27th June and if so what they propose to do about her order.

'Great Snakes!' exclaimed Mr Garfield dropping the letter upon his desk as if it were red hot.

'I know,' agreed Barbie. 'We looked all through the order book and it isn't there, but Miss Waghorn is certain she saw the letter lying on Miss Brown's desk. She remembers the thick white paper and the large writing. She wasn't given the letter to read, and when she asked Miss Brown about it Miss Brown was – rather rude.'

'Great Snakes, this is awful!' cried Mr Garfield. 'This is frightful! June, July, August – it's nearly two months! I'd like to wring that woman's neck. It was a big order, most likely. Look at the address and the 'igh-class notepaper and the splashy writing!' (It was only in moments of stress that Mr Garfield dropped an aitch.)

Barbie had noticed all these pointers herself. 'I know,' she agreed. 'But we haven't lost the order. I could write and explain, couldn't I? Perhaps I should offer to go and see Mrs Scott. What do you think? If I were to go one night and see her, and come back the next night it would only mean one day away from business and it wouldn't really cost very much –'

'No!' cried Mr Garfield, banging the desk with his fist. 'No, Miss France. That's not 'ow Garfield's does things. You write your letter and offer to go and if she says "yes" you'll go regardless. You'll go First Class and you'll stay at the best hotel. You'll do it in style – regardless.'

It was at times like this that Mr Garfield was at his best, thought Barbie admiringly. There was not much to admire in his appearance for he was rather like an owl, with his tufty grey hair and large round spectacles, but he liked to do things in a grand manner. Barbie appreciated that.

'Yes, I'll write at once,' said Barbie.

'Explain everything,' said Mr Garfield more quietly. 'Explain that you've been ill and we've had an imbecile in the office . . . but I don't need to tell you what to say. Thank heaven you're back!'

Barbie wrote, and in due course received another letter on the same thick writing-paper and in the same 'splashy' writing, but in a very different tone. It began, 'Dear Miss France,' and ended 'yours sincerely, Jennifer Scott,' and contained an invitation to stay at Oddam Castle. 'I do not want anything done in a hurry,' Mrs Scott explained. 'It may take several days to discuss the matter thoroughly and decide upon a scheme of decoration.'

Mr Garfield almost purred when Barbie took him the letter. 'You see I was right,' he said. 'They're nobs. I knew it the moment I saw the classy note-paper and the splashy writing. I wonder how they got our name. People like that don't usually read ads.'

'I'm to go?' asked Barbie.

'Well, of course! That's the whole ideer. It would scare me stiff to go and stay at a grand place like that, but you can hold your own. You go and stay and "discuss the matter." Stay as long as she says – and if you want a new dress you can put it down in expenses.' He sighed and added, 'Thank heaven you're back!'

PART TWO

CHAPTER SEVENTEEN

Barbie's job at Garfield's had taken her to a great many places in southern England and occasionally to Wales but it had never before taken her to Scotland, so she was considerably excited at the prospect of visiting Oddam Castle. Her mother's name had been Helen Roy and sometimes, when Barbie felt romantic, she liked to toy with the idea that she was descended from the famous freebooter in Sir Walter Scott's novel. There was no proof that she was (except that her hair was red and her temper somewhat fiery) but there was no proof that she was not. When questioned upon the subject Aunt Amalie had replied vaguely that Helen's family had hailed from Oban but she had never met any of them.

Of course Barbie was not going to Oban – nor anywhere near it – but as she travelled north in the train she could not help wishing that she knew more about her mother.

The train was late in arriving at Ryddelton Station and Mrs Scott herself was waiting on the platform when Barbie got out. Barbie had imagined rather a 'grand personage' (judging from her letters) but there was nothing 'grand' about her. She was much younger than Barbie had expected, with brown curly hair and blue eyes, and she was perfectly natural and friendly. That was Barbie's first impression – later she revised it a little, for there was an air of dignity about the lady, and her light easy manner was the natural outcome of her assured position. She was confident that her word was law (or very nearly) so there was no need to be 'grand.'

'Awfully good of you to come,' she said as they shook hands. 'I hope you're quite fit again. We've got to go over the bridge but they'll bring your suitcase across the line when the train goes on. Which one is yours?'

'All of them,' said Barbie smiling. 'It looks as if I had come to stay with you for six months, but most of it is patterns. I thought it might be a good idea to bring some books of patterns – for curtains and things.'

'An excellent idea,' agreed Mrs Scott. 'It will be fun looking at patterns. I was so glad when you said you would come and stay for several days because it's going to be a bit difficult to do up the Castle without spoiling it. Sounds silly, I know, but you'll see what I mean when you see the Castle.'

'I think I know what you mean,' Barbie told her. Obviously this was going to be a job after her own heart.

'It will be nice having you as a guest,' added Mrs Scott.

This was a tactful way of instructing Barbie what her status was to be. She had wondered about it, for she had been to houses where she was immured in a hastily converted bed-sitting-room and treated as neither fish nor fowl. She did not mind, of course, for it was all part of her business life (it was the way she earned her living) but here at Oddam Castle she was to be a guest . . . and very pleasant too, thought Barbie who had taken a liking to her hostess at first sight.

By this time the three large suitcases had been packed into the car and they were on their way. Mrs Scott was driving herself, crisply and confidently – and rather fast. The country was beautiful; there were high rounded hills covered with heather, purple as an emperor's robe. There was a little river, a cheerful river, silver in the sunshine, dashing along between rocks and stones. There were clumps of trees and old grey cottages with flowers in their gardens. There were a few small, rather stony, fields fenced off from the road by grey stone walls.

'It's different!' exclaimed Barbie impulsively. 'I mean different from what I expected. I thought the hills would be more rugged.'

'They're more rugged in the north. These hills were made by glaciers, they're very old and full of fossils. Are you interested in geology?'

Barbie was interested in everything under the sun.

'Well, you must get my husband to tell you about them,' said Mrs Scott. 'He'll be delighted if you admire them. Some people are disappointed when they see our Border hills.'

Barbie was not disappointed; she liked the easy sweep of them; they reminded her of great green billows in a stormy sea.

Mrs Scott continued to chat, pointing out various places of interest, but Barbie could not give her undivided attention to her companion's words. As a matter of fact Barbie was a little nervous. The road went up and down and zig-zagged round corners like a super switch-back. Mrs Scott knew the road – but Barbie did not. They swooped down a hill, crossed a narrow bridge and careered up an even steeper hill on the other side. If they were to meet a bus . . . but perhaps buses did not come this way . . .

The idea had scarcely crossed her mind when they turned a sharp corner and came upon a large blue bus drawn up at the side of the road. There was room to pass – but only just room and not a foot to spare. Mrs Scott drew up beside the monster and put her head out of the window.

'You've come the wrong way,' she said in authoritative tones. 'This road leads to Oddam Castle and a couple of farms. There's no through road and the bridge isn't intended for heavy traffic. The best thing you can do is to go on as far as the Lodge and turn at the gates. If you try to turn here you'll get bogged.

'Such a nuisance,' added Mrs Scott to Barbie as she let in the clutch and drove on. 'That's the third bus we've had up here in a week. They think it's a short cut. One of them got stuck and the farm tractor had to pull it out of the bog – wasted the whole afternoon.'

'What about a notice at the cross-roads?' suggested Barbie.

'Yes,' agreed Mrs Scott. 'I hate notice-boards, they spoil the look of the country, but if this goes on we'll have to do something.'

All this time the feeling had been growing that she had seen Mrs Scott before, but when she mentioned it Mrs Scott denied firmly.

'I'm sure we haven't met,' declared Mrs Scott. 'I don't claim to be particularly good at remembering people but I wouldn't have forgotten you.'

'Red hair,' murmured Barbie.

'Well – yes – but a very unusual red – and other things. Look, Miss France, there's the castle!' She drew up beside a gap in the trees and pointed across the valley.

The Castle was set upon the shoulder of a hill, it was a square rugged-looking building with a turret at one side and crow-stepped gables; a flourishing virginia creeper covered the whole front. There was no symmetry about it for the windows were of different sizes – some large and some small – and they were at different levels.

'Not beautiful,' said Mrs Scott. 'But there's something rather nice about it. There's been a castle here for six hundred years. It was burnt down twice, once by the English and once by mistake, so it's very higgledy-piggledy inside. There are a lot of little passages and steps up and down and rooms on different levels. Of course we can't do any rebuilding.'

'You wouldn't want to, would you?'

'I could do with another bathroom and some more fixed basins but anything like that is out of the question. The walls are so thick and solid that it costs the earth to burrow into them for pipes. We can't have central heating for the same reason.'

Barbie thought at once of electric radiators, and then she thought she would wait and see. A castle in the wilds, miles from anywhere, was probably lighted by paraffin lamps.

'My husband's family have been here for generations,' continued Mrs Scott. 'We've lived here since we were married, but we never had much money to spend on the old place – just enough to keep it going and no more. Now we've had a little windfall so we decided to spend it like this; new curtains and carpets and things,' added Mrs Scott vaguely.

They drove on past a small lodge and through an entrance gate with big stone pillars and up a gravelled drive. As the road turned and twisted the castle disappeared and then appeared again in a fascinating way . . . then suddenly it was there before them; larger and more rugged than ever.

There were steps up to the front door and as the car pulled up at the bottom of the steps two dogs came bounding out to meet them; a retriever and a spaniel, both black as jet.

'Down Medda! Down Tansy!' cried Mrs Scott, warding them off. 'It's all right, they won't hurt you. They're just excited. Down, you silly creatures!' She led the way into the castle with the dogs leaping round her like mad things.

Barbie found herself in a big square hall with a fireplace at one end and a flight of stairs at the other. The stairs led to a gallery with a carved oak balustrade. The roof was very high and supported by huge beams. Doors led off the hall in all directions. There were electric fittings (Barbie observed) which meant that the castle was not as uncivilised as she had feared. This would certainly make things easier.

In the middle of the hall was a large oak table, a pedestal table which looked like a slice of a very old tree. It was beautifully grained and polished. Barbie, who loved fine wood, fell in love with it at once. She was somewhat distressed to see a large brass tray on the table, two dog's leads and several caps. Mrs Scott added to this assortment by throwing down her driving gloves.

'It looks untidy,' she said, 'but it's a sort of message-board. When Alec comes in he chucks his cap on the table and then I know he's in – and when he sees my gloves he knows I'm in. It's rough and ready but it works. Bet must have gone out because her beret isn't here. I wonder why she didn't take the dogs – '

'She's away to look at the new kittens, that's why,' said a husky voice which seemed to come from the ceiling.

Barbie looked up in surprise, and saw a face leaning over the balustrade. It was a small brown wrinkled face, framed in iron-grey hair.

'Come down, Jardine,' said Mrs Scott. 'You had better get Annie to help you to carry in Miss France's suitcases. Then you can put the car away; we shan't be needing it again.'

'You will so,' declared Jardine. 'The Colonel said I'd need to take the meenister hame efter denner . . . but I'll bring in the luggage. I'm not wanting the lassie's help.'

The face vanished and a moment later a small wiry man came running down the stairs. He shot across the hall and out of the front door like an arrow. If Jardine was as old as he looked he was amazingly active.

'Jardine keeps me in my place,' said Mrs Scott, smiling at her guest's astonishment. 'You see he's been at Oddam much longer than I have. He thinks he's indispensable – and I'm not. I believe he's right,' she added. 'I couldn't tell you what he does – he does everything – and his wife is an excellent cook. His daughter, Annie, is the housemaid and of course she helps to look after Bet.'

'Bet is your daughter?'

'Yes, she's seven. We have a governess to give her lessons but she runs wild in the holidays – very wild, I'm afraid. That's all the indoor staff we've got,' continued Mrs Scott. 'Just the Jardine family and a woman from one of the cottages who comes in and does the rough work. I'm telling you this so that if you can think of any labour-saving devices you can make a note of them. Of course we used to have a big staff,' added Mrs Scott with a sigh.

'Do you use the hall for sitting in?' asked Barbie as she followed her hostess upstairs.

'We can't. There's always a howling draught and one's feet get like ice even in summer. We've put draught-excluders on all the doors but it hasn't made much difference.'

'Screens might help; big brown-leather screens.'

Mrs Scott liked the idea. 'We could have several,' she said thoughtfully. 'They would have to be big – or they would look rather silly – but not too heavy to move about. Where could I get them?'

'We could make them for you in our work-rooms. Not real leather, of course. They would be far too heavy and expensive.'

'Not artificial leather! I shouldn't like that.'

'I think you would – honestly,' said Barbie and, taking a note-book out of her handbag, she rapidly sketched her idea of a screen. 'It would look like this, more or less,' she explained.

Mrs Scott was half convinced. She said, 'Oh yes, I see.'

'We could try it,' said Barbie. 'The best thing to do would be to have one screen made, on approval. No need to have it if you don't like it.'

'That seems a very pleasant way of doing business.'

'It's Garfield's way,' replied Barbie smiling. 'We like satisfied customers.'

'Any other brilliant ideas?' asked Mrs Scott.

'I thought of electric radiators. There's a new kind – very efficient – and they don't use a great deal of current.'

'Oh, we've got lots of electricity. We make it ourselves with water-power, so we can have as much as we want and it costs very little. We have a man who looks after the dynamo – an odd sort of creature but he's been here for years. He does nothing else.'

'Nothing else?' asked Barbie in surprise.

'He's not – really employable,' said Mrs Scott.

Barbie, who was somewhat inquisitive, would have liked to hear more, but Mrs Scott's words had a final ring about them so she did not like to pursue the subject. Probably there was no mystery. The man might be incapacitated by age or infirmity.

She decided (without much grounds) that the man was an old and valued retainer, wounded in the war.

CHAPTER EIGHTEEN

They had been leaning on the balustrade of the gallery, looking down at the hall; but now Mrs Scott opened a door and said, 'This is your room, Miss France.'

It was an attractive room and, although the furniture and hangings were faded and old-fashioned, it had a comfortable look. The bed was a four-poster, it was a double bed; Barbie saw at a glance that it had a modern mattress.

'I hope you'll be comfortable,' said Mrs Scott in the usual manner of hostesses and she switched the bed-lamp on and off to see that it worked.

'It's a *very* nice room,' declared Barbie.

'Nice, but shabby. That's just the difficulty. That's what I meant when I said I wanted the Castle done up, but I didn't want to spoil it.'

Mr Garfield had said, 'Find out how they got our name,' and this seemed a good opportunity, so Barbie asked.

'Somebody recommended Garfield's,' replied Mrs Scott, in a thoughtful tone. 'Let me see—who was it? Oh yes, it was through my brother. He was talking about the Castle to a man called Rupert Something, that he plays golf with, and the Rupert-man said he knew somebody who knew somebody else who was in Garfield's. That was how it was,' declared Mrs Scott triumphantly.

This explanation seemed vague but Barbie understood it at once without the slightest difficulty. Rupert Something (Barbie did not know his surname either) was Nell's latest admirer and Nell had told him about her friend who did interior decoration at Garfield's, so of course when Rupert met a man at the golf club, who mentioned that his sister was looking for a firm of decorators, Rupert had said, 'Garfield's.'

That was the best sort of advertisement: people talking,

thought Barbie . . . and then, quite suddenly, she knew why Mrs Scott had seemed familiar to her. It was not because she had seen Mrs Scott before, but because Mrs Scott was like somebody – somebody with very thick brown hair and very blue eyes.

'Your brother . . .' began Barbie, and hesitated.

'Henry Buckland. Do you know him?'

'I met him once – at a wedding.'

'It's a small world, isn't it?' said Mrs Scott in a casual sort of voice. 'We're always saying that, so it has begun to sound silly, but we're always bumping up against people we know. He's staying here at the moment for some shooting. Henry is mad on shooting.'

'Oh, I see,' said Barbie.

'Dinner is at eight,' added Mrs Scott. 'The Delaneys are coming – they are our nearest neighbours – and Mr Elliot, the minister of Ryddelton Parish Church. Not exactly a "party," just seven of us, but Mrs Delaney usually dresses up. So if you've brought a pretty frock . . .'

Barbie nodded.

'Good,' said Mrs Scott smiling. 'We'll all dress up. Meanwhile you'll have time for a little rest. Do you think you've got all you want?'

'Oh yes, thank you,' said Barbie.

She had a good deal more than she wanted and although she lay down upon the exceedingly comfortable bed it was difficult to rest. Her thoughts were in a turmoil. That odious man – who had been so rude and had made her look such a fool – was actually staying here in the house. What a coincidence! But it was not really a coincidence. There was a clear line running from herself through Nell and Rupert Something to the odious man.

Barbie tried to relax. It was silly to feel upset. Why on earth should she feel upset at the prospect of meeting a man who was merely a chance acquaintance? She had spoken to him at a wedding, months ago. He had said he would call; she had asked him to tea and he had not come. It was rude, of course, but why should she care? Rude; thought Barbie, her temper rising as she remembered the coffee cake and the frock put on for his benefit and Aunt Amalie and herself waiting for the expected guest! Rude, odious man! Of course she was angry!

By this time she had worked herself up into such a state that she almost decided to plead a headache 'after the journey' and to ask if she might be excused from appearing at dinner . . . but that would be silly for he was a guest at the house and she would have to meet him some time. Better get it over, thought Barbie trying to be calm.

She unpacked and put on the new frock (she had taken Mr Garfield at his word). It was cream lace with a copper-coloured sash which exactly matched her hair. The pearls, which Aunt Amalie had given her, were fastened round her neck. As she looked at herself in the mirror and made up her mouth she decided to be quite cool and indifferent to the odious man. She would be completely natural – that was the best way.

It was the best way, of course, but to play the part of being cool and indifferent and completely natural is not easy when one is feeling angry and upset and Barbie was not at all sure that she would be able to do it. She dawdled in her room, trying to calm herself and to decide what to say, and she dawdled for so long that the rest of the party was gathered in the hall when she went downstairs. They were talking and laughing and drinking sherry, but they stopped talking and looked up when she appeared . . . it was natural that they should, but Barbie felt a sudden unreasonable panic.

Mrs Scott moved forward and took her arm. 'Come and meet everybody, Miss France,' she said and performed the introductions.

Barbie was interested to observe that Commander Buckland was considerably disturbed at her appearance. His face went crimson beneath its tan and he was speechless. Obviously he had not been warned of the meeting, obviously he had not forgotten her. This was so satisfactory that Barbie was cured of her embarrassment and was able to say in a cool and indifferent manner that they had met once before at a wedding.

At dinner Barbie found herself sitting at her host's left hand with Mr Delaney on her other side. Opposite her was Mrs Delaney with Commander Buckland on her right. Beyond him was Mr Elliot; Mrs Scott was at the other end of the table.

Mrs Delaney had certainly 'dressed up.' Her frock was more suitable for a ball than for dinner in a country district.

The men were in dinner-jackets.

At first the conversation was fairly general; Colonel Scott explained Barbie by saying, 'Miss France is a big noise in the decorating world. We've managed to get her to come up to Oddam and tell us how to modernise the castle.'

'What an interesting job,' said Mrs Delaney in a tepid voice.

'It is,' agreed Barbie. 'Of course I don't often get such a delightful job as this, but even small houses and flats can be interesting.'

'Oddam Castle will be difficult to modernise,' said Mr Elliot.

Barbie smiled. 'Yes, and getting more difficult every moment. I don't want to change a hair of its head.'

Colonel Scott looked pleased. 'I like it,' he admitted. 'The old-fashioned furniture seems to suit it.'

'Wouldn't you like steel tubes?' asked Barbie in mock surprise.

'Steel tubes are quite demodé,' said Mrs Delaney solemnly.

There is nothing so pleasant as sharing a joke that somebody else has failed to see. Barbie and her host caught each other's eyes for a moment and then looked away.

'Tell us what you do, Miss France,' suggested Mr Elliot. 'I'm afraid I'm very ignorant. If my carpet wears out I go and buy another – preferably at a sale. I don't bother about the colour as long as it's the right size. I suppose that makes you shudder.'

'Do you want me to talk shop?' asked Barbie. She was really replying to Mr Elliot, but Mrs Scott leant forward and nodded.

'Yes, of course we do,' she said.

By this time Barbie was feeling on top of the world so she proceeded to tell them about some of her experiences and as Colonel Scott played up to her and asked her a lot of silly questions there was a good deal of laughter. Once or twice Barbie glanced across the table at Commander Buckland to see how he was taking it. The first time she glanced at him she found that he was staring at her with an odd sort of expression. The second time he was gazing at his plate.

'Are you of Scottish descent, Miss France?' asked Mr Elliot. 'I mean your – er – colouring –'

Barbie nodded. 'Yes, partly. My mother was a Scot. That's

where I got my red hair. Sometimes I like to think I'm descended from Rob Roy MacGregor.'

They all laughed and Mr Elliot said, 'Rob Roy was not a very attractive person. We are told that he was short and thick-set and that his arms were so long that it amounted to a deformity. He was a thief and a murderer –'

'What about your own ancestors, Padre?' asked Colonel Scott. 'They were thieves and murderers –'

'So were yours, Alec,' put in Mrs Scott. 'But you're frightfully proud of them, aren't you?'

'It's a curious thing,' said Mr Delaney. 'Quite a lot of respectable people are proud of being descended from notorious ruffians. It must be far back of course, so that their desperate adventures are seen through a romantic haze . . .'

When the subject of ancestors had been discussed Mr Elliot asked Colonel Scott if he would read the lesson on Sunday.

'Yes, of course if you want me, Padre,' replied the Colonel promptly. 'At least if it's not full of frightfully difficult names. I like that bit about Gideo – you know the bit, Padre. I mean where he told all the chaps in his army "Whoever is fearful and afraid let him return and depart" and smote the hosts of Midian with three hundred volunteers. That's the stuff,' declared Colonel Scott with relish. 'Gideon knew what was what. Give me three hundred dare-devils and I'll guarantee to lick any army under the sun – go through them like butter!'

Commander Buckland, who had scarcely opened his mouth during dinner – except to eat – looked up and said:

> 'He which hath no stomach to this fight
> Let him depart; his passport shall be made,
> And crowns for convoy put into his purse;
> We would not die in that man's company . . .'

'Dear me,' said Mr Elliot. 'The parallel is very striking, very striking indeed. The Sword of the Lord and of Gideon – and King Henry the Fifth – most interesting!'

Barbie said she had forgotten the bit about Gideon and asked where it could be found and Mr Elliot replied, 'In Judges, Miss France, Chapter Seven. The whole story is very curious, for after Gideon had eliminated his faint-hearted followers the remainder were told to drink at the stream and only those who "lapped the water with their mouths" were selected to take part in the battle. One cannot help wondering – '

'They stood, Padre,' interrupted Colonel Scott. 'The other fellows got down on their hands and knees to drink, but the three hundred took up the water and drank it out of their hands. They were alert and ready for a surprise attack, you see. That's the sort of chaps you want in a tight place.'

'I never thought of that,' said Mr Elliot. 'One is always learning interesting things, especially from people with entirely different points of view.'

'Well, that's settled, then,' said Colonel Scott. 'Judges, Chapter Seven. I'll just read it over and make sure there aren't any snags . . . and could we have, "Rise up, O men of God," as one of the hymns?'

Mr Elliot looked slightly surprised, as well he might, for he had intended Colonel Scott to read from the Book of Revelations, but he reflected that too few of his parishioners took an active interest in the services, or the hymns, but just sat and listened – or did not listen – so it was a good thing to encourage ones who showed enthusiasm, like Colonel Scott.

'And I bet those three hundred fellows were awful bores when they were old,' continued the Colonel cheerfully. 'I bet they "stripped their sleeves and showed their scars" and boasted about how many Midianites they had killed.'

It was at this moment that Mrs Scott gave the signal for the ladies to withdraw and Barbie was sorry for she had been enjoying the conversation. She followed her two companions into the drawing-room.

'What on earth is the matter with Henry?' asked Mrs Delaney. 'He's usually so cheerful, but I couldn't get anything out of him tonight. Is it a girl or something, Jennifer?'

'Goodness no, Henry is a confirmed bachelor,' replied Henry's sister smiling.

'Well, there's something – ' said Mrs Delaney vaguely. She added, 'Oh Jennifer, may I play the piano? Your piano is so much better than mine. Don't listen of course. I can play more comfortably when people aren't listening.'

'Yes, of course, Kitty,' said Mrs Scott.

Barbie had made up her mind not to speak to Commander Buckland if she could possibly avoid it, so when Mrs Scott produced a large work-bag full of different coloured wool, and a piece of canvas which she intended to work in cross-stitch, Barbie sat down beside her on the sofa and they got their heads together over the pattern. When the men came into the drawing-room there was no reason to move – in fact there was every reason not to move – so she remained where she was, discussing the needlework and sorting out the wools. Mrs Delaney had opened the piano and was playing quietly. It was a peaceful scene.

'What about bridge?' asked Colonel Scott. 'There are four of us.'

The other men agreed.

Presently Mrs Scott said to Barbie, 'I expect you're tired. If you'd like to go to bed just drift away quietly. No need to disturb anybody . . .'

Barbie nodded and drifted. She was just getting into bed when the light in her bedroom flickered and died out. It did not matter of course but it gave her food for thought. She had decided that Oddam Castle should be warmed by electric radiators but if the supply of electricity was unreliable she would have to think again.

CHAPTER NINETEEN

The next morning was very bright and sunny. Barbie was awakened by the sun shining in through the window; or perhaps by a movement near her bed. She opened her eyes and saw a sprite, perched upon the arm of the shabby old chair and looking at her in a contemplative manner.

'I didn't waken you,' said the sprite. 'I was very quiet – really. I just wanted to see you – and it isn't *very* early.'

Barbie accepted this as an apology and said it didn't matter. 'You're Bet, I suppose,' she suggested.

'Elizabeth Mary Scott,' replied the sprite, continuing to gaze at Barbie with large blue eyes.

She was just about the same size as Agnes Evans, but there was no other point of resemblance. This child was well fed and well cared for. Her limbs were rounded, her cheeks were rosy and she had the friendly assurance of a dog that has never been kicked.

Poor Agnes! thought Barbie rather sadly.

'Jardine said you had red hair,' said Elizabeth Mary Scott after a short silence. 'But it isn't *really* red – not what I call red, anyway.' She added, 'I suppose you wouldn't like to come out. Grown-up people never want to go out before breakfast.'

Nothing she could have said would have accomplished her purpose so quickly. A few moments before Barbie had had no wish to rise from her remarkably comfortable bed – but now, suddenly and inexplicably, she felt it would be extremely pleasant to go out. It did not take her long to dress and soon she and her new friend were letting themselves out of the front door and walking rapidly across the grass.

'Where are we going?' asked Barbie, for it was obvious that this was not just a morning stroll.

'To Bogle's cottage,' replied Bet. 'I want to see him about something *very* important.' She hesitated and then added in a burst of confidence, 'It's about the kittens. Jardine says he's going to drown them – all except one – so Bogle will have to come and take them away. Bogle always does what I tell him. He's not very wise, you know.'

'Not very wise?' asked Barbie who, despite her Scottish ancestry, was unfamiliar with the euphemism.

Bet tapped her head. 'Wanting,' she explained. 'At least that's what people say . . . but he's not as silly as they think. He gets off with things,' she added darkly.

They walked on up the steep hill path and Bet continued to chat in a friendly manner. Barbie listened, but there was a good deal that she did not understand, for although Bet spoke clearly and prettily (in fact very like her mother) she used colloquialisms unintelligible to her English-speaking companion . . . and, just to make things more difficult, Bet failed to realise that Miss France was a stranger to the neighbourhood which she herself knew so well.

Fortunately there was no need for Barbie to take an active part in the conversation so she was at liberty to look about her and enjoy herself. It was a perfectly beautiful morning; the sky was blue and cloudless and the sun was warm. The path wound between rocks and heather – heather which was incredibly purple and buzzing with wild bees. Every now and then the hills drew back from the path and disclosed breath-taking views of other hills peeping shyly over each other's shoulders.

They came quite suddenly to a small grey cottage which was built into the side of a hill and was so like the surrounding rocks that it was scarcely visible. Bet ran forward and knocked upon the door.

There was no reply to the summons, the place seemed deserted, but Bet was undeterred. She knocked again loudly. 'Bogle!' she shouted. 'It's me – and you needn't pretend you're still asleep. The lum's reeking.'

At this there was the sound of a bolt being drawn and the door was opened by one of the strangest-looking creatures Barbie had ever seen. He was a giant of a man, so large that he more than filled the entrance to his house. His head was small and covered with tufts of dusty-coloured hair; his eyes were pale-blue and set closely together.

The conversation which ensued between Bet and Bogle was one-sided as far as the listener was concerned, for the listener could not understand one word that Bogle uttered. This was due partly to his very broad accent and partly to his lack of teeth. She realised this, of course, but all the same it seemed queer and gave a dreamlike quality to the scene.

Bogle was annoyed, that was obvious. He began a rigmarole in a complaining voice.

'Nonsense,' said Bet crisply. 'I didn't wake you. If *you* didn't light your fire, who did? And anyway you're getting lazier and lazier. You let the light go out again last night.'

Bogle evidently denied this.

'Oh yes, you did. Daddy was playing bridge and he was furious. I heard them talking about it. If you don't look out they'll get somebody else to run the dynamo. You wouldn't like that, would you?'

Bogle began to explain.

'Well, you'd better pull up your socks, that's all,' said Bet. 'I'm just warning you – for your own good. See?'

Apparently Bogle saw.

'Now listen,' said Bet. 'Fluffy has had kittens – five darling wee kittens – in the stable loft. You must go and get them and bring them all up here in a basket – and Fluffy too, of course.'

Bogle seemed surprised.

'Because Jardine says he's going to drown them,' explained Bet. 'If you bring them up here to your cottage they'll be safe.'

Bogle began to raise objections to the plan.

'Don't be silly,' said Bet impatiently. 'Of course you can manage it. You must creep in when Jardine's having his elevenses. It will be quite easy . . . and of course I'll pay you for Fluffy's milk.'

An argument ensued but it did not last long, for Bogle knew he would have to do it. That was obvious.

'Mind, I'm telling you,' said Bet significantly. 'If I find you haven't done it there'll be trouble.'

Bogle's pale-blue eyes looked furtively from side to side and he muttered something below his breath. He looked so unpleasant that Barbie was quite alarmed, but Bet was undismayed. She explained again exactly what she wanted him to do and then they came away.

'He's not all that silly,' said Bet as they walked home down the hill together. 'I mean he pretends to be sillier that he is, so that people will say, "Oh, you can't expect poor Bogle to do any work!" and "Poor Bogle, you can't blame him!"'

Barbie thought this quite likely.

'Mummy often says it,' added Bet. 'She says he's un-un –'

'Unemployable,' suggested Barbie.

Bet accepted the word. 'That's it,' she agreed.

'Why does he do what you tell him?' asked Barbie – for this seemed to her distinctly odd.

For a moment Bet hesitated and then she said, 'Oh well – you see – I know something. Oh, Miss France, there's a heron! That big bird is a heron. Have you seen one before?'

Miss France had not seen a heron before, but although she was interested in the bird she was even more interested in the revelation which had preceded her introduction to the bird. Bet knew something – about Bogle of course – so it was blackmail!

Miss France smiled at the thought, for it was unlikely that either Bet or Bogle knew what the word meant . . . and then she frowned, for blackmail is dangerous even if you do not call it by its ugly name.

Meanwhile Bet was skipping along by her side and chattering like a little brook. 'You won't clype about Fluffy, will you, Miss France?'

'Clype?' asked Miss France in bewilderment.

'You won't tell Mummy – or Jardine. You see Fluffy is my very own so Jardine has no right to drown her kittens and I want to keep them all. Rose Anne wants to see them.'

'Who is Rose Anne?'

'That's another secret, but if you promise not to clype . . .'

'I won't clype,' promised Miss France, who had added the word to her vocabulary.

'We're friends,' said Bet, looking up and smiling in a friendly, charming way. 'We're friends – so I'll tell you. It's my very special secret. Rose Anne is my twin. The fairies took her away when we were born and she went to live on the island. Mummy thinks I don't know anything about her, but of course I do. It's a secret, you see. It's fun having secrets. Sometimes I make Bogle take me to the island in the boat and then he goes and fishes and Rose Anne and me have games together. She's the same age as me of course and she likes all the things I like. We play houses in the little hut with the dolls, but we never play hide-and-seek because she doesn't like it either – '

'Bet! You're making it up, aren't you?'

The child hesitated and then she said sadly, 'I thought you'd understand. You've got to have *somebody* to play with.'

'But I do understand. It's a story – like Mary Rose.'

'Oh, do you know that story, Miss France?' cried Bet eagerly. 'It's a lovely story, all about a girl who got lost on an island and the fairies took her away for years and years. Mummy and I were going to see the play last Christmas but Mummy had a cold and Daddy wouldn't come. Daddy said "I'm damned if I'm going to that piece of mawkish nonsense." What's mawkish, Miss France?'

Miss France said 'silly' was near enough.

'Yes, that's what he meant all right,' agreed Bet. 'So then Mummy said, "Don't swear before the child" and Daddy said, "Sorry, but she hears a lot worse from the men at the farm" – which of course I do,' said Bet with a chuckle. 'Mummy would be surprised if she knew what I heard the men saying – and so would you, Miss France. Shall I tell you some of the – '

Miss France said hastily that she would rather not.

'Well, anyway,' said Bet, continuing her story. 'Daddy said he would be sick if he went, and Jardine could take me, but we must come out before the last act because that was enough to make a horse sick. Horses are never sick, you know, Miss France.'

Miss France said she was aware of this interesting fact.

'So we went and it was *lovely*,' declared Bet, leaping two feet into the air at the joyous recollection. 'Oh, it *was* lovely! I didn't want to come away before the end but Jardine said we must. I can't make Jardine do what I want. It's a pity.'

Miss France did not think it was a pity, so she made no comment. As a matter of fact Miss France was somewhat embarrassed at receiving so much information of an intimate nature about the Scott ménage but she had not the heart to silence her informant. Bet was lonely. ('You've got to have *somebody* to play with!' was a *cri de cœur*.)

It doesn't matter, thought Barbie. It's all quite harmless and in three days I shall be gone and never see them again. She was surprised to discover that the thought of never seeing them again gave her a feeling of deep regret.

CHAPTER TWENTY

When Barbie and Bet got back to the Castle they found that the men of the party had breakfasted early and gone out shooting. Shortly after breakfast Mrs Scott took Bet and went off to Ryddelton in the car. She apologised for leaving her guest, but Barbie was only too pleased to be left to get on with her work without fear of interruption. She unpacked the suitcases of patterns, got out a notebook and a measuring-tape and asked Jardine for a step-ladder. Jardine was in his shirt-sleeves this morning and was wearing a green-baize apron, for he had been cleaning the silver. He brought the ladder and hovered doubtfully.

'It's all right: I can manage,' Barbie told him. 'I'm used to this kind of work.'

'It's queer-like wurrk for a leddy.'

'There's nothing queer about it,' declared Barbie smiling. 'I have to earn my living and this is how I do it – that's all.'

She had decided that there was not much to be done about the drawing-room, for it was a period room and if you did anything at all you would have to make a clean sweep. Mrs Scott could have new curtains if she liked but it was not really necessary. The room was large and difficult to heat – it would be very cold in winter – but why use it in winter? There was a room, facing south, which would make a cosy little sitting-room. Of course it needed vision to see this room as it might be, for at present it was dreary beyond words. There was a holly-tree outside the window, which blocked the light; the walls were covered with mustard-coloured paper, and a single electric bulb dangled forlornly from the middle of the ceiling. The room was used as a dumping-place for anything that was not wanted and contained a mass of heterogeneous furniture, two rolled-up carpets and a sewing-machine . . . but its proportions were good and the fireplace was well situated.

Tear up the tree, thought Barbie. Clear out all the rubbish; put in plugs for standard lamps and radiators; paper the walls and lay a fitted carpet and the poor little Cinderella-room would blossom into a charming princess.

The dining-room was even more interesting. It was hung with dark-red wall-paper which obviously had been there for a very long time. Barbie had a feeling that beneath this paper there was wood panelling. If so the paper must come off. Wooden panelling would be perfect for the dining-room at Oddam Castle.

She was standing on the top of the ladder tapping the wall when the door of the dining-room opened and Henry Buckland appeared.

'I say!' he exclaimed. 'You ought to have somebody to hold that ladder!'

Barbie was annoyed. She had decided not to speak to the man, but there was no option. He had crossed the room and was holding the ladder.

'I don't need help,' said Barbie ungraciously. 'I'm used to climbing about on ladders. It's my job. Why aren't you out shooting with Colonel Scott?'

'I came back because I wanted to speak to you,'

Barbie said nothing.

'Couldn't you come down?' he asked.

'I'm very busy,' declared Barbie, tapping the wall industriously.

'Just for a few minutes – it won't take long.'

'I really don't know what you can have to say.'

'You're annoyed with me –'

'Not in the least. Why should I be annoyed? We only met once – at Elsie Mainwaring's wedding.'

'I thought you – seemed rather annoyed.'

Barbie did not reply. She took out her note-book and jotted down some figures. (Afterwards, when she examined her notes, these figures puzzled her considerably.)

'Look here, I wish you'd come down and speak to me!' exclaimed Henry Buckland. 'I can't speak to you up there, it gives me a crick in the neck. Please come down, Miss France.'

The unfortunate thing was that Barbie wanted to come down. She had finished tapping the wall some time ago, and had made up her mind that there really was wooden panelling – right up to the ceiling. Now she wanted to move into the sitting-room and get on with her job. She did not want to comply with Commander Buckland's request, but there was nothing else for it.

'I'm coming down,' said Barbie and descended with agility.

'Oh good!' he exclaimed. 'I just wanted to ask you –'

'I'm sorry, but I can't speak to you now,' said Barbie firmly. 'I've a lot to do. I want to get on with my work.' And with that she lifted the ladder and carried it towards the door.

He ran after her and seized the ladder from her grasp. 'Where do you want it put?' he asked her.

Barbie would much rather have carried it herself but she decided it would be more dignified not to argue so she led the way to the 'Cinderella-room' and opened the door.

'Here?' Henry exclaimed in surprise. 'But this room is never used. Jennifer won't want new curtains in here.'

'If Mrs Scott doesn't want them she needn't have them,' said Barbie and, taking the ladder, she erected it at the window and climbed up.

Henry Buckland looked at her for a few moments in

silence. At last he said, 'Miss France, what have I done?'

Barbie looked down. There was very real bewilderment in the very blue eyes.

'Look here!' he continued. 'I've done something to offend you. It isn't fair not to tell me and give me a chance to explain.'

This was true. Barbie realised that, for her sense of justice was acute. The idea that she was not playing fair disturbed her. Perhaps there had been some mistake. Perhaps he had sent a message and it had gone astray . . . but how difficult it would be to explain! She had met him at a wedding and asked him to tea and he had not come – that was all. How could she explain without making far too much of the incident? The mere idea of trying to explain made her go hot all over. She saw now how trivial it was and what a fool she was to be so angry (my red-haired temper, thought Barbie regretfully); she realised, also, that if she had not liked the man so much she would not have cared a jot whether he came or stayed away; but that did not make it any easier to explain.

'Perhaps I ought to have written to you –' began Henry Buckland after a short silence. 'I mean written and congratulated you.'

'Congratulated me!'

'Yes, Steyne told me about your engagement that day at the club.'

Barbie was so surprised that she could not think what to say, and before she could collect her thoughts the door opened and Mrs Scott came in.

'Henry!' she exclaimed. 'I thought you'd gone to the moor with Alec – and then I saw your cap on the table. What's happened?'

'Nothing,' he replied hastily. 'I just – somehow – didn't feel like shooting – so I came back.'

'Are you ill?'

'Why should I be ill?'

'Perhaps you've got a touch of your old malaria,' suggested Mrs Scott looking at her brother anxiously. She added, 'Yes, you look a bit feverish. You had better go straight to bed.'

'For goodness' sake don't fuss! Can't a fellow decide not to shoot without being ill!'

'Not if the fellow is you.'

'Well, I did,' declared Henry. 'I'm perfectly well – no signs of "my old malaria" as you call it – but I just decided not to shoot.'

'You haven't quarrelled with Alec – or anything?'

'What an ass you are, Jennifer! Have you ever known us quarrel?'

Mrs Scott did not reply. She was cross with Henry, for she disliked having her plans upset. The two men had been despatched to the moor with sandwiches and she had not expected to see them again until tea-time – or after. She had arranged a very light luncheon for herself and Miss France and Bet. It was quite an unsuitable repast for a man . . . but it was no good explaining this to Henry. Here was Henry, which meant that they would have to use the cold roast intended for tomorrow.

Barbie had tried not to listen to the argument and was getting on with the job of measuring the window, but she could not help hearing and she could not help being amused. The two were so like each other that nobody could have failed to see they were brother and sister . . . and the argument could only have taken place between a brother and sister. Later she was to discover that these two were for ever arguing about something but in spite of this they were extremely fond of each other.

'Oh, Miss France!' exclaimed Mrs Scott. 'I don't want new curtains here. We never use this room.'

'I know,' agreed Barbie. 'It was just an idea. You said you wanted ideas for labour-saving, and I thought you might shut up the drawing-room for the winter. This room would make a delightful sitting-room.'

'I don't think – '

'Yes, really,' said Barbie earnestly. She came down the ladder and proceeded to explain her plans for the transformation of the 'Cinderella-room' into a charming, cosy, comfortable sitting-room for the use of the Scott family. It was the real secret of Barbie's success in Garfield's that she could imagine a room transformed and not only see it herself but make other people see it. (Mr Garfield was always saying 'you can put it across.') In this particular case she was so enthusiastic and therefore so eloquent that Mrs Scott's doubts vanished completely and she became quite as keen on the idea as Barbie could have wished.

'A blue carpet – ' began Mrs Scott.

'Or cherry-coloured,' suggested Barbie. 'Somehow I see it as cherry – so cosy and cheerful – and the walls broken-white with a few good pictures from some of the other rooms – and of course there's lots of furniture to choose from. We can collect what we want from the other rooms and see how it fits in and then have it covered to match. That's how to do it.'

Mrs Scott agreed eagerly and the two began to discuss colours and patterns and whether the fireplace should have new tiles . . . Henry Buckland saw that any further private conversation was out of the question and drifted away.

CHAPTER TWENTY-ONE

Barbie had been too interested in explaining her plans to think about anything else and it was not until she went up-stairs to get ready for lunch that she remembered her conversation with Commander Buckland. It had been interrupted at just the wrong moment. He had said, 'Steyne told me about your engagement that day at the club.'

What 'day at the club,' wondered Barbie. She was sure that Edward had not been to the club during the two days at Underwoods (the two days between Aunt Amalie's birthday, when she and Edward had become engaged, and the frightful day when Edward had driven her up to town and she had broken it off). Barbie remembered those two days distinctly. Edward had spent the whole of Saturday in the garden putting up the espalier; on Sunday morning they had all gone to church, and on Sunday afternoon they had lazed in the garden and talked about their plans . . . so when had Edward seen Commander Buckland?

Was Edward still under the impression that they were engaged – and going about telling everybody? If so she would have to write to Edward and make it quite clear that she was not going to marry him. She thought she had made it clear – indeed it was difficult to see how she could have made it clearer – but, knowing Edward, she realised that he was used to getting his own way so perhaps he thought he would be able to persuade her to change her mind.

As she dried her hands on the beautifully soft linen towel with the large red S in the corner Barbie decided that she would have to write to Edward, but first she must find out from Commander Buckland what 'day at the club' he meant.

Unfortunately this plan was difficult to carry out for there was no chance of private conversation. The four of them sat down to lunch in the dining-room and Barbie revealed her idea about the walls.

'Panelling! That would be lovely!' exclaimed Mrs Scott.

Commander Buckland rose and tapped the wall. 'I believe you're right,' he said. 'It sounds like wood underneath.' He smiled and added, 'So that was why you were tapping!'

'That was why,' agreed Barbie and smiled back at him; she had ceased to be angry with the man.

'How can we find out?' asked Mrs Scott.

'Only by stripping, I'm afraid,' replied Barbie. 'But it wouldn't show if we did it behind the book-case.'

'We'll do it directly after lunch,' said Mrs Scott. 'I can't wait to see if it's really panelling. Jardine can help us to move the book-case.'

Of course Bet wanted to know what panelling was, and Barbie explained. She warned her hearers that although it was certainly wood beneath the paper it might not be in good condition or suitable for renovation. Mrs Scott repeated that she 'couldn't wait to see' so the moment they had swallowed the last mouthfuls of their meal Jardine was summoned and the book-case was moved. Barbie fetched her stripping knife and proceeded to peel off the paper while the others looked on. There were several layers of paper – all quite hideous – but at last the wood was revealed.

'It's oak,' cried Barbie joyfully. 'Beautiful oak panelling . . . but it will be a big job to have it stripped and the wood treated. Rather expensive, I'm afraid.'

'We *must* have it done,' declared Mrs Scott. 'I'm sure Alec will agree – even if we have to economise in other ways. Don't you think so, Henry?'

Henry nodded. 'Fancy putting hideous paper over oak panelling! I wonder which of Alec's forebears was responsible for the frightful deed.'

'You'd be surprised how many people did,' said Barbie

laughing. 'At one time it was the fashion to cover up every-thing.'

The afternoon passed quickly. Mrs Scott and her brother were too busy, and too interested in what they were doing, to argue with each other; they crawled about on their hands and knees with a measuring tape while Barbie made notes. Henry was especially helpful, and Barbie was grateful, for without him the job would have taken twice as long to do. Of course there was no opportunity for asking him about 'that day at the club,' but on one occasion when Mrs Scott was called away to speak on the telephone he looked up at Barbie from the floor where he was kneeling and said, 'Have you still got the little gold bell?'

The little gold bell was still on her bracelet. Several times she had very nearly taken it off (the little gold bell was a reminder of the tall stranger who had made a fool of her) and then she had changed her mind. It seemed silly to take it off. Why should she remove the pretty little charm from her bracelet just because of *him*? Now she was glad that she had not removed it for she was no longer angry. There must have been some mistake.

'Yes, there it is,' said Barbie holding out her hand.

She noticed, as she held it out, that the hand was extremely dirty but that could not be helped. Henry's hands were every bit as dirty.

Henry took her hand and looked at the charm. He said, 'You're not wearing a ring.'

'I'm not engaged,' said Barbie. 'Not to Edward or anyone else.'

'Oh, good,' said Henry in cheerful tones.

There was no time to say more. Jardine came in and informed them that tea was ready in the drawing-room.

'The Colonel's back and Mrs Scott is waiting for you,' added Jardine.

'I must wash my hands,' said Barbie and ran upstairs.

It took Barbie all next day to go over the rooms and measure them for curtains and covers; Mrs Scott helped off and on, but the men were shooting with Mr Delaney so Henry was not available. It was Bet who became her chief assistant; following her round, holding one end of the measuring-tape and running to fetch pattern-books or whatever she happened to want. After a little instruction Bet was extremely useful, for her intelligence was well above average – inded Barbie had often coped with grown-up assistants who were much less intelligent than the seven-year-old child.

'Couldn't you stay here, Miss France?' asked Bet. 'I mean you won't have to go back to London when you've finished the work, will you?'

'I'm afraid I must,' replied Barbie, smiling. 'I've got other work to do.'

'You could work here,' said Bet earnestly. 'You could teach me my lessons instead of Miss Robinson and then I would have you all the time. Please do, darling Miss France. I would be frightfully good and we could have such fun together. I know Daddy would do it if I asked him.'

Barbie was pleased – and touched – but she explained that her job at Garfield's was important and she could not give it up all of a sudden to come to Oddam Castle.

'Oh well,' said Bet with a sigh. 'I'll have to wait till I'm grown-up and then I'll come to London and help you – at Garfield's.'

Barbie said Garfield's would be delighted to have her.

'Really and truly?' asked Bet anxiously.

'Yes, if you want to come – when you're grown-up,' replied Barbie with her usual truthfulness.

Having settled the matter of Bet's future career they went on to chat of other matters. Barbie told her young assistant about Agnes – who was the only other child she happened to know – and answered all sorts of curious questions about London. Bet had never been to London so it was a little difficult to describe. In return Bet volunteered information about Oddam Castle and her own affairs, some of it interested her hearer a good deal. It was all mixed up with what they happened to be doing. For instance when they came to a small room next to the bathroom Bet flung open the door and said, 'We must make this specially nice because it's the room Uncle Henry always has when he comes to stay. He always has it because he likes the view. I love Uncle Henry frightfully much, don't you, Miss France?'

Miss France did not answer but Bet did not need an answer. She took the answer for granted.

'Everybody loves Uncle Henry,' continued Bet. 'It's such fun when he's here, and of course he'll be coming to Oddam quite often now that he's got a job in London – instead of in a ship. Do you know what they call him in the Navy? They call him "Force Eight Buckland." Force Eight is another name for a gale. Did you know? I think it's a good name for Uncle Henry because he rushes along like the wind and blows you about and makes you laugh . . . and of course he's terribly brave. He's got the D.S.C. and bar,' said Bet, nodding portentously. 'What do you think of *that*, Miss France?'

This was easy to answer for, like most of her sex, Miss France admired courage.

'Yes, it's splendid,' agreed Bet. 'So you see we must make his room specially nice. It needs new paper, doesn't it? And the carpet is terribly shabby. We'll have to measure it, won't we?'

In spite of all this chat the work went on at a good pace and Barbie's note-books became full of measurements and hieroglyphics which only she could understand.

On the third day Henry Buckland, who had been shooting in the morning, came back to lunch and was received without enthusiasm by his sister.

'I can't think what's the matter with you, Henry,' she declared. 'I've never known you come back to lunch when there was shooting.'

Henry looked a trifle sheepish. 'I thought I could help to measure things – ' he began.

'I'm helping Miss France!' exclaimed Bet.

Mrs Scott smiled at all this enthusiasm and said that no help would be needed as she herself had a free afternoon and intended to help Miss France.

'Oh Mummy – ' began Bet in dismay.

'You must go out, darling,' said Mrs Scott firmly. 'It's a lovely day and you haven't been out all morning.'

'Can't Miss France come?'

'No, Miss France and I will be busy looking at patterns. I've told Annie to take you for a walk. What about a picnic with Annie? That would be nice.'

'It would be horrible,' declared Bet in mutinous tones. 'If Miss France can't come out I'll stay at home and help her – so there!'

Mrs Scott was unruffled. She said pleasantly but firmly, 'Annie will be ready at half past two. Run along like a good girl.'

142

Bet said no more. She did not run, nor did she look like a very good girl, but she went.

'And what are you going to do, Henry?' asked Mrs Scott.

Henry laughed. 'Your steam-roller methods amuse me. You lack subtlety my dear. If you think I'm going to run along like a good boy you can think again. I'm going to look at patterns with you and Miss France – so there!'

Mrs Scott had got her own way with Bet, but Henry was not so easily managed; he had said he was going to look at patterns and he did. The three of them spent the afternoon in close conclave, not only looking at patterns but arranging what furniture was to be assembled for the Cinderella-room. Barbie was amused to find that her name for the new sitting-room had been accepted by the others and already was in common use. Perhaps the name would stick and, years later, somebody would wonder who had called it the Cinderella-room – and why.

At tea-time Bet did not appear and Mrs Scott went to find out whether she was having tea with the Jardines. She returned looking rather worried.

'They think she's gone up to the moor,' said Mrs Scott. 'Alec doesn't like her straying about the moor when there's shooting. He says it's dangerous. What do you think, Henry?'

'Of course it's dangerous!'

'So naughty of her! She knows quite well – '

'Perhaps I had better go and look for her,' said Henry, rising as he spoke.

'You'd never find her. Mrs Jardine says she took a bottle of milk and some biscuits for a picnic. Annie went upstairs to get ready to go with her, but when she came down Bet had gone.'

'Bet didn't want Annie.'

Mrs Scott frowned. 'Annie is a very nice girl.'

'But dull as ditch-water,' said Henry. He smiled and added, 'You don't understand your daughter.'

'I suppose you think you understand her?'

'Better than you do, anyhow, my pet.'

Barbie left them arguing and went up to her room; now that she had her measurements and notes she wanted to draw up a rough estimate of what the work would cost. It was rather complicated because some of the items were essential and others depended upon how much money was still in hand when she had budgeted for essentials. She sat upon the floor with the pattern-books all round her and worked it out.

CHAPTER TWENTY-TWO

The day had been warm and sunny but now the weather deteriorated. Stormy clouds gathered behind the hills and spread quickly across the sky; there was a flash of lightning and a roll of thunder and a spatter of rain on the window. Although it was only half past six the night had fallen and Barbie had to switch on the light. She had scarcely done so when there was a tap on the door and Henry Buckland appeared.

'Miss France,' he said urgently. 'Bet is missing. I wondered if you had any idea – I mean she was with you all the morning. Did she say anything – mention any plan?'

'No – nothing!'

'The others have all gone out to search the moor. I had better go after them –'

'Wait a minute. What about Bogle's cottage? Could she have gone there to see the kittens?'

'No,' said Henry quickly. 'I thought of that first thing. I went up to the cottage, but Bogle hasn't seen her for two days – not since the morning she was there with you.'

'The island!' cried Barbie.

'The island? But there isn't an island – at least there is a small island in the middle of the loch, but nobody ever goes there.'

'Bet goes there.'

'Are you sure?'

Barbie was not sure. She tried to think what Bet had said. 'She talked about an island. I don't know how much was real and how much was "just a story." It was all mixed up with Mary Rose. She said she went to the island to play with a little girl called Rose Anne.'

'Then she knows!' exclaimed Henry in dismay. He hesitated and then added, 'My sister had twins and the other little girl died when they were a few days old. They called her Rose Anne. I thought they should tell Bet about it when she was old enough to understand – but Jennifer wouldn't. Who can have told Bet?'

So it was true, thought Barbie . . . and perhaps the rest of the story was true. She sprang to her feet and seized her waterproof out of the cupboard. 'Bet's there – on the island!' she cried.

'I'll go,' said Henry. 'It's no good your coming in all this rain.'

Barbie was putting on a pair of heavy shoes. 'I'm coming,' she declared.

Henry did not argue – perhaps he realised it would be useless – he went to get his torch and they ran downstairs and out into the storm.

The wind was strong and gusty and filled with fine rain. The trees with their overladen branches bowed before it and creaked alarmingly. It was not really dark but a sort of grim twilight – a queer ghostly light. Every now and then there was a flash of lightning, and a peal of thunder rolled round the hills.

It was difficult to walk, for the gusts came suddenly and with terrific force; it was almost impossible to speak, for the wind took the words out of your mouth and blew them away.

'I should have told you before,' Barbie shouted. 'I didn't know – how much of it was real. I thought – it was just a fairy-tale.'

'You couldn't know,' replied Henry.

After a few minutes they came to the edge of the loch. It stretched before them, dark and forbidding and ruffled with waves which broke upon the shore in white splashes. The path led to a small boat-house. Henry paused here and stooping down moved a stone and found the key.

'She can't be on the island,' he muttered . . . but all the same he opened the door and they went in.

It was sheltered in the little hut and Barbie was thankful to stand there and recover her breath.

'She can't be on the island,' repeated Henry. 'There's the boat.'

The boat lay, rocking gently on the troubled waters; it was fastened with a chain to a hook in the side of the shed.

'Is there only one boat?' asked Barbie.

'Yes. Alec uses it for fishing. She couldn't have got across to the island without a boat.'

'Bogle may have taken her – '

'No, Bogle hadn't seen her. He said he had been at the cottage all day.' Henry turned and added, 'We had better go back – '

'I know she's there!' cried Barbie, clutching his arm.

'How could she possibly be there?'

'I don't know!' cried Barbie frantically. 'I only know she's there – in all this storm – frightened and miserable – soaked to the skin! If you won't come with me I'll go myself.' It was an absurd boast. She had no idea where the island was!

'Look here, Barbara, you've got this island business on the brain. She couldn't have gone to the island and brought the boat back. Don't you understand?'

Even at that hectic moment Barbie noticed he had used her name. It sounded odd to be called Barbara, but she liked it.

'I must go – really,' she declared and began to fumble with the chain.

Henry watched her. He noticed that her hands were shaking, and when she had climbed into the boat she seemed extraordinarily clumsy in unshipping the oars. He was rather annoyed with her for her insistence, but it was obvious that she could not go alone so he jumped into the boat beside her and pushed off.

It was not far to the island and the loch was somewhat sheltered by the surrounding hills so the voyage was not as bad as he had expected. Certainly it was wet and unpleasant – small boats are always wet and unpleasant in the rain – but there was no danger in it for an experienced oarsman. He rowed with short sharp strokes (as sailors row) which drove the boat powerfully through the choppy water. Barbie, less experienced, was considerably alarmed but she said nothing. Quite soon the boat was floating comfortably in the lee of the island.

Henry jumped ashore. He noticed as he did so that there was a stake in the ground and made fast the painter. The stake was new and sound – not weather-worn as he had expected – so it looked as if somebody really did visit the island. Perhaps this was not a wild-goose-chase after all.

'Now look here,' he said. 'You're to stay in the boat

146

There's no object in your coming with me. I'll find the child if she's here. I don't want to have to look for you as well.'

'Yes, all right,' said Barbie meekly. She added, 'There's a hut, I think.' She had just remembered about the hut.

He did not ask how she knew about the hut. 'You're not frightened, are you?' he said. 'It's quite a small island, so I won't be long.'

'Don't hurry – look everywhere,' said Barbie.

She watched the tall figure disappear into the tangled thicket of bushes and trees. She could see the faint glow of his torch and hear his voice.

'Bet!' he shouted. 'Bet, it's Uncle Henry! Bet, where are you? Coo-ee, Bet!'

The storm was passing over and the ragged clouds were flying across the sky. Now and then the moon shone out for a few moments and lighted up the scene. Now and then there was a distant roll of thunder like the roar of a dying beast. The hills had looked friendly in the sunshine, but in this wild weather their aspect had changed. They were not so much unfriendly as indifferent – old, grim and enigmatical. They made one feel that human life was a precarious thing. They made one feel helpless and ephemeral as a butterfly. It was a horrible feeling –

The wind whined through the trees. The water lapped against the sides of the boat. Barbie was cold and rather frightened.

At last, when it seemed as if she had waited for hours, she saw a light glimmering amongst the trees.

'I've got her,' said Henry's deep voice. 'Pull in the boat a bit . . . that's right. Can you take her?'

Barbie held out her arms and received the cold wet bundle. She hugged it to her heart.

'Oh, Miss France,' said Bet in a queer husky whisper. 'I've been years and years on the island – like Mary Rose. He didn't come back. It rained and rained. There was thunder and lightning –'

'It's all right,' said Barbie. 'It's all right, darling.'

'Goodness knows how I found her,' said Henry as he took up the oars. 'She wasn't in the hut. I searched all round. I'd have given up before, but I found a bottle of milk in the hut – it was empty but quite sweet – so I knew she must have been there. Then I found a shoe. I called to her but she didn't answer. Then at last I saw something white amongst the bushes – and there she was lying in a heap! She wasn't unconscious. I don't know why she didn't answer when I called.'

'I couldn't,' whispered Bet. 'I shouted and shouted until I couldn't shout any more. He didn't come back.'

'Never mind, you're safe,' Barbie told her. This was no time for explanations. The child was shivering violently with fright and cold.

'Hold me tight,' whispered Bet in the queer husky voice. 'Hold me tight. I can't help shaking. Hold me tight.'

CHAPTER TWENTY-THREE

The castle was all lit up, but there was nobody in the place except Mrs Jardine. Everyone else was out searching the moor (the police had been summoned to help; the men from the surrounding farms had come with hurricane lamps – they all knew Bet). Henry carried Bet upstairs and then went out to call off the search.

It had been Barbie's intention to put the child straight into bed wrapped in blankets and surrounded with hot-water bottles, but, now that she could see Bet clearly, she realised that they would have to bath her first. She was dirty and bedraggled, her clothes were in rags and she was covered with scratches. Her feet were bare and muddy and her hair was entangled with thorns and pieces of twig.

'Gracious heavens!' exclaimed Mrs Jardine in horrified tones. 'It's like as if she'd been fighting with wild cats. What happened you, Bet?'

'I couldn't help it,' croaked Bet. 'It was the brambles tore my dress. I didn't mean to be naughty. I just wanted to play with Rose Anne –'

They peeled off the soaking wet rags and bathed her like a baby and put her into Barbie's bed. This seemed the best thing to do, for if they had put her into her own bed somebody would have had to sit up with her; it was obvious she could not be left alone. She chattered in an incoherent way all the time.

'I was years and years on the island,' she kept saying in that pathetic husky voice. 'I shouted and shouted, but he didn't come back. There was thunder and lightning. Did you hear the thunder? Don't leave me, Miss France. Promise you won't go away. I thought nobody would ever come – I didn't mean to be naughty – I was playing with Rose Anne but the thunder frightened her away. She left me alone in the dark – it rained and rained and a bear ran after me – a black thing – a bear – and I ran into some brambles – and my shoe came off – and I shouted and shouted. I was years and years on the island – '

'Oh goodness!' cried Mrs Jardine, wringing her hands. 'The bairn's demented. What'll we do! What'll we do!'

Mrs Jardine was almost demented herself, and was doing the child no good by her tears and lamentations, so Barbie sent her away and told her to make a bowl of bread and milk.

'Miss France, don't leave me,' whispered Bet. 'I'll die if you leave me – '

'I won't leave you,' said Barbie soothingly. 'I'm going to sit here and hold your hand – and presently, when you've have your bread and milk, I'm coming to bed – here, beside you – '

Bet did not listen. 'Why didn't he come back?' she croaked. 'He always does what I tell him – why didn't he come back? I saw him fishing, like he always does, and then there was thunder and lightning and it got dark and it rained. I shouted and shouted but he didn't come back and I was all alone. I was all alone in the dark and there was thunder and lightning – '

'Listen, Bet,' said Barbie. 'When I was a little girl I stayed with my Aunt Amalie – and we had a donkey. Most donkeys are called Neddy, but we couldn't call him that because my uncle's name was Ned – so we called him Amos. He had a soft velvety nose and he used to push his nose against me when he wanted a carrot – or an apple – '

She went on talking nonsense. She hardly knew what she was saying. She only knew that she must try to stop that hoarse croaking voice. At first Bet took no notice but after a few minutes tension slackened and the shaking grew less.

'Amos?' said Bet.

'Yes, wasn't that a funny name for a donkey? He lived in a wooden shed at the bottom of the garden. He used to come when we called him . . .'

Barbie was still talking – talking about Underwoods and Amos, talking about driving Amos to the village in the little cart – when Mrs Jardine came back with the bread and milk.

'I don't want it. My throat is sore. I can't eat anything,' said Bet.

'Och, you'll need to take something!' exclaimed Mrs Jardine in dismay.

'I had a sore throat when I was a little girl,' said Barbie. 'Aunt Amalie gave me bread and milk and it went down quite easily.'

'No,' said Bet, turning away her head.

'Let's pretend I'm the mother-bird,' said Barbie in desperation. 'I'm the mother-bird and you're the bird in the nest. Are you a sparrow or a starling?'

'I'm a cuckoo. I'm in your bed, so I must be a cuckoo.'

'Cuckoos are awfully greedy,' declared Barbie, shoving a spoonful of bread and milk into the open mouth. 'Their poor foster-mother has to keep on feeding them all the time – like this –'

Barbie was not very skilful at the job of feeding her fledgling – any mother-bird would have laughed her to scorn – she found it took all her attention to empty the spoonfuls into the open mouth, but somehow she managed and the food went down. Her attention was so deeply engaged that she did not hear the door opening – and shutting again.

'That was Uncle Henry,' said Bet. 'He looked in, and then he went away. Is he angry with me? Is Mummy angry?'

'Nobody is angry,' replied Barbie. 'Would you like to see Mummy before you go to sleep?'

There was no answer. Bet was almost asleep already. Her eyes were closing. 'Amos,' she murmured drowsily. 'Funny name . . . for a donkey . . .'

Barbie looked at her and was comforted, for already the child seemed better and more like her normal self. Her face was not so pinched and there was a trickle of milk from the corner of her mouth. In a few minutes Bet was so deeply asleep that Barbie was able to get up and stretch her cramped limbs without fear of disturbing her.

Soon after the door opened very softly and Mrs Scott came in. She stood for a little, gazing at her child – and then turned away. Barbie followed her on to the landing and found her leaning against the wall with the tears streaming down her cheeks.

'Don't,' said Barbie. 'Please don't. She'll be all right. I'm sure she'll be all right now.'

'If she is – it will be you,' said Mrs Scott incoherently. 'Henry told me. We'd never have thought of the island – she would still be there – Henry told me what you did – and you've fed her and put her to sleep! I can't thank you – I've no words! It's silly to say thank you. There ought to be something else – something that really means something – '

'Don't,' said Barbie. She put her arms round Bet's mother and they stood there together for a few moments in a close embrace.

Presently Mrs Scott released herself and dried her eyes. 'Silly to cry,' she said in a shaky voice. 'I didn't cry when she was lost. I didn't feel like crying till I saw her lying there – with a milky mouth – like a sleeping baby. Oh Miss France! But I can't go on calling you Miss France – '

'What you two idiots need is food,' said Henry, who had come upstairs to find them. 'There's some sort of meal being prepared in the dining-room and Alec is doling out whisky.'

'I'm not hungry,' said Barbie. 'And I can't leave her.'

'Hungry or not you will eat and drink,' said Henry firmly. 'Mrs Jardine will sit with her and call you if she wakes.'

'How can you think of food!' exclaimed his sister.

'I always want food after a battle. I haven't *seen* food since tea-time and it's getting on for one o'clock. If you would come and eat instead of standing there crying it would be a lot more sensible.'

Mrs Scott went on down the stairs, but Henry waited for Barbie and took her arm in a firm grasp. She was shaking all over and her legs felt so weak that she could hardly walk.

'I don't know what's the matter with me,' she said.

'Take it easy,' he replied. 'You'll feel better when you've had some food. Don't think about what might have happened to the child. Just think she's safely in bed and asleep. If we think of "what might have happened" we never get very far. Every time we cross the street we might have been run over . . .'

Barbie knew he was talking to calm her nerve – just as she had talked to Bet – but all the same it had the desired effect. His deep voice and the strong grip on her arm steadied her.

It was after two o'clock in the morning when Barbie crept into bed. Bet stirred and murmured 'Amos' and went off to sleep again, breathing regularly and peacefully. It seemed almost incredible that Bet was unharmed by her terrifying experience but no child who was going to develop pneumonia would sleep like that . . . and the hand which lay on the sheet felt moist and cool. She's all right, thought Barbie. She really *is*. It will be Mrs Scott – but I must remember to call her Jennifer – who will be ill tomorrow – if anybody is ill.

Bet slept peacefully, but for a long time Barbie could not sleep. She was too tired and excited . . . or perhaps it was that queer meal which they had eaten in the big red dining-room: soup and cold fowl and whisky. Henry had said he always felt hungry after a battle, and she saw what he meant. Her three companions had looked like the survivors of a battle and she herself had a strange dazed sort of feeling as if it were not quite real. The Scotts had thanked her with quite unnecessary gratitude – or so Barbie thought – and they all called her Barbara which added to the feeling of unreality. She was further embarrassed by the necessity of calling companions by their Christian names.

There had been moments when they all talked at once and laughed in a hectic sort of way, and moments of silence. Colonel Scott had broken a moment's silence to say, 'The police were frightfully decent.'

'Did they get a meal or something?' asked Jennifer vaguely.

'Jardine saw to that,' said Henry. He paused and then added, 'She's a strong little creature.'

'Pneumonia,' said Jennifer with a little gasp.

'No – honestly,' said Henry. 'I wouldn't worry too much.'

'Does anybody know how it happened?' asked Colonel Scott.

Barbie knew. 'It was Bogle,' she said.

'But Bogle told Henry – '

'I know – but it *was* Bogle.'

'Don't let's talk about it tonight,' said Henry quickly. 'We can sort it all out in the morning. Let's go to bed.'

There was one last memory which was in Barbie's mind

when at last she dropped off to sleep. It was the feeling of Henry's hand beneath her elbow helping her upstairs – and the sound of his voice saying, 'If you want anything in the night come to me. You know where my room is, don't you? It's next the bathroom. If she's ill or you're worried don't waken Jennifer – just tap on my door. I shall wake in a moment.'

CHAPTER TWENTY-FOUR

Barbie was awakened by a slight movement beside her in the bed. She opened her eyes and saw a pair of blue eyes looking at her – a pair of blue eyes in a rosy face.

'I didn't waken you – honestly,' said Bet in her normal voice. 'I was as quiet as a mouse. You wakened yourself. I've been awake for hours and hours. When I woke up I thought it was all a dream, but I wouldn't have been here if it was a dream – so it must have been real.'

'Let's pretend it was a dream,' said Barbie yawning.

'Do you think we could?'

Barbie felt sure that Bet could pretend anything – and said so.

'You mean Rose Anne,' said Bet doubtfully. 'But that's different – and I'm never going to pretend her again. I'm never going to the island again and I'm never going to talk to Bogle again or ask him to do anything.'

Barbie said she was glad to hear it.

'Will Mummy be angry about my dress?'

'About your dress?'

'It's all torn,' explained Bet gravely. 'I shouldn't have worn it – I should have worn my shorts. I put on my very best dress to go to the picnic with Rose Anne – and it's ruined. I don't believe Mrs Jardine will be able to mend it.'

Barbie wondered what to say.

'Was it true about Amos?' asked Bet.

'Yes,' said Barbie.

'Tell me more about him.'

'Not now,' said Barbie, yawning again uncontrollably.

There was a short silence and then Bet said, 'It's nearly

ten and I haven't had any breakfast!' With that she jumped out of bed and made for the door.

Barbie had intended to keep her in bed, of course, but obviously there was nothing the matter with her. If they kept her in bed she would have more time to think about what had happened, so perhaps it was better not to make a fuss. Barbie herself got up more slowly, she was stiff all over, but when she had had a bath and dressed she felt none the worse. The house seemed very quiet but when she went downstairs she found Jennifer having breakfast in the dining-room.

They both exclaimed at the same moment. 'You should have stayed in bed!'

This coincidence banished the slight embarrassment and made them smile. Neither of them was very hungry; they drank their coffee and talked about Bet.

'She's a tough little thing,' said Bet's mother. 'I suppose it's because she runs about all over the place in all weathers – and drinks such quantities of milk. I often feel sorry for children in towns.'

Barbie thought of Agnes and agreed that children living in towns had a very poor time compared with Bet.

When Jennifer and Barbie had finished their coffee they went out into the sheltered courtyard and relaxed in deck-chairs. It was a beautiful morning; the sky was blue and the hills looked friendly again . . . it was almost incredible to think that last night the wind had howled and the rain had fallen in torrents. The only evidence of last night's storm were twigs and branches which had been wrenched off the trees, and pools of water in the gutters.

Presently they were joined by the two men who had been out already. Colonel Scott sat down wearily, but Henry looked round the little group with a smile.

'All present and correct,' said Henry. 'I've just seen your dear little nuisance. She seems on top of the world.' He added:

'Never was heard such a terrible curse,
But what gave rise to no little surprise
Nobody seemed one penny the worse.'

'Nobody – except the jackdaw,' said Colonel Scott. 'The jackdaw – you'll remember – was a good deal the worse.'

'Bogle?' asked Henry.

'Yes. How did you know?'

Henry did not answer, and Colonel Scott continued: 'Bogle went off the deep end last night and fought two policemen who were searching the moor near his cottage; he must have thought they were after him or something. At anyrate he was so violent that they were obliged to arrest him in self-defence. He managed to escape from them and they let him go, but he fell into a peat-bog and broke his leg so they had to bring him down to the hospital. He's there now, raving like a lunatic. The nurses are terrified to go near him. I saw him for a minute – they thought I might be able to calm him down – but the sight of me made him worse. He's absolutely round the bend. Dr Fraser says they'll have to send him to Dumfries.'

'Oh no!' cried Jennifer. 'Bogle couldn't bear it. He likes to be free. He *has* to be free. You know that, Alec!'

'His leg will have to be properly set and put in plaster.'

'Oh, poor Bogle!'

'Poor Bogle tried to murder your daughter,' said Henry.

'But that's nonsense!' exclaimed Jennifer.

'He took her to the island and left her there in all that storm.'

'He forgot to go back,' declared Jennifer. 'Bogle forgets things. You can't blame him. He's not like other people and he's terrified of thunder – I'm sure he forgot all about it.'

'I think Jennifer is right,' said Colonel Scott.

'Of course I'm right! Bogle is devoted to Bet; he would do *anything* for her! It's quite pathetic.'

Barbie had listened to all this without speaking but now she said: 'Bet knows something about him – some secret.'

They all looked at her now: the two Scotts in bewilderment, but Henry with dawning comprehension.

'What on earth do you mean?' asked Jennifer.

It was difficult to answer. She hesitated.

'Unless I'm very much mistaken Barbara means blackmail,' said Henry. He chuckled and added, 'That would account for everything, wouldn't it? In fact it's the key to the mystery. Shall we ask Barbara to tell us all about it?'

'But I've told you! Bogle has a secret.'

'Which Bet has discovered?'

'Yes.'

Henry began to laugh uncontrollably.

'How can you laugh!' exclaimed Jennifer.

'I can't help it,' declared Henry. 'If only you could see – your own faces! It's all clear now. Bogle got tired of being blackmailed so he marooned his blackmailer.'

'We must ask Bet,' said Colonel Scott. 'We must get to the bottom of it.'

Henry had taken out his handkerchief and was wiping his eyes. He said, 'If you take my advice you'll get Barbara to ask her. Barbara has learnt more about Bet in three days than you've learnt in seven years. I've always told you that you didn't understand your daughter.'

There was a stricken look upon Jennifer's face.

'Oh no,' cried Barbie. 'I mean of course I will if you like! I mean children often tell things to strangers – everybody does – I expect you've done it yourself.'

'Yes, that's true,' said Colonel Scott.

'If you don't mind me saying so I think Bet is lonely,' continued Barbie. 'That's why she gets into mischief – and – and makes up stories. Hasn't she got a little cousin – or some child who could come and play with her?'

'We've talked about that, often,' said Colonel Scott. 'Unfortunately we don't seem to have any relations or friends with small children. I wish we had.'

'Barbara knows a child,' said Henry.

'What!' cried Barbie in surprise.

'That child who lives near you in London,' explained Henry. 'Bet told me about her. Wouldn't she do?'

'Oh no, she wouldn't do at all.'

'Perhaps her parents wouldn't let her come?'

It was not that, of course. Barbie felt certain that Glore would be only too pleased to foist her daughter on to the Scotts for as long as they wanted – or longer – but Agnes would not do. Barbie could not imagine Agnes here, at Oddam Castle. She tried to explain this to the Scotts.

'I don't see that it matters,' said Colonel Scott. 'If she's the miserable little waif you describe it would do her all the good in the world to come to Oddam. What do you say, Jennifer?'

Barbie expected Jennifer to say no, quite firmly, but Jennifer said, 'Poor little creature, we might have her to stay for a bit and see how she gets on.'

'That's settled then,' said Colonel Scott. 'We'll send Jardine to fetch her.'

Barbie began to laugh hysterically: Agnes was to come; it was settled; they would send Jardine to fetch her.

'What's funny?' asked Henry.

'You can't settle things like that – all in a moment.'

'Why not?' asked Colonel Scott.

Barbie felt as if she were being pushed into a corner. 'Oh, I don't know,' she said vaguely. 'There are all sorts of things to be considered. She's a very quiet child. She hasn't got much to say for herself . . .'

'Bet talks enough for half-a-dozen children,' put in Bet's uncle.

'And her mother is rather awful,' added Barbie. 'Mrs Evans might be a nuisance.'

'How could she be a nuisance?' asked Jennifer.

For a moment Barbie hesitated – thinking of Glore – and then she realised there was no need to bother about that. If Glore were troublesome Jennifer would brush her off like a fly. And then Barbie thought: no, not like a fly, because a fly returns to buzz and annoy. Jennifer would brush off Glore like an intrusive earwig which scuttles away and hides beneath a stone! Not unkindly but with calm authority Glore would be told exactly what to do (as the wandering bus-driver had been told). Oh no, there was no fear of Glore being a nuisance at Oddam!

Barbie said doubtfully, 'I'll see when I get home. There will be a lot to arrange. Agnes hasn't got any suitable clothes.'

'She can wear Bet's clothes, can't she?' asked Colonel Scott impatiently. 'If that's all the trouble – '

'It isn't,' said Barbie hastily. 'I don't know – I mean I'm not sure that Bet would like her.'

'Why not ask Bet?' suggested Henry. He paused and then added, 'Where is Bet? We haven't lost her again, have we?'

Jennifer rose quickly, and was about to hurry away, when Bet was seen approaching across the lawn. She was carrying a basket and was closely followed by a large grey cat.

'There,' she said, putting the basket on the ground. 'There are Fluffy's kittens. I had to go and fetch them from Bogle's cottage, but you won't drown them, will you?'

'No, we won't drown them,' said Colonel Scott.

They watched her taking the kittens out of the basket.

'Five!' exclaimed Jennifer in horrified tones.

'Yes, but she loves them all – and so do I,' said Bet hastily. 'Jardine said he would drown them and that's why I made Bogle take them, but now Bogle is in Hospital so they'll have to come home. It's all right, Fluffy,' she added. 'They're all safe and sound. I told you I wouldn't hurt them, didn't I?'

When she had delivered the kittens to their anxious mother she delved into the bottom of the basket and produced a parcel of dirty grey flannel tied up with a piece of cord, and putting it down upon the flagstones unrolled it. The parcel contained a pile of miscellaneous articles which glittered in the sunshine.

'What on earth is that?' exclaimed Colonel Scott.

'It's mostly glass, I think,' said Bet, turning it over. 'Look, here's a piece of red glass. It's nice and shiny, isn't it? I expect that's why Bogle liked it – and here's half a silver spoon – and some blue beads – and a broken wine-glass. Oh goodness, here's your ear-ring, Mummy! You lost it that day when we had a picnic on the moor.'

'The jackdaw's treasure!' murmured Henry. 'Now we know all about it, don't we?'

'Not quite all,' said Colonel Scott.

'I suppose I ought to have told you before,' said Bet, looking up at them appealingly. 'I'm sorry I didn't, now, but honestly I thought it was just rubbish. I didn't know Mummy's ear-ring was here. I thought it was just things he'd found in the rubbish heap. Honestly I did. You see, it was one day when I was playing Indians and stalking him and I saw him sitting on his doorstep with the parcel beside him on the ground. He was playing with the things and polishing them to make them shine. I thought it was all just bits of broken glass and things like that.'

'Is that all you know?' asked Colonel Scott.

Bet nodded. 'Yes, I'm not going to have any more secrets – ever. Bogle kept the parcel in the shed where the dynamo is. It was hidden under the floor. That's why he didn't want anybody to come and look at the dynamo, you see, in case they found it.'

'Well, that proves you can't blame Bogle,' said Jennifer

with a sigh. 'Poor Bogle is just a – just a jackdaw.'

Henry had been poking about with his finger amongst the rubbish. 'I'm not so sure,' he said. 'Is that just a piece of broken glass – or what?' There was a glittering object in the palm of his big brown hand; a tiny thing which sparkled in the sunshine with rainbow lights.

'A diamond!' exclaimed Barbie involuntarily.

'That's what I thought. It looks uncommonly like a diamond to me.'

'It can't be!' cried Jennifer, taking the sparkling object from his hand. 'It can't be a diamond. But it is a diamond! Look, Alec!'

'It's a diamond all right,' agreed Colonel Scott. 'It has been taken out of a setting. You can see the little scratches – '

'And here's another of the same breed,' said Henry. 'It strikes me that our jackdaw is rather clever. I mean if you happened to have a little hoard of stolen gems you might do sillier things than hide them amongst a pile of broken glass.'

'Where could Bogle have found them,' Jennifer exclaimed.

'Your guess is as good as mine,' replied Henry. 'The police will have to solve that problem.'

'Will they put Bogle in prison?' asked Bet in horrified tones.

'No,' said Colonel Scott. 'At least – that depends – '

CHAPTER TWENTY-FIVE

So much had happened during the last two days that Barbie felt as if she had been staying at Oddam Castle for weeks. She had almost forgotten what she had come for – it had been pushed into the back of her mind – but now that life was returning to normal she realised she would have to complete her job and go back to London. The Scotts pressed her to stay for at least a week – more if she could – and Henry added his persuasions. His leave was nearly over and he would be going back to London himself, to his job at the Admiralty, so it would be much better for her to wait and go with him.

'I must go tomorrow,' said Barbie. 'It's very kind of you

but I'm a business woman. I've got all the measurements; I'd just like to go over them and show you the patterns and make the final decisions. Could we do it this afternoon?'

'You should rest, Jennifer,' said Colonel Scott. 'You look all out. Henry and I had better take this stuff over to the Police Station. Why not look at Barbara's plans and patterns after tea?'

This arrangement suited Barbie for it gave her a little more time (she knew how important it was to have everything properly prepared) so she brought down the pattern-books and arranged them in the drawing-room. It made a very good show-room and she was pleased with the effect. There were just a few more measurements to be made and then it would all be ready; she borrowed the ladder from Jardine and took it into the Cinderella-room.

Barbie had been feeling tired but she was so interested in her work that the sleepy feeling wore off quite quickly.

She had almost finished measuring the window when Henry came in.

'I thought you were going to the Police Station with Colonel Scott!' Barbie exclaimed.

'Well, I didn't,' he replied. 'Alec is quite capable of dealing with the matter himself. I've been trying for days to get five minutes alone with you; but, if Bet wasn't hanging around, you were discussing patterns with Jennifer. I wish you'd come down,' he added. 'It gives me a crick in the neck talking to you up there.'

Barbie chuckled.

'It is rather funny,' agreed Henry. 'History repeats itself – but it feels like a week since last time.'

'It feels like a month to me.'

'Please come down, Barbara.'

'I can't – honestly – I'm not just being difficult. I must have all my measurements completed before tea.'

'When can I speak to you?' he asked. 'There's something I want to know.'

There was something Barbie wanted to know – something she wanted to ask him – but for the moment she could not think what it was.

'When can I speak to you?' repeated Henry. 'If you're going away tomorrow there will be no time. There will be tea – with all the Scott family – and then your show, which

I have just seen arranged with admirable efficiency in the drawing-room. Then there will be dinner, I presume, with the Scott family, of course. After dinner more chat with the Scott family – and so to bed. See what I mean?'

Barbie saw. She remembered now what she wanted to ask him.

'Give me ten minutes,' she said. 'Go away and come back in ten minutes.'

'Can't I help?'

'No,' said Barbie.

Henry went away for exactly ten minutes and then came back. He shut the door behind him, and Barbie came down from her perch.

Barbie had decided to get in first with her question – but so had Henry.

'It's just something I don't understand,' said Henry quickly. 'You see Steyne told me that you and he were engaged to be married – and you say you're not engaged – but he showed me the ring.'

'There wasn't a ring!'

'But he showed it to me! It was that day at the club when – '

'I don't know what you mean,' declared Barbie in bewilderment. 'You keep on saying "that day at the club" . . . and Edward never gave me a ring. I was engaged to him for two days – that's all. Then I – broke it off. I just – decided I had made a mistake, you see. People do sometimes, don't they? So if Edward said we were engaged it wasn't true – and he couldn't have shown you the ring because there never was a ring.'

'I saw it,' said Henry. 'Steyne showed it to me. It was a large emerald in an old-fashioned setting. He had it in his pocket in a little white case. He said he had intended to buy you a new ring but this had been his mother's engagement ring and you had said you would rather have it because of its associations, so he had it cleaned and repaired for you. It was very sparkly.'

Barbie gazed at Henry; she could not speak.

'It does matter,' said Henry. 'I mean it has nothing to do with me. I only mentioned it because – '

'But it does matter!' cried Barbie. 'I must know. When did he show it to you?'

'The day after the Mainwaring wedding.'

'It couldn't have been! You've made a mistake!'

'No, I haven't made a mistake,' said Henry. He had been watching Barbie's face which had suddenly become very pale and pinched. He dragged forward an old battered sofa and threw the window open.

Barbie subsided on to the sofa. 'I felt rather queer,' said Barbie in a faint voice. 'It's – so – horrible.'

'What's horrible?'

'About the ring – and all he told you. The ring wasn't Edward's ring. It didn't belong to his mother – or anything. It belongs to Aunt Amalie – at least I suppose that was the ring he showed you.'

'You mean it was all lies?'

She nodded. 'Edward tells lies. That was why I couldn't marry him. I simply can't bear lies . . . and the worst of it was he didn't understand; he wasn't ashamed or anything . . . but of course you don't know what I'm talking about.'

Of course Henry didn't. How could he?

Barbie tried to remember exactly what had happened. She said slowly, 'It was the first time Edward came home to Underwoods after I was ill. Aunt Amalie was wearing the emerald ring and Edward admired it. He noticed the stone was loose and offered to take it and have it repaired, so she gave it to him. That was in April. It took ages to have it repaired. He didn't give it back to her until the day Nell came down to lunch at Underwoods – it was the end of June. I remember distinctly because –' she hesitated. She remembered because Nell had said Edward would have liked to put the ring on *her* finger. 'Anyhow I remember distinctly,' added Barbie.

'Are you quite sure about the date?'

'Quite sure.'

'The emerald wasn't loose when I saw it. Steyne showed it to me the day after the Mainwaring wedding. I know that quite definitely, because that was when he gave me your message about not coming to tea.'

'About not coming to tea?'

'Yes. I was practising some putts on the last green and he came over to me and explained that you and he had just got engaged and that under the circumstances a stranger would be *de trop*. He did it very nicely of course –'

162

'He would!'

'You mean that wasn't true either?'

'Of course it wasn't true.'

'But you were engaged to him.'

'Not then,' said Barbie. 'Oh dear, it's so difficult. It wasn't all lies. It was lies mixed up with truth – which is the worst kind of lies, because you can't disentangle them.'

'Let's try to disentangle them.'

'I suppose we had better,' said Barbie miserably. 'Elsie's wedding was in June and Edward and I weren't engaged until a month later. We got engaged on Aunt Amalie's birthday. We had fizz for dinner and drank each other's healths.' She hesitated and then added, 'What was the object? It seems pointless. Why did Edward say we were engaged when we weren't?'

'To warn me off,' murmured Henry.

Barbie was not listening. She was trying to follow the tortuous workings of Edward's mind. 'And why did he show you the ring?' she added. 'That was a most extraordinary thing to do, wasn't it?'

'It didn't seem extraordinary at the time. He just took it out of his pocket in a casual sort of way.'

'But why?'

'If he hadn't showed me the ring I wouldn't have believed him,' said Henry. 'I think he knew that. The ring sort of clinched it. Seeing is believing. When I saw the ring I couldn't help believing that you and he were engaged to be married. It made me very angry.'

'Angry?'

'Yes, very angry. I knew it was all wrong.'

'I don't understand,' said Barbie helplessly. 'What was wrong?'

He was standing beside her, looking down at her, but now he pulled up a dilapidated old stool and sat down on it so that their eyes were on a level. How blue his eyes were!

'Listen,' said Henry. 'We're all in a fog, and the only way to get clear is to start at the very beginning. I knew it was all wrong for you to marry somebody else because you belonged to me. You belonged to me,' he repeated with absolute conviction. 'The moment I saw you in that crowded tent I knew you were the One. I asked a fellow who you were and he told me. I seized two glasses of fizz and a

163

piece of cake – as a sort of excuse to speak to you – and
was just trying to barge my way through the crowd whe
you disappeared through the flap. Of course I followe
I'd have followed you to Timbuktu if necessary, but
wasn't necessary – there you were, sitting on the seat und
the tree! It was almost too good to be true.'

Barbie gazed at him. Her heart had begun to thump. Sh
was breathless.

'I didn't exactly fall in love with you at first sight,' con
tinued Henry thoughtfully. 'It wasn't like that. I just kne
for certain that you were my woman. You were the woma
I was going to marry; the woman I'd been looking for al
my life. When I talked to you I was more sure than eve
– and I thought you felt it too. I'm being quite frank, yo
see. There's been too much misunderstanding already.
thought you – felt something.'

He paused and looked at her.

'But – this is mad,' said Barbie in a whisper. 'We scarcel
– know each other – '

'I know you,' he said confidently. 'It's written on you
face; it shines out of your eyes; I can hear it in your voice
First of all you're honest. That's terribly important to me
You're real gold all through. You're brave. You're fu
– yes, you're tremendous fun. Above all you're kind and –
and comfortable. You're all the things I want my wife t
be.'

Barbie's eyes were pricking with tears. She said, 'But I'v
got a bad temper.'

He chuckled.

'I have, really. It's my red hair.'

'I adore your red hair,' said Henry.

'This is mad,' she said. 'It really is – mad.'

'It's sane and sensible,' said Henry, taking her hands i
his. 'When two people find each other – Oh Barbara, I d
love you so frightfully! You dear, sweet, beautiful darling
Oh Barbara, say you love me – just a tiny bit. If you don
love me I shall go to China or Singapore or somewhere. Sa
it quickly,' said Henry frantically. 'Say it's all right. Ju
say it's all right – ' He went down on his knees on the dir
floor and put his arms round her.

'I thought we were being sensible,' said Barbie. She was ha
laughing and half crying – and to tell the truth was not muc

164

more sensible than he was.

'Say you love me,' he implored. 'You do – don't you? I can't believe that a feeling like this only works one way. It couldn't come – like this – unless there was a sort of something in both directions. There is, isn't there? Say yes! Please say yes.'

She said breathlessly, 'There is – something –'

'I knew it! I knew you felt it!' cried Henry joyfully. 'When are we going to be married? Let's fix the day –'

The idea of 'fixing the day' brought Barbie to her senses. She pushed him away firmly. 'No,' she said. 'No, Henry – honestly – you're going too fast. You're like a hurricane – or something –'

'But look at all the time we've wasted! We might have been married by now!'

'No – really – please, Henry. Please be sensible!'

'But you love me, don't you? I mean it's going to be all right?'

His eyes were gazing into hers anxiously. He was waiting for her answer.

'I think – it's going to be – all right, but we must be – sensible,' said Barbie with a little catch in her breath. 'It's so – important, isn't it? So important. You must give me time – to be sure. I made a mistake before.'

'That was different.'

'Yes, but I must be sure. We must wait and see.'

'Barbara, I don't understand!' he exclaimed. 'Why must we "wait and see"?'

She tried to explain. 'We must wait and see whether it lasts over into my ordinary world,' said Barbie earnestly. 'This isn't my ordinary world. For the last few days I've been living in a sort of dream. Everything is so different. Oddam Castle doesn't seem quite real – and the old hills – and the storm – and the bright sunshine – and all the things that have happened. It isn't *real*.'

'But life is more real here than it is in London. There's nothing artificial about it. Isn't it more real to go out in a storm and look for a lost child than to stand in a queue for a bus?'

'Not to me,' she replied. 'To me the last few days have been like – like living in the middle of a play: Mary Rose and The Tempest and – and Treasure Island – and –'

Henry had begun to chuckle.

'Well, it's true,' said Barbie smiling. She added, 'When I arrived Jennifer told me that this was a very quiet place; she hoped I wouldn't find it dull.'

'Barbara, you're marvellous!'

'And that's another thing,' said Barbie, quite serious again. 'That's another thing that makes me feel as if I weren't really me. You all call me Barbara. In my real life nobody calls me anything but Barbie. It isn't that I don't like you calling me Barbara – I do like it – but it makes me feel a different person.'

'I shall call you Barbie,' said Henry after a moment's thought.

'Not here,' said Barbie quickly. 'I mean Jennifer would notice and think it odd.'

'All right – not here – but we're getting off the subject. The question is – '

'No, we aren't getting off the subject. It's all part of the same thing. I must wait and see whether this – this Midsummer Madness lasts over into my own ordinary world. Don't you understand, Henry?'

She saw that he did.

'So what?' he asked anxiously.

'So we wait and see. Not long, you know, but just till we meet in London and talk it over sensibly. You can come and see me at the flat.' She paused for a moment and then added, 'But be sure to come. Don't get put off by anybody telling you fairy stories.'

'Nothing will put me off – nothing on earth,' declared Henry.

The bell was ringing for tea. Barbie rose and tried to tidy her hair and collect her scattered wits. She remembered that the Scotts would be waiting in the drawing-room for her to show them the patterns and tell them about her plans.

'You must go out, Henry,' she said hastily. 'I simply couldn't do it if you were there.'

'But I haven't had any tea!'

'I can't help that – it's business. Please go out, Henry. How would you like it if I insisted on being there and talking to you when you were standing on the quarter-deck steering your ship into harbour?'

Henry had never stood upon the quarter-deck steering his ship into harbour but he knew what Barbie meant. As he went away obediently he reflected that as a Naval Officer's wife she would have a real deal to learn.

CHAPTER TWENTY-SIX

It was 'early to bed' that night for everybody at Oddam Castle, for they were all worn out, but just as they were leaving the drawing-room Jardine appeared and announced that there was a 'pairsonal call on the telephone for Miss France.'

'For me!' exclaimed Barbie in surprise.

'Take it in the dining-room,' said Jennifer.

Barbie was even more surprised when she heard Aunt Amalie's voice—a faint far-away voice but definitely Aunt Amalie's.

'Darling, is something the matter?' cried Barbie in alarm.

'No, dear. Everything is quite all right. I just want to ask you something. I got your address from Mr Garfield. Can you hear me?'

Barbie said she could.

'You seem a long way off,' said Aunt Amalie. 'But never mind. I just want to ask if you can remember the name of Edward's friend—the one who borrowed the hundred pounds.'

Barbie was so staggered at the unexpected question that she could not reply.

'Try to remember,' said the far-away voice persuasively.

Try to remember! As if she could possibly forget! 'Hasn't the money been repaid?' asked Barbie.

'Yes dear, he's paid it back, but I want to know his name.'

Barbie thought wildly; but she could see no way of avoiding the question. Aunt Amalie had rung up on purpose to ask and it was obvious that she intended to get an answer. After another slight hesitation Barbie answered truthfully. 'Edward said his name was Tony Chancellor.'

'Tony?'

'Yes.'

'Anthony, I suppose?'

'I suppose so.'

'That's all I want to know,' said the far-away voice. 'I'm sorry to have bothered you. How are you getting on? Not doing too much, I hope.'

Barbie said she was getting on splendidly and feeling perfectly fit. Then she said, 'Aunt Amalie, why do you want to know about that man? If the money has been repaid it's all over and done with.'

'Edward is coming down tomorrow night,' explained Aunt Amalie. She added hastily, 'There are the pips! Goodbye darling, take care of yourself –'

'Golly!' said Barbara softly as she replaced the receiver.

Her mind was in such a turmoil that she stood there for some minutes trying to think it out. Why on earth had Aunt Amalie wanted to know the man's name? Why? thought Barbie. Why on earth! And what would happen now! Well, I can't help it, she thought.

Three hundred miles away Amalie was putting down the receiver at her end of the line. Now she knew all about it. She had known before, really, but her talk with Barbie had confirmed her knowledge. Barbie's reluctance to answer her question, and the way she eventually had answered, confirmed it beyond all doubt . . . 'Edward said his name was Tony Chancellor.' It was not a natural way of answering. Then afterwards Barbie had said, 'Why do you want to know about the man? It's all over and done with.' This was a warning not to inquire further.

Amalie decided to say nothing to Edward. It was the easiest way. It hurt to know that Edward had deceived her, and hurt all the more because it was so unnecessary, but she must just get over it as best she could. There was nothing to be gained by having a quarrel with Edward.

Edward arrived in time for dinner; he was as gay as ever, charming and affectionate and full of amusing stories. He had brought a present for Amalie – a book which she had mentioned that she wanted but had not been able to get. It was a delightful book about Alpine plants with beautifully coloured plates but Amalie wished he had not brought it.

After dinner they went into the drawing-room and Penney faded away in her usual tactful manner.

'May I smoke, Amie?' asked Edward.

'Yes of course. You always smoke,' she replied.

'But I always ask, don't I?' said Edward smiling at her.

Quite suddenly she was sorry for Edward – terribly sorry. He was so charming. He was so kind. There was just this one dreadful flaw which spoilt everything. It was like a disease, thought Amalie, gazing at him. You could not blame anyone for having a disease. You tried to cure them. Was it any good trying to cure Edward?

'Amie, why are you looking at me like that?' asked Edward.

'I wasn't,' she said hastily. 'I wasn't looking at you in any – special – way.'

'You were. There's something the matter. Oh yes, there is. I know you so well. I've suspected – ever since I arrived – that there was something. You had better tell me and get it off your chest.'

She could not speak.

'Come on, darling,' said Edward, sitting down and smiling at her encouragingly. 'You had better tell me. Are you worrying about Barbie and me? You needn't worry. Barbie has gone to Scotland on business (I discovered that from Garfield's) so I can't do anything at the moment, but when she comes home I shall trot along to the flat and see her – and we'll kiss and be friends.'

'I don't think – she will.'

'Why? Has Barbie said anything to you?'

'Not really. She didn't explain why you had – quarrelled.'

'It was utterly ridiculous,' declared Edward. 'Barbie has a frightful temper. She flares up at nothing – and sulks.'

Until this moment Amalie had been perfectly calm but quite suddenly she was very angry. She said, 'That's nonsense, Edward. She's a little hasty sometimes but she never sulks. I don't like to hear you speak of Barbie so unjustly.'

'I'm not unjust. She took the huff over nothing. I don't know *now* what it was all about.'

'Is that true, Edward?'

'What do you mean?'

'I wonder if it was anything to do with Mr Chancellor.' She had not meant to say it, but she was so angry and the words burst out before she could stop them.

'So she *did* tell you!' exclaimed Edward furiously. 'She told you all about it – after saying she wouldn't! After saying you weren't to be told because it would hurt you!'

'Barbie didn't tell me anything.'

'Who did, then?'

'Nobody,' said Amalie. 'Nobody told me. I just guessed that there was no such person as Mr Chancellor.'

For a moment Edward hesitated and then he laughed. 'Goodness!' he exclaimed. 'What a fright you gave me! How on earth did you get such an extraordinary idea? Toby Chancellor was at school with me.'

'At school or at Oxford?'

'At school of course,' said Edward, but he said it uncertainly.

'And is his name Toby – or Tony?'

Edward had become rather pale. 'Amie dear, what's all this *about*?'

Amalie was still angry. 'You can't remember,' she said. Then she added, 'My father always used to say liars should have good memories.'

Edward rose and walked to the window. It was dark outside and the curtains had not been drawn. He stood there looking out and for a few moments there was silence.

'You're unkind,' he said at last in a husky voice. 'I love you better than anybody else – and I can't – bear it.'

'Oh Edward!' she cried. 'I love you too – that's why I'm angry. Why didn't you tell me the truth? Why didn't you ask me for the money? You knew I would have given it to you. Why did you make up a long story . . .'

'I don't know. I just – thought of it. I said it to please you.'

'To please me?'

'Well, it *did* please you, didn't it?'

'Oh Edward!'

'I like pleasing people,' he said defensively. 'I like things to go smoothly and everyone to be happy. I like to be liked. Is that wrong?'

'You like to have everything your own way.'

'But if it's the best way – best for everyone –?'

'Not if you have to tell lies to get it.'

'I didn't tell lies.'

'You told me a long detailed story about a man who doesn't exist.'

'That isn't lies,' declared Edward. 'It isn't lies when

you tell your secretary to say you've gone out if Mr So-and-So calls. It was just like that, Amie. Like saying you're out when you don't want to see a fellow – or admiring a girl's frock when you think it's ghastly. Everyone does it. Do you tell the truth all the time? Does Barbie? Of course not.' He had been down in the depths but now he was perking up again and becoming quite cheerful. 'Of course not,' he repeated. 'If you told the truth all the time you soon wouldn't have a friend in the world. It's the same in business. You wouldn't do much good in business if you didn't use your wits and play up to people a bit. Why only the other day . . .'

He went on talking and she listened in dismay. She thought, but this is dreadful! He can turn black into white. He doesn't know the difference. He has no moral sense . . . and this is Ned's son, the little boy I loved and mothered! And Ned was the soul of honour – straight as a die! It must be my fault. Perhaps I didn't bring him up properly. This is dreadful!

She was so upset that she ceased to listen to what he was saying and it was not until his voice stopped that she realised she had not heard.

'You understand, don't you, Amie?' said Edward after a short silence. 'You remember I was to try it for a year and see how I got on and how I liked it – and of course the year is up in October.'

'You mean you've decided to give up your partnership in the firm?' asked Amalie incredulously.

'That's what I've been telling you.'

'I thought you liked it.'

'Oh, I didn't mind it at first, but it wasn't really what I expected. I didn't expect to get landed with a lot of office work. I like going about and meeting people – that's my line. The other partners are such stick-in-the-muds that they don't realise that. They don't realise how valuable I am. Anyone can sit in an office and tot up figures but very few people can go out and make valuable contacts and bring in new clients.'

'Have they told you to – to – '

Edward laughed. 'Oh, they haven't sacked me – if that's what you mean. It was mutual.'

She wondered if it were true. She realised with a shock of horror that she would never again believe what Edward told her without wondering if it were true.

'Of course I'll get my money out of them,' continued Edward. 'At least it's your money, but you won't mind if I keep it, will you? It's easier to get a really good job if you can put down some capital.'

'What are you going to do?' she asked him.

'That's the question,' said Edward jauntily. 'What am I going to do? If I can persuade Barbie to be sensible I shall get another job in this country, if not I shall go abroad.'

Amalie gazed at him. 'Persuade Barbie to be sensible!' she echoed. 'You mean to marry her?'

'Yes, of course.'

'But you've just said she was bad-tempered and sulky and –'

'Oh, she's not all that bad,' declared Edward. 'I'm very fond of Barbie – always have been – and of course there's Underwoods. I suppose you thought I didn't know that Father had left it to Barbie. I've known about it for months. I thought I'd like to see exactly how Father had left his money, so I paid a visit to Somerset House – you pay your bob and you can see anyone's Will. I was pretty angry at first I can tell you.'

'And then you decided to marry Barbie!'

'Amie!' he exclaimed in horrified tones. 'You don't really think that about me! You know I've always loved Barbie – ever since we were children – I've never thought of anyone else. Look, Amie, look at that!' he added, taking something out of his pocket and holding it out to her. 'That will show you! We cut it in half when we were children. Barbie has lost her bit, but I've always kept mine – all these years.'

It was half a silver sixpence.

Seeing is believing (as Henry Buckland had found). Whether or not it was true that Edward had treasured his half of the sixpence 'all these years' nobody but himself would ever know, but Amalie did not doubt the evidence of her eyes.

'Oh Edward, I'm sorry!' she exclaimed. 'Oh Edward! What a pity it all is! What a dreadful pity!'

'A pity!' he echoed in surprise. 'But if Barbie sees that – if I show her my half of the sixpence –'

Amalie shook her head. She said wearily, 'I don't understand you, Edward, but I think I do understand Barbie. Perhaps it's because we're the same kind of person – underneath.'

'Amie, listen!'

'No,' she said rising. 'I can't listen any more tonight. I'm – too tired. I don't know when I've felt so – awfully – tired.'

The feeling of utter exhaustion had come quite suddenly. She was so tired that the thought of going upstairs and undressing and getting ready for bed dismayed her . . . but she called Penney and Penney came and put her arm round her and together they went slowly up the stairs.

Edward stood in the hall and watched them (he had offered to help Amie up the stairs but his services had been refused). He had a feeling of depression and loneliness. He had a feeling that his best friend had deserted him. It was a horrible feeling while it lasted . . . but it did not last long.

CHAPTER TWENTY-SEVEN

The first night of Barbie's homecoming she and Nell sat up till all hours talking. Barbie did most of the talking and there was so much to tell that her throat was quite rough by the time she had finished. She told Nell all that had happened, starting from her arrival at Ryddelton Station . . . but she did not mention Henry Buckland. Barbie had decided not to tie herself in any way, not even by mentioning his name to Nell. When Henry walked into the flat – walked into her own everyday life – she would know for certain whether he was really and truly the One. There was another reason, too. She had 'gassed' to Aunt Amalie about Henry Buckland, preparations had been made for him – and he had not come. This time there would be no 'gas' and no preparations, so of course he would come.

Of course he would come. It was only now and then at odd moments that Barbie was beset with doubts. It was as if Something said to her, 'Supposing he doesn't come? He said he would come before – and he didn't. What will you do if he doesn't come?' 'Of course he'll come,' said Barbie to the Something.

Nell was a little half-hearted about the plan for Agnes. 'Oh, Barbie, I don't know . . .' said Nell. 'Of course it would be marvellous for her, but supposing they didn't like the poor little creature and sent her back? It would be worse then, wouldn't it? Agnes would have had a taste of Paradise.'

'Wouldn't it be better to have had a taste of Paradise than never to have known anything but *that*?' asked Barbie, pointing in the direction of the Other Flat.

'And there's Glore,' added Nell. 'Glore might make herself a nuisance.'

'Not to the Scotts,' said Barbie confidently. 'The Scotts can look after themselves . . . and from now on we're going to look after ourselves too. Kind but firm is the recipe for dealing with people like Glore.'

Barbie had a good opportunity of trying out her recipe next morning, for Glore's usual knock was heard as they were finishing breakfast.

'Don't bother, leave it to me,' said Barbie, gulping down the last mouthfuls of coffee and rushing to the door.

'Oh Miss France, you're back!' exclaimed Glore. 'Did you have a nice holiday in Scotland?'

'It wasn't a holiday, it was business, but I enjoyed it thoroughly.'

'Is Nell in?'

'She's finishing her breakfast. We're rather late this morning.'

'Oh,' said Glore. 'Oh well, I've just come to borrow your electric iron. Mine is out of order.'

Barbie smiled kindly. 'Your iron has been out of order for weeks, hasn't it? The best thing to do is to take it to the electrician – the one at the corner is quite good; he'll put it in order for you.'

'Oh!' said Glore.

'Take it along this morning,' said Barbie . . . and she stood there, still smiling kindly in a Jennifer Scott manner.

'Oh, well – yes – I could, I suppose.'

Having settled the matter satisfactorily Barbie produced a letter. It was written upon thick paper and was addressed to Mrs Evans in large bold hand-writing (hand-writing which Mr Garfield would have recognised).

'Here's a letter,' said Barbie. 'It's from Mrs Scott – the lady

I was staying with in Scotland. I haven't time to talk about it now.'

'What is it?' asked Glore eyeing it with suspicion.

'Take it and read it,' said Barbie. 'It explains itself. I must fly or I shall be late. I'll be home at six if you would like to come and talk to me about it.'

'But Miss France –'

'I really must fly,' declared Barbie and she thrust the letter into Glore's hand.

Barbie was a little late in arriving at Garfield's and Mr Garfield was waiting for her. They went into his office, and together they examined all the measurements and patterns, and Barbie explained her notes. She told him what the Scotts wanted done and what she had advised.

It took a long time to go through everything and when they had finished Mr Garfield sat back in his chair and looked at her. 'You've excelled yourself, Miss France,' he said solemnly. 'Yes, you've excelled yourself. It couldn't be better. What a head you've got!'

'We can do it soon, can't we?' said Barbie anxiously.

'We can do it soon – and we will. It's a big job of course – all those chairs to be upholstered and everything – but we'll put it through quick. Top priority – see? We'll put it in hand straight off and what's more we'll cut the prices. Good advertisement, you see. Opens new ground. People coming in and seeing the place and saying, "Where did you get it done?" and then saying, "Garfield's. They did it straight off in 'alf no time – and it wasn't expensive, neither."'

(Barbie could not imagine the Scotts saying this, but she took the point.)

'Really, I don't know when I've been so pleased about a job,' declared Mr Garfield. 'We've had bigger jobs of course, but this is special. It's what I call romantic. An old castle in the mountains! Would they let us use it in our ads?'

'No,' said Barbie with conviction.

'Oh well, you can't have everything,' said Mr Garfield philosophically. 'I can't see why they should mind, but some people *are* a bit shy.'

The matter was now settled so Barbie collected her note-books and prepared to go.

'Just a minute, Miss France,' said Mr Garfield getting

up and beginning to walk about the room. 'There's another thing I wanted to see you about. It isn't a new idea; I've been thinking about it for some time. What about a partnership? Garfield and France sounds pretty good to me. If you can raise a bit of money to put into the business I won't say no, but if you can't – well it can't be 'elped, that's all.'

Barbie was astonished. It was a very good business and in the last few years it had expanded enormously; she knew that, for she had access to the books. She had often wondered why Mr Garfield did not take a partner with a little capital and enlarge the premises, but she had never thought of herself. A partnership in Garfield's! It was beyond her wildest dreams.

She said feebly, 'Mr Garfield, do you really mean it?'

'Would I say it if I didn't mean it?' he exclaimed.

'No, of course not,' said Barbie hastily. 'It was silly of me but I was so surprised. I never thought of such a thing for a moment. As a matter of fact I think I could raise some capital, my aunt would lend it to me, but ...'

'But what?' asked Mr Garfield.

Barbie hesitated.

'My goodness!' exclaimed Mr Garfield, gazing at her in dismay. 'My goodness! You aren't thinking of getting married, are you?'

'Nothing – is settled.'

He flung himself into his chair. 'That's the worst of women! 'Ere am I, offéring you a partnership in the best Interior Decorating business in town and you chuck it aside like an old glove!'

'Oh no, I don't!' cried Barbie .'I'm terribly pleased and grateful – but I don't quite know – '

'Like an old glove,' repeated Mr Garfield bitterly. 'Why, Miss France, you're a genius in this line of business – a genius, that's what you are – and you chuck it all up because some bloke wants you to keep 'ouse for 'im – cook 'is dinner and mend 'is socks!'

'Nothing is settled,' repeated Barbie. 'And even if I do – get married – I might stay on.'

'I've 'eard that tale before,' said poor Mr Garfield, his aitches flying in all directions. 'That's what they all say, "I might stay on." They stay on and then they find it interferes with 'is comfort – or they're going to 'ave a baby – or something. I know.'

'I'm sorry,' said Barbie, blushing like a rose. 'I really am awfully sorry. Perhaps you wouldn't mind waiting for a day or two. Nothing is settled yet – and please don't say anything about it to anybody.'

Somehow she managed to get herself out of Mr Garfield's office and fled.

There was a great deal to arrange, for if Oddam Castle was to be 'top priority' other work would have to be shelved. Some of it could be shelved quite easily, but other work could not. Barbie had so much to think about that she forgot her appointment with Glore, and when she got home she found Glore waiting for her on the landing.

'Oh, Miss France!' exclaimed Glore. 'I thought you were never coming. I've been waiting for ages.'

'Ten minutes,' said Barbie, glancing at her watch and assuming the Jennifer Scott manner in which she meant to conduct the interview. 'Come in, Mrs Evans, and sit down. Perhaps you'd like a glass of sherry.'

'I'd rather have gin,' said Glore. 'And I do wish you'd call me Glore. It sounds funny calling me Mrs Evans. Everyone calls me Glore. Agnes does too. Mummy is such a silly name, isn't it?'

Barbie was not anxious to call her visitor Glore and was even less anxious that her visitor should call her Barbie (she was aware that Agnes called her mother by the ridiculous name and did not approve of it at all. In Barbie's opinion 'Glore' was very much sillier than 'Mummy'). Thus thinking, Barbie did not reply, but busied herself pouring out the drinks.

When they had both sat down Glore said, 'I've read the letter. It's funny isn't it, Miss France? I mean it seems queer. I suppose you told them about Agnes.'

'Mrs Scott explained all that in her letter didn't she?'

'Yes, but it seems queer. I've been thinking all day and really I don't think I could bear to part with Agnes.'

'In that case there's no more to be said about it. We'll just write and explain to Mrs Scott that you – '

'Oh, but it wouldn't be right!' said Glore hastily. 'I mustn't think of myself, must I?'

Barbie said nothing. Her impression was that Glore never thought of anybody but herself.

'It seems funny,' repeated Glore. 'I mean letting Agnes go all that way to people I don't know anything about. It would be better if I went with her and stayed for a day or two and saw how she got on. If I did that they wouldn't have to send that gentleman to fetch her.'

'Does Mrs Scott suggest that?' asked Barbie.

'Well – no, but I thought –'

'If Mrs Scott had wanted you to go to Oddam she would have invited you.'

'Oh!' exclaimed Glore, rather taken aback.

'I'm afraid you'll either have to say yes or no,' said Barbie. She smiled and added, 'That's the sort of person she is.'

'Would they be kind to Agnes, Miss France?'

'They would be very kind indeed. The Scotts are delightful people and if you decided to let Agnes go to Oddam Castle they would treat her as their own child. I can promise you that.'

Barbie smiled encouragingly for she was pleased with Glore, and for the first time a little sorry for her. Unfortunately Glore spoilt the good impression with her next question.

'I was wondering if they would pay,' said Glore. 'I mean if Agnes is going to be a companion to that little girl . . . I mean companions get paid, don't they? I wouldn't want them to pay Agnes, but they could pay me, couldn't they? It will be lonely without Agnes.' She took out a dirty little handkerchief and wiped the corners of her eyes very carefully – so as not to smear the mascara.

'They won't pay anything except the expenses,' replied Barbara with conviction. 'Agnes would be clothed and fed and educated free of charge. It seems to me a most generous offer.'

'Well, I don't know,' said Glore. 'It will be lonely without Agnes. She's my own little girl, you see. She's my ewe-lamb, Miss France. Of course you wouldn't understand what it's like to be a mother. I don't know how I could bear it – really I don't.'

Nothing annoyed Barbie more than hypocrisy. It would have given Barbie great satisfaction to walk into Glore and tell her exactly what she thought of her, but fortunately she managed to refrain. Instead she said coldly, 'Well, we had better write to Mrs Scott and refuse her offer. Shall I do it, or will you answer her letter yourself?'

'Oh no!' cried Glore in alarm. 'No, really! I mean I mustn't be selfish. I must think of Agnes, mustn't I? It would be nice for Agnes to go.'

'You needn't decide tonight,' said Barbie. 'You can think it over and let me know what you decide. It will be time enough if we send Mrs Scott a wire tomorrow morning.'

Barbie rose and added, 'I've got a lot to do.' And Glore (who usually was impervious to hints) rose and departed.

But before Barbie had shut the door behind her she turned and said, 'Oh, Miss France, perhaps you ought to wire tonight. I mean they might hear of someone else, mightn't they? It would be a pity if . . .'

'Yes, it would,' agreed Barbie. 'I'll wire tonight, shall I?'

'I think you'd better,' said Glore.

Glore would have been surprised if she could have seen what happened when the door closed behind her. Miss France threw her hat in the air and danced a jig.

CHAPTER TWENTY-EIGHT

Nell was very much interested to hear of the latest developments, for by this time she was quite as keen as Barbie on the plan. The two friends chatted about it in their usual uninhibited manner as they washed up the supper dishes. It had been decreed from Oddam Castle that the child was to be handed over to Jardine at Euston Station in time for the night train to Scotland on Thursday evening, and Barbie was particularly anxious to take Agnes herself so that Glore and Jardine should not meet. She did not think Glore would make a good impression upon Jardine. Of course Nell saw the point at once and with commendable unselfishness offered to take Glore to the latest American 'Musical' on Thursday evening.

'She won't go,' said Barbie with a sigh. 'She's sure to want to go to the station with Agnes.'

'I think she'll go,' replied Nell. 'If I offer to take her she won't be able to resist it.'

'She'll smell a rat.'

'No, she won't. I'll just get tickets and say you don't want to go and ask if she would like to come with me.'

'Nell – really!' exclaimed Barbie, half shocked and half awed by the machiavellian scheme.

Nell was right; Glore could not resist the invitation. She did not hesitate for a moment.

'It's no good us both going to the station, is it?' said Glore cheerfully. 'Pity to waste the ticket. I mean if Miss France *wants* to go to the station . . .'

Barbie nodded.

It was settled as easily as that.

Glore's way was to take an ell when an inch was offered. She had found it paid. 'I'll send Agnes over at half past two,' she said. 'That will be all right, won't it? She can have her tea with you and it'll give me a chance to do some shopping before I meet Nell at the theatre. I mean if you're going to take her to the station you might as well have her for the afternoon.'

This was more than Barbie had bargained for, but she was so stunned by the woman's impudence that she agreed to the plan.

'Was any mother ever so callous?' said Barbie to Nell, when their visitor had taken her departure.

'Lots are,' replied Nell. 'Some are worse. You've only got to read the daily papers. Look at that woman who shut her child in a dark cupboard for two whole days – and the one who strangled her baby.'

'But they were different!'

'What do you mean – different? Their neighbours didn't know what was happening until it all came out. Murderers don't wear the mark of Cain on their foreheads.'

'Nell, you're making my blood run cold!' exclaimed Barbie with a shudder.

'My blood has run cold several times,' said Nell in thoughtful tones. 'Sometimes at night – when I couldn't go to sleep – but in the morning I always decided I was a perfect fool. Anyhow it's all right now,' she added cheerfully.

No more was said upon the subject, and of course there was no difficulty in Barbie getting the afternoon off. Mr Garfield would have given her practically anything she asked for (he was willing to give her half his kingdom if only she would accept it) so Barbie was ready for Agnes when she appeared at the door of the flat at half past two.

The idea was that Agnes would not need any clothes for her visit to Oddam Castle because she could wear some of Bet's – and Bet had plenty – but the child had to travel in clothes. When Barbie thought of her arriving at the castle in those peculiar garments she decided that it wouldn't do. All Agnes's clothes had been bought at sales off the bargain counter; they were not only unsuitable for a child of eight years old but they were shabby and not very clean . . . and now that Barbie looked at her critically, she realised that Agnes herself was not very clean.

Agnes had a button in her hand; she held it out and said, 'Glore hadn't time to sew it on for me. She said you would. It's come off my coat.'

Barbie was so angry when she saw the button that she threw discretion to the winds. The only thing to do was to take Agnes shopping and buy her some suitable clothes. She explained this to Agnes, and off they went.

At first Barbie had intended to buy Agnes a coat in place of the yellow cloth coat (with the scrubby-looking velvet collar and the missing button); but the dress beneath the coat was bright-blue satin, trimmed with lace, and the shoes Agnes was wearing had holes in the soles . . . so Barbie let herself go. She bought a pair of cherry-coloured shorts and a white pullover, brown leather lacing-shoes and white socks; she bought a brown tweed coat and a cherry-coloured beret and some much-needed underwear as well. Having spent so much money on her protégée Barbie decided that the child's hair would spoil the whole effect, so she whirled Agnes into the nearest hairdresser and had the absurd pony-tail cut off and the dark hair trimmed closely to what proved to be an exceedingly well-shaped head.

All this time Agnes had said practically nothing, for she was a silent child, but it was obvious that she did not approve of the new garments (she preferred something more 'fancy') and when she saw the pony-tail of hair lying upon the floor she shed tears and had to be pacified by a bag of toffee. After this they returned to the flat, laden with parcels.

There was still one little job to be done, perhaps the most important; Barbie put Agnes into the bath, scrubbed her all over thoroughly and washed her hair.

The result was astonishing – Barbie was more than satisfied

– never had time and money been so well spent. Clean and tidy and dressed in her new clothes Agnes looked like a different creature. She did not look like Bet, of course, but she looked like the sort of child you might expect to see in Bet's company – which she certainly had not done before.

'You'll do,' said Barbie with a sigh of exhaustion.

Agnes was surveying herself in the long mirror. 'Goodness, I don't look like me!' she exclaimed.

'You look like a very pretty little girl.'

'Do I?' asked Agnes, gazing at her reflection in wonder.

'Yes, don't you think so yourself?'

For the first time Agnes smiled (Barbie had never seen Agnes smile before and she was surprised, for the smile lighted up the little face and filled it with intelligence).

'It's a pity Glore can't see me,' said Agnes. 'I'd like Glore to see me, Miss France.'

'But you're pleased that you're going to Scotland, aren't you?' said Barbie hastily.

Agnes nodded. 'It'll be nice for Glore to get rid of me so that she can go to Montreal.'

'Montreal!'

'It's a town,' said Agnes. 'I don't know where it is, but she's going there with Mr Banks.'

This was the first Barbie had heard of it and she was considerably alarmed, for if Glore went off to Canada she might disappear completely and never come back. What then would happen to Agnes? Jennifer Scott had said they would have Agnes to stay for a bit and see how she got on. She had said no more and no less.

'When is Glore going?' asked Barbie anxiously.

Agnes did not know. In fact Agnes knew nothing whatever about her mother's plans except that she was going to Montreal with Mr Banks.

They had a very belated tea – it was more like supper – and Agnes was quite cheerful; indeed it seemed that her new outward appearance had changed her inwardly as well. Barbie tried to prepare her for her visit to Oddam Castle (she had tried to describe London to Bet but this was even more difficult).

'Will I have to wash the dishes?' asked Agnes.

'No,' replied Barbie. 'You'll just have to play with Bet and have lessons with Bet – that's all. Bet's cat is called

Fluffy and she's got five kittens. I expect Bet will give you one . . .'

Barbie went on talking about Oddam and the pleasures in store for Agnes until it was time to go to Euston.

CHAPTER TWENTY-NINE

Jardine was waiting for them in the station-yard and just for a moment Barbie did not know him. She had seen him in his working clothes; she had seen him in his shirt-sleeves with his green-baize apron, but this was a dapper little man in an exceedingly well-cut navy-blue suit and a bowler hat. Barbie could not help smiling, for Jardine in his London clothes looked exactly like Mr Bolfry – even to the neatly-rolled umbrella. He could have walked on to the stage exactly as he was and played the part to perfection.

'You're nice and airly, Miss France,' said Jardine, approaching and removing his bowler hat. 'I was hoping you'd be airly. Leddies are a wee bit apt tae leave things tae the last meenit.'

'This is Agnes,' said Barbie when she had shaken hands with him.

Jardine looked at Agnes critically and nodded. It was evident that he approved of her (what he would have said or done if he had seen her at half past two that afternoon Barbie could not imagine).

'She's a wee bit peaky,' said Jardine. 'But that's not tae be wondered at – living in London. It's an awfu' place! Mistress Jardine'll soon fatten her up. Are ye a guid traiveller, Miss Agnes?'

Agnes gazed at him.

'Are ye seeck in the train?' asked Jardine putting the question differently.

Agnes shook her head.

'That's fine,' said Jardine with a sigh of relief.

This realistic approach to his duties as a courier-nurse-maid pleased Barbie considerably and she followed him on to the long platform with an easier mind.

Everything had been arranged in the usual Scott manner,

the tickets had been taken and sleepers reserved. The sleepers were at the far end of the platform and the attendant was waiting for them and greeted Jardine as an old friend.

Agnes and Jardine got into the train and Barbie was about to follow them when she felt a touch on her arm, and turning, saw Henry Buckland.

'Yes, it's me,' said Henry, seeing her surprise.

'But I thought you were staying at Oddam till Sunday!'

'Couldn't stick it out,' exclaimed Henry. 'I was afraid you might meet some other fellow or something. I came south with Jardine last night and I've been searching for you all day. I went to your flat this morning and rang and knocked but nobody answered; then I went to Garfield's and they said you had taken the afternoon off. I went back to the flat and rang and knocked till I was tired. By that time I was like a maniac; I thought I had lost you again! Then it struck me that you might come to the station with the child – so here I am.'

For some reason this sad tale pleased Barbie quite a lot.

'I've been busy,' she said, smiling at him.

'Doing what?' asked Henry suspiciously. 'Interior decorating – or out with some fellow?'

'Neither,' replied Barbie with a chuckle. 'If you must know I was – exterior decorating.'

'Oh, Miss France!' cried Agnes, appearing suddenly with Jardine at the door of the train. 'Oh, Miss France, I've got a dear little bedroom all to myself with a light over the bed. Mr Jardine says you can come and see it.'

'How decent of him!' said Henry. 'Can I come and see it too?'

'It'll be better not,' said Jardine firmly. 'She's a wee bit excited. She'll just say good-bye to Miss France and we'll get her teeth washed and off tae bed. It's better to get her off tae bed before the train starts.'

Henry was about to reply in a joking manner but Barbie looked at him quickly and he took the hint.

'All right,' he said. 'I'll wait here for you, but don't be long – and for Heaven's sake don't get carried off to Scotland in the train. I've had enough trouble pursuing you round London.'

As they walked back down the platform together Henry took her arm. 'Where shall we go and feed?' he asked. 'My club is a nice quiet place. What about it, Barbie?'

She noticed that he had called her Barbie and was pleased that he had remembered. Incidentally it made her feel more like herself. It was lovely to see Henry again. He had come. She had known he would come, of course – but she had not expected him to come so soon – and he had pursued her all day – and now they were together. Barbie's heart was singing with happiness.

They had supper at Henry's club. It was so late that there was nobody else in the dining-room, except an old gentleman who was immersed in an evening paper, so it was easy to talk, and although it was only four days since they had seen each other there was a lot to talk about.

Barbie was anxious to hear all about Bogle and the diamonds, but Henry could not tell her a great deal for the poor jackdaw was too ill to be questioned. Four large diamonds and a ruby had been discovered amongst the broken glass and these had all been taken from an old-fashioned pendant which formed part of the 'loot' stolen from a hotel in Ryddelton about eighteen months ago. The gems had obviously been prised from their setting by an unpractised hand and the police had a theory that the thieves might have dropped the pendant when they were making their escape and Bogle had found it and removed the stones himself.

'It's only a guess,' said Henry. 'I doubt whether we shall ever know for certain. They're all doing their level best to whitewash the jackdaw. I think he's a black-hearted villain, myself.'

Barbie was not sure what she thought about it. She had only seen Bogle once – for a few minutes – and certainly had not liked him, but whether or not he was entirely responsible for his actions she could not tell.

'Don't let's bother about Bogle,' said Henry. 'I want to hear what you've been doing. It's your turn to talk.'

It was Barbie's turn to talk and, after a slight hesitation, she told Henry what Agnes had said about her mother going to Montreal, for the matter was worrying her a good deal.

'What can we do?' asked Barbie. 'Mrs Evans is such an extraordinary woman. She might – just – disappear. Is there any way of preventing her?'

'We'll do nothing,' said Henry promptly. 'It will be all the better if the mother disappears. If I know anything about

185

Jennifer she'll keep that child – and I know a good deal about Jennifer. She's tough on the surface but soft underneath. I can't see Jennifer sending that child back to an unsatisfactory home . . .'

'But Henry, you don't mean – '

'And I can't think why you said she was a neglected little waif, plain and miserable; she's a very nice-looking child. There's something very attractive about her. She's neat and tidy. What I call well-groomed,' added Henry.

'Well-groomed,' said Barbie, chuckling appreciatively.

'What's the joke?'

'I've spent all afternoon grooming her, that's all. It's been rather exhausting, but if you're satisfied . . .'

She began to laugh, and Henry laughed too – and insisted on hearing the whole story. It was a good story and Barbie told it well. She had not realised at the time how funny it was, but telling it to Henry made her see the joke. It had all begun with the button in the grubby little hand . . .

'That button made me see red,' declared Barbie. 'It was the last straw! To think any mother could send her child like that – with a button off her coat! Glore could have taken a needle and thread and sewn it on in a minute.' Barbie hesitated and then added, 'Perhaps a man couldn't quite understand – I mean perhaps you think it was silly to make such a fuss about a button.'

'I don't,' said Henry quickly. 'The button was a symbol. I shouldn't dream of appearing on duty with a button off my jacket. It's the same sort of thing.'

Presently Henry leant forward and said, 'Barbie, have I lasted over into your everyday life?'

She nodded.

'You mean it's all right?'

She met his eyes steadily. 'Yes, Henry.'

He put his hand over hers, which was lying on the table, and gave it a little squeeze. He could do no more, for the old gentleman at the next table (who resembled a benevolent walrus) had put down his paper and was watching them with interest.

'He's deaf,' said Henry. 'He's an old admiral and as deaf as a door-nail. Barbie, darling, darling, darling! I love you frightfully!'

'I don't think he's as deaf as all that,' said Barbie rather breathlessly.

'Oh yes, he is! I wish he were blind! Darling Barbie, when did you *know*?'

'I think I've known all the time. I was just – trying to be sensible. I was just – waiting for you to come.'

'You knew I would come.'

Barbie hesitated for a moment and then said, 'Yes, I suppose I did – really – or I would have accepted Mr Garfield's offer.'

'Mr Garfield's offer!' cried Henry in horrified tones.

'Not marriage,' said Barbie hastily.

'Not marriage?'

The dismay, writ large upon Henry's face, made Barbie laugh. 'Just – a partnership – that's all – ' gasped Barbie.

'A partnership in Garfield's!'

She nodded.

'I say, that's pretty good, isn't it?'

She agreed. As a matter of fact she was rather pleased that Henry should realise how good it was. 'But I can't do both,' she added with a mischievous twinkle. 'I can't accept Mr Garfield's offer and marry you as well, so if you still want me – '

'I want you,' said Henry earnestly. 'I want you as my wife and my partner and my friend. I wanted you the very first moment I saw you – and a hundred times more now. When can we be married, Barbie?'

'Not too soon – '

'Couldn't it be too soon. Barbie, darling, please – '

'The admiral is looking at us,' murmured Barbie.

'I think he's a bit short-sighted – '

'Henry, do be sensible!'

Henry muttered something about admirals under his breath.

'We must be sensible,' declared Barbie, clinging to the word. 'We really must be sensible. I don't want to grasp at happiness. I've said I'll marry you but there are things that must be settled first. I don't want to let anybody down.'

'You mean Garfield's. But if you want to go on working at Garfield's there's no reason why you shouldn't.'

'Wouldn't you mind?' asked Barbie in surprise.

'Of course not,' he replied. 'I want you to be happy.

I don't want you to give up anything that you like doing. We're going to be partners,' said Henry earnestly. 'Why should I ask you to give up something you enjoy?'

He paused and looked at her, but she said nothing.

'It's your Thing,' he continued. 'You love the work and you're very good at it – I could see that by the way you went about your job at Oddam – and somehow I can't imagine you sitting at home, idle. You wouldn't be happy.'

'It would be a bit – dull,' admitted Barbie. She hesitated and then added thoughtfully, 'I couldn't take the partnership, but I think Mr Garfield would be quite pleased to let me work with him part-time.'

'That's settled then,' declared Henry. 'It's an excellent plan – and of course it means we needn't wait. We can be married at once.'

'No, we can't, Henry. There's Nell to be considered. I can't just walk out of the flat and leave Nell stranded. I can't, really,' said Barbie in earnest tones. 'Poor Nell was alone in the flat all the time I was ill, and it was miserable for her. We shall have to find someone else to share the flat with Nell – and it won't be easy.'

'Surely she would understand – '

'Oh, she would understand,' agreed Barbie. 'She's frightfully unselfish, but that's all the more reason why I can't let her down. Nell isn't just an ordinary friend; she's very special. As a matter of fact I wouldn't be here at all if it hadn't been for Nell. I should have died in that hospital if she hadn't got Dr Headfort and made them send me to Underwoods.'

Henry gazed at her in silence.

'You see, don't you?' urged Barbie. 'You wouldn't want me to let her down, would you, Henry?'

'N'no,' said Henry doubtfully. 'But couldn't we – '

'And then there's Aunt Amalie,' continued Barbie. 'I'll have to break it to her gently. I believe the best way would be for me to take you to Underwoods so that she could see you. She's old,' explained Barbie. 'You can't rush people when they're old; they like things done in a leisurely sort of way – and I expect she'll want us to be married at Shepherdsford.'

'Oh, help! Not a posh affair like the Mainwaring's!'

Barbie looked thoughtful. 'Not unless she wants it awfully

much . . . but Aunt Amalie has been so good to me that I wouldn't like to upset her.' For a moment Barbie hesitated, wondering whether she should tell Henry that some day Underwoods would belong to his wife, and then she decided that this was not the time. Later, when he had met Aunt Amalie and talked to her and had seen Underwoods she would tell him everything.

'Supposing Lady Steyne doesn't like me?' asked Henry in sudden apprehension.

'She'll love you,' replied Barbie smiling at him very sweetly – and she looked so enchanting that it was all he could do to refrain from kissing her then and there.

'I say,' said Henry in a husky voice, 'you don't want coffee, do you? Let's go to your flat, Barbie. There won't be any admirals in your flat, will there?'

'There will be nobody in the flat,' Barbie told him.

'That will suit me down to the ground,' declared Henry, signalling to the waiter to bring his bill.

Barbie gathered up her gloves and bag and rose from the table. She said, 'It will all be quite easy except finding another girl to share the flat with Nell.'

When Barbie said there was nobody in the flat she was quite mistaken; Nell had got home early and at that very moment was sitting upon the sofa with Dr Headfort. His arm was round her, and her head was on his shoulder, and they were very comfortable indeed.

At that very moment Nell was saying, 'Yes, Will, I know. You've said all that before, but finding somebody really nice to share the flat with Barbie won't be easy, and I can't leave her in the lurch.'

She added:

'I am not of that feather to shake off
My friend when he should need me.'

Will Headfort immediately replied, ' "Beware the fury of a patient man." '

'You're cheating,' said Nell suspiciously. 'I don't believe that's Shakespeare . . . and anyhow you're not patient. That's just the trouble.'

'I've been patient for ages,' declared Will. 'You promised

you would tell Miss France when she came back from Scotland –'

'I meant to – honestly – but Barbie hasn't been like herself. There's something wrong with her.'

'Do you mean she's ill?'

'N'no,' said Nell thoughtfully. 'Just – sort of – queer. Sometimes she's a bit too cheerful, and sometimes she stands quite still and stares at the wall. This morning I heard her muttering to herself and she was saying, "Of course he'll come." '

'In love,' said Will, who knew the condition only too well. 'Yes, but who?'

Will hesitated and then he said, 'If it's that cousin of hers she had better be careful. Edward Steyne has got the reputation for being not very straight – and if you once get that reputation in the City you're done for. Nobody wants to do business with a man unless he's trustworthy.'

'Oh!' said Nell. 'Oh dear . . . but I'm not surprised.'

'Not surprised?'

'I knew he was a bit of a twister. Barbie knows too – that's why she broke off her engagement – so I don't think she would change her mind and marry Edward. In fact I'm sure she wouldn't, because she hates lies.'

'She must be in love with somebody else,' said Will hopefully.

Nell shook her head. 'Barbie doesn't know anybody else.'

'I wish you didn't know anybody else,' said Will Headfort with a sigh. 'That new chap, Percy Something; I don't like him.'

'Goodness, you aren't jealous of Percy!' exclaimed Nell in surprise.

'I'm jealous of everyone who looks at you; and of course everyone looks at you: taxi-drivers, waiters, porters,' said poor Will. 'Everyone looks at you because you're so beautiful. I wish I were a poet instead of a dull old doctor so that I could tell you how beautiful you are.'

'Darling Will,' said Nell. 'I think you are a poet –'

'No. I'm not – but I understand poetry now. For instance I always thought it was rather silly for Romeo to say, "O, she doth teach the torches to burn bright," but now I understand what he meant. It isn't a metaphor, it's absolutely real. Juliet lighted up his world – as you do mine.'

'Oh Will, nobody has ever said anything to beautiful to me before!'

'Not Percy?' asked Will. 'Not Rupert or Phil or – '

'Nobody ever!' declared Nell, holding up her mouth to be kissed.

He was kissing her when the door opened and Barbie came in – with Henry.

THE END

Fontana Books

Fontana is best known as one of the leading paperback publishers of popular fiction and non-fiction. It also includes an outstanding, and expanding, section of books on history, natural history, religion and social sciences.

Most of the fiction authors need no introduction. They include Agatha Christie, Hammond Innes, Alistair MacLean, Catherine Gaskin, Victoria Holt and Lucy Walker. Desmond Bagley and Maureen Peters are among the relative newcomers.

The non-fiction list features a superb collection of animal books by such favourites as Gerald Durrell and Joy Adamson.

All Fontana books are available at your bookshop or newsagent; or can be ordered direct. Just fill in the form below and list the titles you want.

FONTANA BOOKS, Cash Sales Department, P.O. Box 4, Godalming, Surrey, GU7 1JY. Please send purchase price plus 7p postage per book by cheque, postal or money order. No currency.

NAME (Block letters)

ADDRESS

While every effort is made to keep prices low, it is sometimes necessary to increase prices at short notice. Fontana Books reserve the right to show new retail prices on covers which may differ from those previously advertised in the text or elsewhere.